THE
PERFECT
NEIGHBORS

Rachel Sargeant grew up in Lincolnshire. *The Perfect Neighbors* is her third novel. She is a previous winner of *Writing Magazine*'s Crime Short Story competition and has been shortlisted for various competitions, including the Bristol Short Story Prize. Her stories have appeared in *My Weekly* and the Accent Press Saucy Shorts series. Rachel has a degree in German and Librarianship from Aberystwyth University and a Masters in Creative Writing from Lancaster University. She spent several years living in Germany where she taught English and she now lives in Gloucestershire with her husband and children.

@RachelSargeant3
www.rachelsargeant.co.uk

RACHEL SARGEANT

THE
PERFECT
NEIGHBORS

**KILLER
READS**

KillerReads
an imprint of HarperCollins*Publishers* Ltd
1 London Bridge Street
London SE1 9GF

www.harpercollins.co.uk

This paperback edition 2018

18 19 20 21 22 LSCC 10 9 8 7 6 5 4 3 2 1

First published in Great Britain in ebook format by HarperCollins*Publishers* 2017

Copyright © Rachel Sargeant 2017

Rachel Sargeant asserts the moral right to
be identified as the author of this work

A catalogue record for this book
is available from the British Library

ISBN: 978-0-00-828660-6

Set in Minion by Palimpsest Book Production Limited, Falkirk, Stirlingshire

Printed and bound in the United States of America

For more information visit: www.harpercollins.co.uk/green

To Fergus, Gillian, Jenny, Peter and Karen

PART ONE

1

The spotlight is set into the ceiling so prisoners can't get at it. Helen's head hurts from the glare but she doesn't shield her eyes. The moment she closes them, the images will flood back. Jagged photos in a digital picture frame, moving upwards and sideways, repeating and holding. She doesn't know which one will torment her first. If she's lucky, it's the child's cello, on its back, neck broken, blood smeared around the sound holes.

But it could be the blood-cherry cheesecake. Or the matted, pink-black belly fur of the dead dog. Or the gaping crew-neck sweater oozing its obscene innards onto the parquet floor. *Or Gary*.

She sits on the edge of the bed, her arms cradling her knees. If she could focus on the cello, the rest might fade. She must grab the sticky instrument; drag it into view; admire the thickening stains on the polished wood; remember the small, expert hand that once pressed against the fingerboard; and strain to hear the soothing sound of his playing. But it won't be enough to block out the other images. Seventeen days so far and nothing has dimmed.

She stands up and paces the floor, her joints grating from lack of exercise. They let her walk in the yard at the back of the police

3

station, but the snow piled at the fence reminded her of the cell so she asked to go back in. White room. White loo in the corner, no seat or lid. The only stab of colour is the green button by the door. She presses it.

"Please, sit yourself. Your lawyer will visit you in a little time," the desk sergeant tells her through the intercom.

No point in arguing; it's doubtful his English is up to it and, even after eight months in the country, she's still another expat Brit who can't be bothered to learn German.

She flops onto the bed. The mattress smells like Marigold gloves. Washing-up, Gary doing the drying. But another view of Gary invades – folded ankles, empty expression, crimson shoulder. She fights the vision and tries to see Gary at their kitchen sink. Tries to make him smile. Make him speak. She curls up, exhausted by the effort.

The door bolts deactivate but she stays foetal. It's the lawyer, Karola. The ruddy-faced neighbour who keeps spaniels in her back garden and waves at her on Mondays when they put their dustbins out. She's Frau Barton to her now, the only bilingual German-trained lawyer the school can find at short notice. These days she's more used to picking up dog poo than counselling women charged with murder.

Helen rolls towards the wall.

"Why didn't you mention Sascha Jakobsen?" Karola asks.

The name shoots through Helen. She says nothing.

"He's told the police that you were with him at the outdoor pool in Dortmannhausen."

Helen sits up. "He said that?"

"The police searched the frozen pool site again. You'd better tell me everything," Karola says, perching on the bed. Dark trouser suit, darker soul.

Helen draws her legs up, away from her. "There's nothing to tell."

"How long have you known Jakobsen?"

Why ask when she knows the answer? The school is a goldfish bowl and they both swim in it. Karola Barton knows every bit of her business. All the neighbours do, all the neighbours that are still alive.

Helen says: "It wasn't like that."

Karola stands up. The crease of her trousers is plumb-line vertical. "What was it *like*, Mrs Taylor?"

2

Monday, 5 April

Eight Months Earlier

Gary squeezed Helen's hand. "Excited?"

She said nothing. Was she excited? New start in a new country. As a full-time wife. She managed a smile and nodded.

They drove off the A road – the *Landstrasse* as Gary called it – into a grey, built-up area. She thought of the coach trip she'd made with a Year 10 class to Bulgaria; communist-built apartment blocks on the outskirts of Sofia.

Gary pulled up at traffic lights and pointed. "And behind there is the Niers International School."

Through the spike-topped metal fence on the right she made out rows of full bicycle stands. It looked like a provincial railway station.

"But you can't see it properly from here," he added.

A pot-bellied man in a dark uniform was standing by a sentry hut, the wooden roof scabby and cracked.

"You have guards?" she asked.

"Don't mind Klaus. We have two full-time security men to

patrol the site. The parents like it. Except our guys spend most of the time playing toy soldiers in their little house."

Helen laughed until she noticed *Ausländer Raus* spray-painted on a bus shelter. "Does that mean what I think it means?"

The light went green, and they turned left.

"Foreigners Out – but you hardly ever see that stuff. Most of the Germans love the international school," he said. "Lots of locals work here in support roles, and the parents spend good money in the town."

He'd told her about the parents before. Most worked for big international companies in Düsseldorf, and others were rich locals prepared to pay for an English-speaking education. And some were teachers.

"Think about it, Helen," Gary had said when they sat down with their pros and cons sheet on one of his weekend visits, agonizing over where to live. "Not yet, but in a few years, if we have children, it could be their school. There are so many perks, as well as the salary."

That had been the clincher: Gary could earn more staying out here than the two of them put together in the UK. Helen had stopped being stubborn in light of the cold hard figures. She quit her job and put her house up for rent.

He went over a speed bump, and she felt the seatbelt rub against her collarbone.

"Have you noticed the street names?" He pointed at one, multisyllabic, a jumble of Ls and Es. "Can you read them?"

She shook her head. They had been driving non-stop since Calais. The traffic signs after the border into Germany had become a strident Teutonic yellow. Here the street names were in white, more like British ones, but they were unpronounceable.

Gary crawled along at 20 mph and seemed unfazed by the need to slalom his way around parked cars, playing children, and speed bumps. She glanced at his profile – round cheekbones,

7

smooth jaw, patient eyes. Who would have thought affability could be so magnetic? Her stomach settled.

"What are you thinking?" he asked.

"About Birmingham." Where they first met.

At the teachers' conference in the university bar after the speeches, he'd been the gentle-faced man in the noisy crowd. The one everyone wanted to talk to. A kind of jig took place as people vied for a position next to him. And when he caught her looking and smiled, Helen – never normally part of a pack – took it as her cue to join the reel. By the end of the evening she and Gary were the only people still dancing.

"No regrets?" he asked.

Was she still scared about the move? It had taken her long enough to make up her mind. She stroked his arm and smiled. Not scared now; a little apprehensive, maybe.

"Nearly there," he said. "You'll love the neighbours. Polly and Jerome are great. They live across the way with their two girls. Jerome Stephens is head of science."

After a couple more turnings he made a right into Dickensweg, a cul-de-sac of identical semi-detached houses. Unlike the grey of the Bulgarian patch they'd driven through, the houses had been painted lemon in the last decade and, as if by some unwritten rule, all the cars were parked on the left side of the road. Bicycles, trailers, and pushchairs were propped up against almost every front door as if soliciting at a car boot sale, and large yellow dustbins lurked on front lawns like Tupperware daleks.

A pink-faced man with big, white hair climbed out of a red sports car. Gary beeped the horn and gave him a thumbs up. "That's our next-door neighbour, Chris Mowar. He's head of art."

The man crossed the road in front of them, bowed theatrically and disappeared into a house on the other side.

"Is everyone round here head of something?" she asked.

Gary nodded. "We've got the head of geography at number 4, although he's hardly ever at home, and the school's public relations manager at number 1. And the head teacher, of course."

He touched the brake and pointed up the street. "Through that copse is Hardyweg, where the rest of the heads of department live. The *weg* bit means way. Dickens and Hardy. The town council re-named the streets in honour of the school thirty years ago. A nice gesture, don't you think?"

Helen smiled. It did sound nice, welcoming. She felt mean for thinking the street looked shabby.

Three boys, dressed in T-shirts, shorts, and wellies, were playing with remote-controlled trucks in the road. Maybe they didn't feel the cold. Helen zipped up her jacket.

Gary braked again. "I'd better not run them over; they're the head teacher's kids."

The boys waved at the car and moved out of the way. Gary waved back and drove to the end of the road. Instead of another pair of semis, there was a large detached house with a magnificent wisteria that framed the front door, and sunny yellow shutters at every window. *Number Ten* declared the carved wooden plaque, with no sign anywhere of the ugly metal house numbers that Helen had seen on the other walls.

Warmth sped through her. Moving here was the right thing. They couldn't have maintained a long-distance marriage for much longer. She was bound to get another teaching job. It might not be head of PE again but there would be something. In the meantime she could enjoy living in this beautiful house.

Gary reversed into the turning circle and moved back down the street.

"That one's Damian and Louisa's. Number Ten, that's what we call it, like the prime minister's place. We're at number 5."

"Damian and Louisa?"

"The head and his wife. Remember I talked about them."

Helen swallowed her disappointment as he pulled up opposite a house displaying a lopsided metal 5, weed-ridden flower beds and a knocked-over bin. Twenty yards from her husband's boss and his executive home.

3

Tuesday, 6 April

Something disturbed Helen. The warm mound under the bedclothes beside her was fast asleep. She turned over.

The ringing noise sounded again.

"Gary." She nudged the duvet. "Doorbell."

She'd woken up once already, and Gary had been standing by the window. Too tired to ask him what he was doing, she had gone back to sleep. Now he snuggled further down the bed.

"Gary?"

She climbed out and padded around in search of her robe. She slipped it over her naked body and headed downstairs. The doorbell rang again.

A perfect woman stood on the doorstep – sleek shoulder-length hair a shade of chestnut that only a top salon could make look natural, and flawless made-up skin. The woman's eyes did a tour of her tousled hair, bare face, and ancient towelling dressing gown. Helen tugged at its hem but could do nothing to stop it ending mid-thigh.

"I'll come in so you don't catch cold," the stranger said, stepping into the hall. She closed the front door and filled the air with eau de Chanel. Helen found herself apologizing for being in bed at eight thirty. Heat spread across her neck and cheeks. Why the self-conscious idiocy? It was her home now and she could sleep all day if she wanted.

"You've had a long journey, Helen. It's understandable," the woman said.

Helen tugged at her dressing gown again; the woman knew so much about her. Were they all nosy neighbours here? God, she hoped not.

"I've called round to let you know that I'm throwing your welcome party tonight. It's seven for seven thirty. You don't need to bring anything, this time. I've got Polly helping me, and Mel, of course, bless her." She rolled her eyes. Without waiting for a response she opened the door to leave.

"But where …? I didn't catch your name?" Helen called.

The woman turned. "Hasn't Gary mentioned me? I'm Louisa." She headed down the path, stepping over the weeds between the paving slabs.

***

Helen squeezed Gary's hand as they walked over the road to Louisa and Damian Howard's house that evening. "Should we have brought something? It seems rude to turn up empty-handed."

"Don't worry about it. Louisa likes to make a fuss of new people. I suppose it's what head teachers' spouses do." He pulled her towards him, smiling. "Come on, I can't wait to show off my gorgeous wife."

One of the children she'd seen in the road the previous day, a boy of about eight, opened the door.

"Hi, Toby," Gary said.

The child was wearing a white shirt and black bow tie. "Super to see you," he said, as if quoting from a script. "Let me take your coats. Oh, you haven't got any." He looked at a loss at this departure from what he'd rehearsed.

"Don't worry, mate," Gary said, patting his shoulder.

The hallway was vast and had the most amazing smell – some kind of herb. No sign of the functionally beige carpet that plagued the floors in Gary's place. Louisa and Damian must have ripped theirs out and put down vinyl. When Helen looked closer, she realized it was solid wood. So this was Number Ten. She found herself placing the words in capital letters.

"Gary, darling." Louisa appeared in the hall and kissed Gary on both cheeks. She was wearing tailored brown trousers and a cream chiffon blouse, every inch a prime minister's wife and living up to her house name.

She eyed Helen's jeans. "You wear casual so well," she said as her head moved in the general direction of Helen's in an air kiss.

Helen stiffened but Louisa seemed oblivious to the offence she'd caused. "Toby, poppet," she said, "move your school bag; it's a deathtrap when you leave it on the stairs. Put it in the cellar and then get ready for the recital."

"Yes, Mummy," Toby groaned.

The wooden floor continued into the lounge, a sumptuous cream rug at the centre. Did all head teachers live like this or only those in international schools? A gold and yellow striped wallpaper adorned the far wall. The French windows were draped in blue velvet curtains, half closed, but Helen could make out a trampoline in the large back garden beyond. The other lounge walls had modern art prints mounted on them. Sliding doors through to the dining room were pushed back to reveal an elegantly laid table.

"I know those doors are ghastly," Louisa said, appearing behind her with a bowl of salad. "Our next project is to have them removed and the surrounding wall knocked out. It's difficult for Damian when he has to entertain important visitors in such a tiny space, isn't it, darling?" She patted the arm of a tall, blond man who had walked in with two glasses of champagne.

"It seats twelve, Louisa. It's fine. You must be Helen. I'm Damian." He turned the sigh he'd aimed at his wife into a smile at Helen. He gave both women their drinks and kissed Helen on the cheek. The kiss was chaste but his hand stayed on her waist. Damian Howard struck her as someone who might spend a lot of time kissing other people's wives.

"Darling, why don't you take Gary to choose a beer? I'm sure he'd prefer it to champagne. Helen, come and meet Jerome and Polly. Jerome's our head of science." In a slick manoeuvre Louisa separated her husband from the new female guest. She ushered Helen over to a couple who had just arrived.

Jerome shook Helen's hand.

His wife, who was holding a baby monitor, smiled in greeting. "Gary's told us so much about you. It's super to meet you at last," she said. She was wearing jeans. Had she been on the receiving end of Louisa's "casual" jibe too?

"Do you think I could put this down?" she asked her husband, holding up the monitor. She turned to Helen. "We're next-door – at number 8 – so we'll hear the girls on the baby alarm if they wake up. That's the marvellous thing about living here. You always know who's about."

Helen nodded but was surprised these middle-class parents left their children under the supervision of a piece of Mothercare kit.

The doorbell rang and Louisa brought another couple into the room. It was the man Helen had seen climbing out of the red sports car. He took her hand. "I'm Chris Mowar and you must be my new lady next door. It's going to be a pleasure."

He held onto her and his shiny eyes scrutinized her face. She decided it was time to tug her hand away, but as she did so, he let go, making it look as if she had pulled harder than necessary. She had the unpleasant sensation that she'd reacted exactly as he had wanted her to.

"This is Mel," he said, as if introducing someone he'd met in the hallway.

The woman tried to balance the large plate she was carrying in her left hand to free her right for a handshake but she couldn't manage it. Beads of moisture gathered on her hairline. When Damian appeared with Gary's beer and more champagne on a tray, she tried to give him the plate of food she'd brought.

"Sorry, Mel, I'm just the bartender. I'll put your drink over here."

"I can hold that plate while you have your drink," Helen said.

Mel shook her head. She must be about thirty-five years old, around the same age as her husband, Chris, but he'd aged better despite his white hair. He dressed better too; his silk shirt must have had a tidy price tag. But looking at Mel, Helen wondered whether Louisa had told her as a joke that this was a Vicars and Tarts party. Dimples of cellulite showed on her thighs through overstretched leopard-print Lycra.

When Louisa came back, Mel offered her the plate.

"Hot cross buns. Lovely," Louisa said. "Put them in the kitchen."

Polly looked down at her baby monitor. "It's Purdy I'm more worried about. She's chewed her way through two cushions this week already."

"Purdy is their Dalmatian," Damian said, topping up Helen's glass. "We're a doggy street. Karola Barton at number 1 gave up a legal career to breed springer spaniels. At the last count, she and Geoff had six in kennels in the back garden. And we've got a dog although Louisa makes such a fuss of him he thinks he's our fourth son. He's in the music room at the moment." He nodded towards a door beyond the dining room. "No doubt he'll join us for the recital."

Before Helen could ask what he meant, Louisa tapped a spoon against her glass. Everyone fell silent and she made her announcement: "It's super to see you here to greet our newest arrival, Helen. Please join me in giving her a traditional Niers School welcome."

The guests erupted into applause. It was like being received into a religious cult. Helen's glance stayed on the parquet floor until the ovation subsided. When Louisa stopped clapping, the others did too.

"And now the boys are going to perform for us," Louisa said. "Toby has been begging me to let him play 'Kalinka', haven't you, Toby?"

Toby gave a bemused smile and opened the door beyond the dining table to the music room. Out bounded an enormous polar bear of a dog. It sniffed round the assembled guests, its wagging tail slapping their legs. Mel Mowar gulped and backed into a coffee table.

Louisa grabbed the dog's collar and pulled him across the floor. "For goodness' sake, Mel, you know Napoleon won't hurt you. He's just being friendly. Everyone, go through to the music room."

Mel's breathing sounded erratic, but no one paid her any attention, not even her husband Chris.

"Shall we go through?" Helen whispered to her.

Mel gave a relieved smile.

The tiny music room was kitted out with an upright piano, a bookcase of music scores and now three small boys, sitting behind a cello, violin, and tambourine. As the guests squeezed in, the smallest boy waved his tambourine at them.

"Murdo, don't play until I nod," Louisa told him.

"Noh, noh," the boy said.

Helen decided he was younger than he looked, and cute. She smiled.

Louisa's elegant fingers glided over the keys. It was obvious that Toby hadn't begged to play the piece at all. She'd chosen it to show off her musicianship.

Helen glanced at the bookcase, at the TV in the corner, at the other guests in the cramped room – anywhere to avoid watching the self-satisfied expression on Louisa's face. There was a small window out onto the garden. Something caught her eye at the back fence. A dot of orange light and a dark, moving shape. She squinted hard for a better look.

When Louisa tackled a tricky chord, Jerome Stephens stepped forward to applaud and obscured Helen's view of the garden. She tilted her head and saw elbows and hands on the back fence. A face appeared, spat out a cigarette and vanished.

She was about to warn her hosts, when Toby came in on the cello. It would be rude to interrupt the child; she'd wait until the end. She'd expected him to be rubbish, assuming that Louisa was a deluded, selectively deaf mother who couldn't hear the screeching tune being murdered on the half-size instrument. But Toby could play. He wasn't Jacqueline du Pré but he was better than the kids who performed solos at the school where Helen used to teach. And they had been teenagers; this was a boy of eight. When he finished she clapped as enthusiastically as the other guests.

Louisa announced that they would play the last part again so that Toby's brothers could join in. She hit the piano keys harder this time. Leo, the middle child on the violin, hadn't inherited his brother's talent. Napoleon retreated to the dining room to escape the highpitched whining. Louisa nodded at Murdo but he continued chewing his tambourine. He joined in the applause at the end.

"Why didn't you play, Murdo?" Louisa asked. "Didn't you see Mummy nod?"

Damian ruffled his youngest son's hair. "It doesn't matter, matey. Let's have supper."

Helen opened her mouth to tell them about the intruder, but the view from the window was serene and the idea seemed ridiculous. Had she really seen someone on the fence? It was getting dark outside and she was two glasses into the Howards' quality champagne. When she saw Gary looking at her quizzically, she smiled and followed him into the dining room.

She was sure of two things: Louisa would seat her as far away from Damian as possible and she'd end up next to Mel's husband Chris. She was right on both counts. Chris was to Helen's right and beyond him was Polly, still holding her baby alarm. Louisa took her place at the head of the table, on Helen's left. Damian was at the far end, but still managed to smile in her direction every time she looked up. She found herself blushing.

When Chris put down his glass and asked, "So, Helen Taylor, tell me about yourself," she didn't want to answer. There was something unnerving about him, as if he might use whatever she said against her one day.

"Not much to tell. What about you?" she said. "What do you teach?"

"I'm head of A and D. That's Art and Design. Hardly rocket science but it passes the time until my project is complete." He faced her but raised his voice to address the whole room. "Have you heard of Michael Moore?"

Before she could answer, Louisa leaned forward. "He's an American documentary maker. Chris intends to follow in his footsteps."

Chris shook his head. "Louisa, my darling, a Chris Mowar Production doesn't *follow*. What I'm working on will turn the documentary film industry on its head."

"Chris has a big plan to expose con men but I think it's been done before," Louisa said, looking at Helen.

"Not with the treatment I'm giving it." Chris tapped the side of his nose. "It's all about the long haul. Con men take their time to exploit people's weaknesses. They'd exploit yours," he said, leaning back in his chair and staring at Louisa.

"How droll you are," she said and gave a forced giggle.

Chris stretched out his arms. "Take this room, for instance, with its statement yellow wallpaper."

"It's savannah and gold. What about it?"

"Whatever you want to call it, it's not school-issue. You've practically rebuilt this house from the inside out. A con man could send the whole thing tumbling down."

Louisa didn't reply. She concentrated on picking a crumb off the table and depositing it on the side of her plate. The only sound was Napoleon chomping on his bone under the table.

"So, Helen, what do you think of our little neighbourhood?" Damian called down the table. She wondered if he was asking to deflect the spotlight from his wife. But Helen was now the one feeling the heat. Polly and Jerome looked at her. Louisa was watching too.

"It's delightful," she said, banishing *parochial* from her mouth.

"This street is a real community, like Britain in the 1950s," Damian said.

"Even though we have some foreigners in our midst." Chris laughed.

"Poor old Manfred," Polly said, moving the baby alarm nearer to her plate. "He must miss his cottage."

"He was jolly lucky the German Government gave him a house in perpetuity. We get our rented houses but once we leave the school we're on our own," Jerome said.

"But isn't that the point?" Polly replied. "He was given that house for life. Whatever the rights and wrongs of that arrangement, the school shouldn't have demolished it."

"I think we'd better explain to Helen," Damian said. "Manfred Scholz lives at number 2. He's our groundsman – looks after the school site. One of the perks of the job was his own cottage inside the campus. We wanted the land to build a new gym so he and his wife had to be re-housed in Dickensweg."

"He's a super chap. Dignified," Jerome added. "But probably time the old boy retired."

"He's been lonely since his wife died but I do what I can to include him," Louisa said.

Chris folded his hands behind his head. "If you ask me, he's no lonelier than he was before. With all that obsessive cleaning, the only way to get attention from a Hausfrau is to lie on your back covered in dust."

Helen was shocked at the open insult to the German locals.

She glanced across the table to Gary. He stopped smiling and winced. She thought it was apologetic; it damn well ought to be. What kind of neighbourhood had he brought her to?

After dessert, Louisa took coffee orders. Helen stacked the plates and followed her into the kitchen. The room was space age: white units, black granite tops, built-in cooker. She opened the bin to scrape the plates and saw a heap of hot cross buns at the bottom. So that's what Louisa thought of Mel's food offering.

"Where shall I put this?" Mel appeared with leftover gateau.

"Bio bin," Louisa said.

"I'll do it." Helen took the plate from Mel to prevent her seeing inside the bin.

Jerome came in to say goodbye; he was leaving before Polly to be with their girls. When Helen went back to the dining room, there was no sign of Gary, Damian, or Chris.

"They've gone to the den, in the cellar," Louisa explained. "It's very much Damian's lair; it stops the men making the lounge untidy." She gave a little giggle. It sounded like a hiccup.

She invited the women into the lounge but didn't ask them to sit down. As if at some late-night cocktail party, they stood in the middle of the room. Helen longed to sink into one of the cream sofas which beckoned her like a bubble bath. The herbal scent that she'd encountered in the hallway was stronger here.

Louisa noticed her sniffing. "It's lavender. I'll give you a sample before you leave. I'm a qualified aromatherapist, but only work part-time now that I'm chair of the Parents' Association and on the Board of Governors."

"I don't know how you do it all," Polly said.

"I try," Louisa said and smoothed down a chiffon sleeve.

Helen glanced at her watch. Midnight. How much more of Superwoman could she endure? She excused herself to go to the loo and went to find Gary.

***

20

The cellar in Gary's house was about as attractive as a multi-storey car park, but when she stepped over Toby's school bag and descended into Damian's den it was like heading into a nightclub. Red tiles on the walls and another wooden floor. The first room was decked out like a cinema with a huge flat-screen TV, easy chairs, and a popcorn machine. She could hear the men in the room beyond. As she approached, she heard Chris's voice.

"You need to lighten up, mate. Club Viva's in the past. What's done is done."

And Gary's reply, "Steve texted me again."

They were standing around a pool table, holding cues. Gary rubbed the bridge of his nose.

They looked shocked when they saw her, as if she'd caught them in the act of something. Was it because a female had invaded their beer den, or something else?

Gary coughed awkwardly. "Are you ready to go, love?" he asked, resting his cue against the wall. "It's time we called it a night."

Whenever they caught up with friends in England, he'd party into the small hours until she dragged him away. But tonight he seemed ready to leave his colleagues. Maybe he wasn't as fond of his neighbours as she'd assumed. The thought of how in tune the two of them were was exhilarating. She couldn't wait to get him home.

***

They made love for the first time since her arrival and she fell asleep in his arms. She woke in the night. Was Louisa at the bloody door again? But it wasn't the doorbell; it was a staccato tapping noise. Her mind flickered to the face at the Howards' back fence. An intruder? No, she was being hysterical. The sound must be from next door; Gary had warned her that the walls

21

between the two semis were thin. Chris must be filming night shots for his documentary.

But the sound was coming from their spare bedroom, the one Gary had set up as a study. She realized she was alone in the bed.

"Gary?" There was no one else in the house to disturb, but she whispered as she went to him. In the light of the computer game on the screen, he looked grey and there were hollows under his eyes. He was hitting the hand-held controller with his thumbs.

"You'll be wrecked in the morning. Come back to bed," she said.

He jumped when she spoke. "Sorry, I forgot you were here." He sighed and rubbed his eyes.

He'd got up both nights since she had arrived in Germany; now he didn't even remember she was there. "Are you happy about us living together?"

He reached out for her arm. "How can you even ask that? It's what I've wanted ever since we got married. I can't sleep, that's all. It's nothing that you've done."

"You looked serious in Damian's cellar tonight," she said. "What were you talking about?"

"Can't remember now. Politics probably. Men don't only talk about football you know."

"What's Club Viva?"

In the light of the computer screen, Gary's face grew paler. He thumbed the games controller, ignoring her question.

"Gary?"

"Actually that was football talk," he said and forced a chuckle. "You caught us out. Did you enjoy the evening?"

"Polly and Jerome were nice," she conceded. "And Damian was friendly." She thought of his lingering smiles across the table. Too friendly maybe. "Is he a bit of a, you know, wanderer?"

Gary's eyes shot up from the computer screen. "How would I know?" He sounded defensive, then he shrugged. "Why would he

22

play away when he's got Louisa? She's great, isn't she? What did the two of you talk about?"

Helen sighed. "I listened more than talked. Are you coming back to bed?"

"I'll just finish this," he said, a desolate look in his eyes.

Fiona

"You're on the home straight now," Dad said. "Come July we'll have a graduate in the family."

He lifted my heavy suitcase onto the bed and winced, letting out a sharp breath.

"Sssh, Dad, don't tempt fate." I put my arms round his neck and kissed him, pretending not to notice the twinge when I pressed against his chest.

Mum found some wire coat hangers in the empty wardrobe and opened the suitcase. "I wouldn't be surprised if you get an Upper Second. Your French is so good after your year in Lyons." She started putting my clothes on the hangers.

"Thanks, Mum, but how do you know? You don't speak French," I said, taking over the unpacking.

She kissed me on the nose and we giggled.

Dad rattled the bookcase. "You'd best put your big books on the bottom so it doesn't wobble over." He walked to the window. "Nice view of the bins."

Mum joined him. "She doesn't need a view. She'll either be working or sleeping when she's in here."

"How far is it to the student bar?" Dad said, standing on tiptoes to peer out. "We could check out the route with you before we go."

"No, thanks," I said quickly. I wasn't in with the in-crowd at the best of times, but arriving at the uni bar with my parents would make me the uncoolest student outside the computer science faculty.

"Do I take it you want your personal chauffeurs to hop it before we damage your street cred?" Dad said. He was smiling, but there was that penetrating twinkle in his eyes. Even when he'd been ill he had kept his unerring ability to read me like a kiddies' comic.

I hugged them both, breathing in the smell of them.

"See you at Christmas," Mum said.

We hugged again, not knowing that Christmas would never come.

4

Gary pecked her on the neck, shoved a slice of toast in his mouth and headed for the kitchen door.

"I was thinking I might paint the lounge this week. Any preference on colour?" Helen called after him.

He came back in. "Up to you as long as we paint it back to magnolia if ever we move out."

"What about the Howards' house? They've virtually taken a bulldozer to it. Will they have to put it back when they leave?"

"Eventually. I don't know who the landlord is – some German Herr Money Bags no doubt – but we have to leave things as we find them. I can't see Damian quitting Niers International in a hurry. Where else would you have every child's dad in full employment? A bit of a difference from the comp you worked in."

Helen said nothing but wanted to point out he'd never been to her school. Shrewsbury Academy had more than its fair share of success stories.

"Number Ten is something, isn't it? Louisa has a real eye for design," he said. "You could try a bit of painting if you want to." He gave her another peck and left.

Helen dropped the breakfast pots in the sink and wondered what she could do that wouldn't involve an unfavourable comparison with the decor queen across the road.

She and Gary had spent the previous week like tourists: Cologne Cathedral, a boat trip on the Rhine, and *Kaffee und Kuchen* in several chintzy cafés. Days wrapped in the mist and drizzle of a North German spring, but burning with the same light as their Jamaican winter honeymoon. They'd discovered the Caribbean together, but here Gary was her personal guide, showing off, proud and impatient for her approval. And she'd given it, teasingly at first, watching uncertainty flicker in his eyes before letting her kiss reassure him.

She pointed the tap at the dirty plates. Her mind wandered to the welcome briefing she'd endured the previous Friday. The school employed a nurse, a smart, thirty-something German woman called Sabine, who doubled as the staff and pupil welfare officer. She'd invited Helen and two new teaching assistants into her treatment room. Helen sat between the two gap-year Australians, facing a medical examination table. Above it was an instruction poster on how to conduct a smear test.

Over instant coffee and custard creams, Sabine told them, in her impeccable English, about registering with a local doctor and what school facilities they were entitled to use. When Helen had asked when the school swimming pool was open to staff and families, Sabine shook her head. "It's only for the children. The nearest indoor swimming pool is over the border at a Center Parcs in Holland." A door banged shut in Helen's head; she lived for her daily lane swim, but not if it meant dodging round splashing holidaymakers.

"Of course, there's the open-air pool in Dortmannhausen village," Sabine added. "We Germans don't swim outdoors unless there's a heatwave, but one of the British wives got a campaign going and persuaded the *Kreis* authorities to open it from early May, so you won't have to wait long."

Now Helen grabbed the tap and let water gush over the crockery, some splashes hitting her. May was still three weeks away. She opened the herbal oil that Louisa had foisted on her at the dinner party and coughed at its biting, acidic scent. She added a few drops to her bowl and watched the pale liquid spread in the running water and mingle with her crockery. It looked like pee. She grabbed the bowl and emptied it.

She watched out of the window as various neighbours set off for school, some on bikes, some walking. She stepped back from the window when Louisa swept past in an enormous four-by-four, powerful enough to cross the Serengeti plains. She slammed the herbal oil bottle into her pedal bin.

By nine the cul-de-sac was deserted. She must have missed Chris next door at number 7 although his sports car was still parked in the street.

She tipped out the rest of her coffee. Now what? Mop the floor? Rearrange the fridge? She could ring Mum. They'd exchanged several texts and she'd sent a postcard from Cologne, but they hadn't spoken since she left Shrewsbury. If she phoned, Mum would read her mood from a thousand miles away. And she'd say that thing she always said. Like she did when they came back married from Jamaica. Like she did when Helen announced she was giving up her job to join Gary in Germany – "Just as long as you're happy." It was the soundtrack through the unauthorized version of her life. When she refused to eat peas; when she chose swimming over ballet; when she changed universities halfway through her degree. She decided to wait a few more days before ringing, do it when she was settled.

A key rack on the wall caught her eye. She picked up the key labelled "Shed".

***

28

Inside the concrete construction at the bottom of the garden she discovered a decent set of tools and a lawnmower. She thought of the manicured shrubbery around Louisa's house and her competitive instinct took hold. But something about being in the back garden unnerved her, and not just the yapping dogs in the nearby kennels. A dark copse of trees grew behind the gardens in Dickensweg, separating them from the gardens of the next street. It joined up at right angles with the wood behind the Howards' fence. The whole estate enjoyed a similar leafy arrangement. Her skin prickled. An intruder could pass through the network of copses and climb into any garden unnoticed. She gathered her tools and headed to the front of the house.

She stabbed the spade into the flower bed under the kitchen window but only broke off the stalks of a few weeds. She dug harder, but the dense greenery fought her off and she couldn't reach the soil. Another lunge, and the bones in her arms juddered as the spade hit bedrock. Rubbing the sweat off her forehead, she contemplated how else she could tackle the task.

"Slacking already?" Chris said, coming out of his front door. His voice made her bones rattle more than the bedrock had done.

"Not working today?" she asked. School would be well into the registration period. Didn't the head of A and D have a form class?

He stepped across their joint path towards her. "Tough job turning your garden into Number Ten."

She felt him sizing her up. She knew what he saw: damp fringe, ruddy cheeks, traces of snot and grass stain where she'd rubbed her nose.

"A bit of weeding," she said.

He shook his head. "It's more than that. You're a competitive woman." When she didn't respond, he continued, "Gary's told us all about your coaching and your swimming career. You like to be the best, don't you?"

She lifted the spade again, undecided on whether to sink it

into the soil or to bring it down on his head. How dare this stranger pronounce on her life? "I don't know what you mean."

"Louisa likes to be the top wife round here, that's all I'm saying." He sauntered towards the sports car, gave her a wave and drove off.

She dug faster, scratching and gouging, and turned over a good third of the bed before she heard a car pull up.

"I see Gary's got you earning your keep."

In any other tone Helen would have taken the comment as a jokey conversation opener but this voice was as piercing as Chris's eyes had been.

"Morning, Louisa," she managed to say. The top wife climbed out of the Serengetiguzzler. Pastel pink tracksuit, spotless trainers, full make-up.

"I stopped to ask whether you wanted to come for a run but I can see you're busy. How about tomorrow at nine thirty?"

"I'm not much of a runner," Helen said, blurting out the first thing that came to mind.

"Gary said you ran three miles a day when you lived in England."

What the hell else had Gary said? "Maybe, once I've settled in."

"Make it soon. It's bad for the metabolism to stop exercising. You'll put on weight."

"I'm sure the gardening will compensate," Helen said, not snapping.

The door of number 7 opened and Mel backed down the step with a pushchair. She was wearing the same leopard-print leggings that she'd worn at Louisa's party the previous week.

Glad of the distraction, Helen called out: "I didn't know you had a baby. Who's this then?"

The pushchair was empty. Helen assumed the child was still in the house, but Mel's strained features instinctively told her there was no child.

For once she was glad of Louisa, who said: "Is that another pushchair for HFN? What a knack you have for finding them. Pop it in the boot and I'll take it up later."

Mel's face bulged with colour. "I'll walk it round. Thanks."

"If you're sure you can walk that far," Louisa said and added for Helen's benefit, "Mel suffers from shortness of breath."

Helen gave Mel a smile. "What's HFN?" she asked for something to say.

"Home Front Network. The Elementary division of the school starts at nursery age, but we do our bit for pre-school families too. Some young mothers, living so far from their home countries, become a bit overwhelmed and need a helping hand to get organized. I'm the branch chair," Louisa said.

Helen pitied the harassed mums who found Louisa Howard on their doorstep offering to organize them. "Are you a volunteer, too?" she asked Mel.

"Mel is an absolute stalwart but we prefer volunteers who are mothers themselves. Unless you've had a baby, you can't know what you're dealing with." Louisa clasped her hand to her chest, no doubt an *I Endured Childbirth* gesture.

Mel, who'd been admiring the pavement, walked off without saying goodbye. Helen got the impression she'd heard Louisa's pronouncement before and knew she'd reached the end of it. She trudged along Dickensweg, shoulders hunched over the pushchair. An elderly man came round the corner, tipped his felt hat to her and went towards the door of number 2.

"Manfred, come and meet your new neighbour," Louisa called out to him.

If the man was irritated at being summoned, he didn't show it. He walked towards them. Although he was tall, he stooped so he didn't tower over Helen the way many German men did. He lifted his hat in greeting, revealing a smattering of liver spots at his hairline. How old was he? Seventy? Nearly eighty? He gave her a firm handshake.

"*Angenehm*. Pleased to meet you," he said.

"Where have you been this bright and early?" Louisa asked.

"Every morning I go for a healthy walk along the river." As he spoke in his thick guttural accent, he gave off the tinny fumes of alcohol.

"I'm glad you're keeping busy. Do let me know if I can do anything for you. You're always welcome here."

Welcome in his own country? What a cheek. He must have caught Helen raising her eyebrows but his face remained impassive, his own heavy eyebrows and thick moustache doing much to conceal his expression. When Louisa turned away from him, he took this as his dismissal and headed back up the street.

"He does his best, poor chap, a bit of a drinker," Louisa said. "Don't worry, he can't understand; his English is pretty ropey. Anyway, must dash if I'm to fit in five miles before lunch. Let me know when you're ready to join me. Remember what I said about the weight." She climbed back into her car.

Helen was sure Manfred had hesitated on his porch, listening. His English sounded pretty competent to her.

By noon she'd turned over the front bed. The street was silent. Sun glinted on the shutters at the Howards' house, reflecting their yellowness onto an open upstairs window at number 8. She shuddered, imagining the same colour might be projected on her own house. A crow cawed and swooped at the window. It clung onto the bottom of the frame, claws scrambling and scraping, wings flapping. Its beak banged against the glass, fighting with its own image. Pulse racing, Helen dropped her spade and backed to her front door. The battling bird lost its footing and flew off. She went back to work but, as she dug, kept looking around, unable to shake off the feeling that someone was watching, standing over her.

She was glad when it was three o'clock and busy in the street. Mothers, bikes, and children used the path by Louisa's house to cut through to the next cul-de-sac. Also striding up the road without the pushchair, at a pace which Helen previously assumed wasn't possible for her, was Mel. She turned up her path and didn't acknowledge Helen.

As well as clearing the flower bed, Helen mowed the lawn and pulled out the weeds between the paving slabs. Her shirt stuck to her underarms and her back was stiff, but she was happy-knackered; a good day's work. She sat on the step with a coffee as some teenage girls moved through Dickensweg towards the cut-through. They tapped into their mobile phones. When Chris's sports car roared up, the girls flocked around it, all their texting forgotten.

"Have you decided yet, sir?" one said, flicking her greasy side fringe behind her ear.

Chris brushed his hand through his own thick, white hair. "I'm still working on the casting."

"What are you looking for?" a tall, elegant girl asked. Helen thought she was stunning.

Apparently so did Chris. "Strong features like yours might work."

The girl lost her poise as the compliment reduced her to a giggling teenager. The girls crowded closer and all talked at once. Chris fed them with non-committal but encouraging one-liners: I have to get the balance right; everyone has a chance; I'll let you know when I screen test.

As he walked past Helen, he said: "We only have to do the back gardens, you know. School maintains the front between May and October. Another three weeks and they'd have done it for you."

She stamped the mud out of her wellingtons before going indoors. *Prick*, she stamped, *prick, prick, prick*.

***

That night her sleep was fitful. But as well as Gary's frantic tapping on the games controller through the left-hand wall, other noises invaded her dreams. The face at the Howards' back fence morphed into the crow at the Stephens's window. Her heart raced and she sat up in bed until the dream left her. When fully awake, she ached her way to the bathroom, her back and knees complaining about the gardening. The sounds from her dream were louder through the wall. She sat on the loo, releasing her stream slowly to keep it quiet. A nosy git like Chris Mowar would get off on hearing her pee. She heard a cough, a gasping, empty-out-the-lungs noise, and sloshing sounds. She pressed the flush; Chris was making too much noise next door to hear her.

5

Mel's heart raced when the Barton couple at number 1 stepped out of their front door with their pack of yapping spaniels. But they turned left onto the main street, the dogs pulling against their leads to sniff the grass verge. Mel sighed with relief and knelt by Chris's car to continue cleaning the tyres.

"*Guten Tag*," a voice said, hard and guttural.

The young man was gaunt, scruffy-looking. He must have come from the copse that ran between their cul-de-sac and the one behind. She'd seen him once before, hanging around the edge of the wood, and she'd stayed indoors until he'd walked off. Now he squatted beside her and said something in German.

She didn't know what he said, but she could smell him, taste him, tobacco. She leapt to her feet and felt her skin draw bone-white. Black dots floated in front of her eyes.

He stood up and put his hand in his jacket. She flinched. He pulled out a packet of cigarettes, opened it and offered her one. She stepped further away, her eyes darting between the man and the packet. She wished Chris was here; he'd know what to do.

35

The man shrugged, lit a cigarette for himself and pocketed the pack.

What now? She was working a cotton bud between her fingers. Her fists were tensed in front of her although she knew she'd be no match if he got nasty.

He pointed at the cotton bud. "You British won't get your wheels dirty."

A deep heat rose up her throat and she felt dizzy. Hearing him speak English made him more threatening.

He ran his fingernails over the bonnet, not quite hard enough to leave a scratch. "Expensive car," he said. "You like driving it?"

He stared at her. The cold intensity of his eyes pushed her into answering. "It's my husband's car."

But she wished she hadn't; her response only made him ask something else. "Where does he drive you?" He drummed his fingers on the bonnet and turned them into a fist when she didn't answer. "To the Rhineland?"

She watched his fist and shook her head.

"Or the Mosel or the Sauerland? Or the Black Forest or the Ahr Valley?" He fired off the place names like bullets.

She carried on shaking her head. When would this end?

"You must go somewhere."

"I …" she faltered.

His eyes narrowed and he snarled: "Or is only England good enough?"

She flushed crimson, panic rising. The man looked unstable; she'd have to say something. How was she going to get away? She couldn't run into the house; he'd see where she lived. Maybe if she'd accepted the cigarette, he'd have stalked back to the copse and left her alone. Her refusal had made him angry.

"We go to Austria, to the Grossglockner, in spring. The Whitsun holidays." She held her breath. Why had she said all that?

His eyes pierced her, made her shake. It was better when he spoke. Why was he silent?

"The neighbours. We go with the neighbours," she blurted out.

A dog barked up the street, the couple returning with the spaniels. The man darted into the trees and disappeared.

6

Helen and Gary sprawled on the sofa, replete after the roast pork they'd prepared and eaten together. She'd phoned her parents before lunch. It turned out to have been an easy, excited call. They'd booked a cruise to celebrate Dad's sixtieth in December.

She moved onto Gary's knee and kissed him. They snuggled together. He still had the soapy clean fragrance from his morning shower but some of the Sunday cooking smells had seeped into his T-shirt.

He returned the kiss and said: "I've worked out why you're in a good mood: the outdoor pool opens tomorrow."

"I can't wait. With all the free time I've got now, I can set myself a proper training schedule. I could aim for a decent time over 100 m crawl. What do you think?"

"I love it when you talk athletic." He pulled her down and manoeuvred himself on top. Contentment came over her as he unbuttoned her shirt. Things were great; she adored Gary, Germany was fine.

The doorbell chimed, and Gary dropped to the floor, struggling with his zip, "bugger" coming loud through clenched teeth.

"I'll go." She could guess who it was. She fastened her shirt but resisted the urge to scoop stray hairs into her ponytail.

Louisa. "It's the wives' breakfast at my house tomorrow. I've put you down for a dozen cookies. Aldi ones will do if you can't bake."

"I've arranged to go swimming tomorrow."

Louisa paused, and Helen savoured her hesitation. She felt like she had when her squad had won the Midlands swim championships. Triumphant.

But her victory didn't last.

"I hope you're going to the village pool. I managed to get 400 people to sign my petition and I convinced the town hall officials to open it for us."

As Helen listened to Louisa's account of how she asserted herself, she gripped the door, longing to slam it in her neighbour's community-spirited face. Eventually Louisa remembered she had more breakfast invitations to deliver and left.

"Is there nothing that bloody woman doesn't do?" Helen asked Gary. "Do all the neighbours kowtow to her?"

"I've heard her coffee mornings are fun. All the wives who don't work are happy to help. And it's thanks to her you'll get to swim tomorrow."

"I think I'll drive to Center Parcs instead."

"Don't be silly; it's thirty kilometres away. Not even someone as stubborn as you would hack off their own nose in spite."

Fiona

"Hi, it's me." I was out of breath after dashing from the languages block to get a signal.

"Shall I phone you back?" Mum said. "Save your credit."

"I've got a lecture now. I just wanted to tell you something." I cradled my mobile under my chin and got out my lit folder. "Do you remember that extended essay I had to write when I was in Lyons?"

"I think you mentioned it. Eight thousand words, wasn't it?"

"That's the one," I said, almost dropping the folder in my excitement to get my words out. "I got a First for it."

"That's brilliant."

I propped the folder against the wall. "Listen to what my tutor said: 'This is one of the best undergraduate analyses I've read. I have high hopes for your results this year.' Can I tell Dad now?"

"He's having a nap, love, but I'll tell him later."

"Is he all right?" I couldn't keep the alarm out of my voice. He'd slept in the daytime during his treatment. But he was better now, wasn't he?

"Of course. He's just taking it easy."

"If that's all it is …"

"Definitely. Stop worrying. So are you celebrating in the uni bar tonight?"

"I don't think I've got time." I still had a business case study to finish and some vocab to learn.

"You can give yourself one night off."

"I suppose I could go to the George." Liz and Cheryl preferred the pub to the uni bar. I tagged along last week but left when the engineering lads moved in for a flirt. I had an essay to write anyway.

"Go on, love," Mum said, "you never know, you might meet the man of your dreams."

7

Monday, 3 May

Cold pinched Helen's arms and thighs as she stepped out of the changing room into the open air. It turned to tingling, comforting heat as she slid into the water. She dropped under the surface and set off at a gentle crawl.

It felt like home.

She quickened her stroke, her hands cutting deep through the water. Of course, Gary had been right to insist she came to this pool, but he'd called her silly and stubborn. He'd never said that to her before, not even when she wanted to stay in England. Their marriage, so serene during the weekends they spent in Shrewsbury, was changing. She looked up at the clock by the exit. The last 200 metres were not far off her personal best.

The exertions of the early lengths caught up with her and she slowed her pace. There was no sign of Louisa's 400 petition signatories and they couldn't all be at the wives' breakfast; even Louisa's catering had its limits. On the far side of the pool was an elderly couple, floating from one end to the other, the full 50 metres, at a rate too slow to be classed as swimming. The woman was on her front with her flowery swimming cap so high out of the water she was almost standing up. Her husband was on his back, also head high, as if sitting in a favourite armchair.

The only other swimmer was a man who, with the whole pool to swim in, chose to carve out lengths a mere three feet away. He was constantly in her field of vision, keeping pace. Just like Louisa – wherever she turned, she found her. Louisa must have sent her envoy to the pool to stalk her. She smiled to herself, knowing how ridiculous she was being. She upped her speed to shake him off but was surprised he didn't stay with her for a second length. She slowed down, despite all her competitive training telling her not to, and finished the length at a leisurely rate.

When she looked back, he set off from the far end swimming butterfly. His technique was good: arms sweeping wide and low, allowing his shoulders to clear the water, conserving energy. He was veering to the left, towards Helen, as his stronger arm pushed deeper. She should move out of his way but she was annoyed at the invasion of her space and stayed put. His left arm reached the wall about six inches from her shoulder.

"*Entschuldigung*," he said, lifting his goggles. "*Mein Fehler*."

"I don't speak German," she replied although she was pretty sure his unfamiliar words were an apology.

His shoulders stiffened. "You are from the international school." It sounded like an accusation. He climbed out of the water and slipped on the flip-flops he'd left on the poolside.

He walked towards the shower on the grass area behind the pool. Tall and rangy. In swimming trunks his arms and chest were sleek with good muscle definition. In clothes he would appear skinny. How old was he – 21, 22? He'd fill out with age. He turned around in the shower and saw her looking. She blushed. He came back and squatted on the poolside behind her. "You are from the school," he said again.

"I've just arrived from England," she conceded.

His shoulders relaxed. "So you are new. Do you like it?"

"I'm looking forward to getting to know Germany."

"Germany. But not the school?" He shook his head. "It's okay you mustn't explain. I work there also, IT support, but I live here in the village. My name is Sascha Jakobsen." He had an accent, although he pronounced "village" with a v rather than the w favoured by most Germans trying out the English word.

He pushed the wet fringe out of his eyes. A tiny wave of something unexpected rippled through Helen's body. He was waiting for her to introduce herself but to talk for longer would stop them being strangers and she sensed danger in that.

"Bye then," she said, preparing to glide away.

"*Tschüs*," Sascha said. He walked towards the changing room.

Helen launched both arms over the water and dolphin-kicked her legs. He wasn't the only one who could swim butterfly. She wondered whether he was watching her but told herself to stop.

8

When Gisela went to get the second bottle of *Sekt* from the kitchen, she saw Sascha on the balcony. He was hanging out his trunks and towel. It wasn't that long ago he would have left them in his bag on the floor, expecting that his washing would reappear clean and dry on his bed. But he no longer expected that of his mother; he no longer expected much of her at all.

He turned round, and she darted into the lounge. With the first bottle already inside her, she had to grab the doorframe to keep herself upright. She fell into an armchair and hid the new bottle under a cushion. She lit a cigarette and inhaled so hard that she hacked up phlegm.

He put his head round the door on the way to his bedroom. "Hallo, Mama."

Gisela coughed again, for longer this time. The two of them inhabited the same apartment but different worlds. He never greeted her, so why now?

She felt for the neck of the bottle under the cushion. Her mouth was so parched it hurt but she couldn't open the *Sekt* because he'd hear the cork pop. She crept over to the *Schrank* wall unit and eased out the bottom drawer. *Verdammt!* The vodka wasn't there and neither were the miniature fire water bottles she'd bought at Lidl. Sascha! She should hammer on his door and demand an explanation. I'm the parent here. But when she heard his door open, she jammed the *Schrank* drawer half shut.

"I'll make coffee," he said, coming in to help her with the drawer. He slid it back into place and left the room, whistling.

She slumped into her chair. *Heilige Maria Mutter Gottes* (Holy Mary Mother of God), since when did this scowling young man whistle? Judging by the wet swimming things, the *Freibad* must have opened for the season. Perhaps he was exhilarated after exercising in the fresh air. Good. He spent too much time brooding in his bedroom or in the car.

He came back into the room, smiling, and she felt a pang of fear. "Have you been to the school?" she asked.

His face hardened. "Why would I go there?"

"I just thought …"

"What did you just think?"

"Nothing. How was your swim?"

"I met a woman."

"Oh?" There'd been no one since Julia, since he'd cancelled dates with her to park outside the metal fence of the Niers International School instead.

His face remained hard but he said: "She'll be useful, maybe open doors for me."

9

Helen got home on a high after the swim, her blood buzzing with exercise hormones. And then the drudgery of her new life settled on her shoulders. She spent the afternoon signing up at the school library. She had trouble tracking it down; for all its solid frontage, the school had camouflaged its library in a Portakabin at the back of the campus. Eighties temporary units neglected into permanence.

She found the Elementary School's second-hand uniform shop first and went in to ask for directions. Sabine, the school nurse, was working behind the counter. Helen laughed and asked her if she did every job in the school.

"I'm usually only here on Friday. It should be the head's wife's shift today but she has a breakfast party. Do you know Louisa?"

Helen's whole face clenched. Of course, Louisa volunteered in the school shop. She thanked God that the wives' breakfast had given her a narrow escape.

"I know her slightly," she said. She turned to leave but noticed a pretty velvet top hanging from the rails.

"Try it on," Sabine said. "We don't just sell second-hand uniforms, we have clothes for everyone. It was Louisa's idea."

Helen dropped the blouse sleeve as if it was on fire.

47

When she finally found the library, the assistant told her she had to get her membership form signed by her husband before she could borrow any books. "You're his dependant. School rules." Helen stuffed the form in her pocket and stormed outside, silently vowing to order her books from Amazon.

"I'll come to yours at eight." A voice she recognized was coming from the other side of the Portakabin.

Damian Howard. For once she'd be pleased to see a neighbour, this one in particular. As head teacher, he could make the stupid library assistant give her a ticket. But she stayed out of sight when she realized he was on the phone.

"I can only stay an hour ... Shelly, Sweetheart, please. It's better than nothing ... You know I do. I can't wait ..." His voice was getting nearer.

She moved away briskly in case he came round the corner. Something told her Shelly Sweetheart wasn't a pet name for Louisa.

***

Later, back at home, she wanted to plant up the front flower bed with the marigolds she'd bought from Aldi but, when she peered out of the kitchen window to check the street was clear of nosy neighbours, she saw Damian and Chris in conversation by Chris's car.

There wasn't a day that went by when Chris, or Mel, didn't polish the sport car's paintwork. A wave of irritation came over Helen: Gary was still at school whereas Chris was long since home.

And Damian was home too. Head teacher and family man, who made private calls in work time. She'd wait until he'd gone back to his side of the road. The thought of making social chit-chat with him made her sick.

But she stayed at her window, watching. Damian faced Chris, his fists clenching while Chris ignored him in favour of washing the car. Helen was turning into a curtain twitcher and she hated herself for it. But she was fascinated. There was no sign of the peace and harmony that Gary swore reigned supreme in Dickensweg. She thought for a minute that Damian was going to thump Chris. Hating herself even more, she opened the window to listen.

"What about it?" Damian snapped.

"I want to make some changes." Chris was still polishing the car.

"You bastard," Damian said and walked away.

"Don't forget I've got the Chateau Petrus at eight," Chris called after him.

Helen pulled back from the window. She'd heard of Chateau Petrus. It was a wine that cost over five hundred pounds a bottle. Where did Chris get the money for expensive plonk? And why offer to drink it with a man he'd just argued with? She wished she'd opened the window sooner.

When Chris had gone indoors, she took her box of plants to the flower bed under the kitchen window. As soon as she knelt down and turned the soil with her trowel, a feeling of comfort came over her. She was deriving as much pleasure from gardening as she did from swimming. But the pool had the advantage of being five miles from Dickensweg.

"Hi, Helen" Louisa's voice said above her.

Helen jumped. The woman could join the SAS with those ambush skills. She gouged a deeper hole in the soil.

"I should have told you about the garden centre in Dortmannhausen," Louisa said. "So much better than the bargain packs the supermarkets do. I stocked up two weeks ago."

"And you've been hardening them off ever since."

Louisa hesitated, as if unsure whether Helen intended an insult or a compliment.

Before Louisa could re-start, Mel came out of her house, looking like Andy Pandy. Helen couldn't think beyond the ancient TV puppet's romper suit that was a dead ringer for the blue and white thing Mel was wearing.

"Murdo wants his Mr Tumble boxers for school tomorrow. Will you have my load ready tonight?" Louisa called out.

Mel nodded and came across to Helen, "Have you got any washing or ironing?" It was the first time Helen had heard her volunteer a question. "You will have to pay me but I'm quick."

The last thing Helen wanted was a neighbour rummaging through her washing, but at least Mel had the gumption to run her own business. And going back inside to find washing would give Helen an excuse to get away from Louisa.

She told Mel she had some of Gary's shirts to iron. "Come in the house and I'll get them."

"I'll wait here."

"Don't be silly. Come in and I'll show you what needs doing."

Mel hesitated but Louisa took her arm. "In you go, Mel. Helen doesn't want her dirty laundry aired in public."

Helen was prepared to ignore the double meaning but anger rose inside her when Louisa followed them into the house uninvited. She went upstairs to find the shirts. When she came back down, Mel was peering into the drawers of the hall cabinet and Louisa was looking on. Mel snatched the laundry from Helen and made for the door.

10

The water rippled as Helen lowered herself into it, the misty atmosphere absorbing her splash. She was tempted to float there like the old couple the day before, to clear her mind. But she couldn't shake off the sticking, spiky thoughts she had about her neighbours. She stretched into a steady crawl, upping the pace after two lengths.

What the hell was going on last night? Some kind of Stepford Wives' pantomime? Mel was certainly dressed for comedy. And the blatant way she rifled through Helen's hall, was that some kind of prank with Helen as the butt of the joke? She jabbed her hand deep below the surface, challenging the water's resistance. But the water won and broke the rhythm of her stroke.

Or was Mel the stooge? It was more likely that Louisa rather than Mel wanted to nose around. Was the whole "have you got any ironing" set-piece a scam masterminded by Louisa? Helen rocked from side to side as she tried to get control of her arm pulls. There was something not right about that woman, about both women. She wouldn't be giving Mel ironing again however well she did it. And it wasn't any wonder Damian was playing away. Louisa must be hard to live with.

Creepy Chris must know what Damian was up to. Helen slowed her leg kicks to give her arms time to settle. That would explain Damian's angry body language by Chris's car last night. Maybe he'd caught Damian on his phone to Shelly Sweetheart like Helen had. Was he threatening to tell Louisa?

The lot of them had been in their expat bubble so long they'd forgotten how normal neighbours behaved. She would never become like them. Thank God she had this pool to escape to. She pushed her hand down and this time hit the catch point. The water worked with her and her rhythm came back. She kicked hard and stepped up the pace. She settled into a twenty-length speed swim.

She was resting when the young man – Sascha – got in beside her. Already flushed from her swim, her face got even hotter.

"How many laps have you made?" he asked, fixing his goggles on his forehead.

She knew her distances to within five metres but she couldn't think. "I've … just started."

He took off his goggles and fiddled with the strap. "We could make a few laps together."

Her gut told her to decline and glide away; to accept would land her in the heat of something she couldn't control. But, before she answered, he said: "I'll get the *Schwimmbretter*. I don't know the name in English."

He pulled his lean body up onto the poolside and headed over to the cage of swimming floats. A baby brother, nothing more.

She matched him over several lengths but, when they sprinted the final four, she hadn't raced so hard in months and thought blood would burst through her eardrums. She gulped for breath and put her head down for the last push. When her fingertips reached the wall, he was already standing up.

"*Unentschieden,*" he panted. "We both won."

"A draw? How chivalrous," she said, heart racing.

"*Schiffalrus?*"

"It doesn't matter. Let's swim."

Their last set degenerated into a leisurely breaststroke as they lifted their heads to recapture the air that racing had taken out of them. He told her he'd captained the school swim squad. She played down her own swimming career, saying she'd won the odd race now and again. For the first time in weeks she didn't feel the need to assert her capabilities. Her companion accepted her as an equal. Condescending Louisa and belittling Chris faded out of her mind and she relaxed.

***

Sascha was waiting by her car when she came out to the car park. They'd said their goodbyes poolside. A chill crossed her shoulders and she fastened her jacket. Why was he still here?

"Are you going back to school?" he said. "The office needs me in work. It will save much time if you drive me there."

A lift to a stranger? She hesitated. She'd enjoyed their swim but it had to end there. She could lie, say it wasn't her car but Gary's England footie badge on the windscreen would give her away.

"I'm not going straight home," she said.

"Of course. You don't know me. I shouldn't ask." He tucked a strand of wet hair behind his ear. The gesture was cute, innocent. She reminded herself he was just a boy. And he worked at the school like Gary. He was one of them. There'd be no harm in giving him a lift.

She climbed in the driver's seat and leaned over to open the door for him. She immediately regretted her decision. Burnt tobacco invaded the air. Drawn cheekbones, Adam's apple, zip-up jumper bobbled with age, her passenger looked spare and eager. He didn't belong in Gary's car.

She kept her eyes dead ahead as she set off, feeling like a learner driver on the German highway. She hadn't driven with a passenger apart from Gary since she arrived. She gripped the steering wheel with both hands. The pool was beyond the village and there were wheat fields on both sides. She imagined Sascha studying every ear of corn as she crawled past. When the silence grew too awkward she asked him how long he'd worked at the school.

For a moment he didn't answer, then he said: "How are you finding it? Living there?"

Her foot slipped on the pedal. The needle on the speedometer nudged up. She found a sort of answer. "Fine. I've cleared the front garden, but there's competition in our road. One woman's managed to trail a whopping great wisteria round her door."

"Wisteria," he mouthed.

"It's a purple climbing flower that sort of hangs …"

"I know what it is." His shoulders stiffened. Then, aware of her looking, he relaxed into his seat.

She drove the rest of the way in nervous silence.

They reached the turning for the school and she drove past the community noticeboard. For once not defaced by graffiti, there was a poster for half-term activities. Gary would have a week off school so they could go away. He was always talking about the lakes in Southern Germany. Time for themselves. Away from Dickensweg. She glanced at her passenger. Away from everything.

She drew up to the traffic lights and signalled right for the school campus.

"Wait," Sascha said. "I want to see the garden you told me about, with the wisteria."

Offering this man a lift to work was one thing, but driving a complete stranger past her house was something else. As the lights changed, she flicked her indicator to the left and decided she would drop him outside Louisa's garden. She would remember another errand and ask him to walk to his office. Drive off without him ever finding out which house was hers.

"So you live at number 5," he said as they went past the mown lawn and cleared flower bed that betrayed which garden had enjoyed her attention. But he seemed to lose interest in her answer. His eyes fixed on the house at the end. He got out of the car, walked up the path to Number Ten and cupped one of the wisteria blooms in his hand.

Helen went after him. "I'm not sure the owners would like that."

"She will get angry."

"She? Do you know her?"

He let go of the wisteria petals and moved back to join her on the path. He took out a cigarette.

Louisa's front door flew open. "What the hell are you doing? Get away from here. Now."

Helen gasped. She'd been on the receiving end of Louisa's bossiness before but this was fury. Then she realized that the woman's rage was aimed at Sascha.

"This is my country," Sascha said. His voice sounded calm but his hands trembled as he brought his lighter up to his cigarette.

"You've got three seconds to get out of here then I'm calling the police. They'll arrest you for unlawful access," Louisa said.

"How is it unlawful?" He aimed a ring of smoke in Louisa's direction. "Helen brought me here."

"*You*. I welcomed you into our street and this is how you repay me."

Helen's limbs twitched as Louisa's anger turned on her.

Sascha blew another smoke ring towards Louisa. The veins in his neck started to bulge.

"Get out of here," she shouted.

He clenched his fists, and for a moment Helen feared he'd attack Louisa, but he threw the cigarette into one of the shrubs and disappeared up the cut-through.

"What was that about?" Helen asked, but Louisa, murderous below her make-up, stared her down. She felt hollow and shaky and was relieved when the woman stormed back inside and shut her door, causing the wisteria trellis to quiver.

11

Gisela squatted with the dustpan and brush, and overbalanced. She put her hand down and felt a pricking sensation somewhere at the end of her arm. She ignored it and focused on sweeping up the broken glass. Her heart raced when the door opened and, like a child, she braced herself for the reprimand.

It came quickly. "*Verdammt*! *Schon wieder*! And you've cut yourself. Come and sit here." Sascha reached into the First Aid cupboard.

He grimaced as he tied a bandage around her hand. His mouth was clamped shut and his eyes were angry. Her head thumped with alcohol and shame. It should be her role to tend the family wounds. What a *scheiß* job she'd made of that. Their seeping scars could never heal.

She slurred. "How was your swim? Did you see your girl?"

He tore the end of the bandage. "Leave it alone," he growled.

12

"What the hell were you thinking?" Gary said when Helen broached the subject that evening. "Didn't your mother tell you not to talk to strangers?"

His coldness shocked her. She thought after a meal and a glass of wine he'd listen. But he sounded as mad as Louisa.

"He said he worked at the school, in IT."

"Come on, Helen. If he'd said he was the deputy head would you have believed him?"

"I would expect Louisa to say something like that, not you."

"I'm just scared for you, Helen."

"Scared?"

He shrank away. "I mean concerned."

She folded her arms. "I'm a big girl, I can take care of myself. And he was harmless."

"Don't be stupid, Helen. You can't just trust people. He could have done anything. Any man can …" His voice tailed off. "Some men."

"Who is he anyway? What's he done to get you and Louisa so paranoid?"

Gary looked away again. "I don't know him."

He had replied too quickly. Was he lying?

Helen turned towards the hall. "I'll go and ask Louisa."

Gary grabbed her arm. "Don't." His fingers were digging in. He realized and let go. "Sorry, I didn't mean … It's probably best if you give Louisa some space for a while."

"So tell me why that man sent her into meltdown?"

"It sounds like the same man who trashed her garden a few months ago. He pulled up all the plants and smashed the fountain in the pond. He was about to hack down the wisteria in the front when they came home. It cost Damian a fortune to put it right."

She thought of the first time Sascha had spoken to her, blunt and accusing when he realized she was English. She could see that anger turned on a British garden. "Did they call the police?"

"Damian told him to get lost. As far as I know he hasn't returned until today, although I think I saw him parked up outside school once."

The face she saw at the Howards' fence, was that Sascha? She ought to have told Gary but it seemed a bit late to mention it. "Will they call the police now he's come back?"

"No idea." He looked away.

He was doing it again, shutting her out. She was sick of him withholding things. "I'll ask Sascha when I see him at the pool," she said.

"God, Helen, you know his name? You need to keep away from him. You can't go there after this. He might be dangerous."

"I was alone in the car with him and he was fine until we got to Number Ten. Whatever his quarrel with the Howards, it doesn't involve me."

"Of course it involves you. You're part of this community whether you like it or not. We owe it to our neighbours to show some solidarity."

He sounded like Louisa again. Helen was surrounded by the neighbourhood mafia and Gary was doing his best to join it. Her resentment boiled over. "Why don't you show me some solidarity?

Don't you dare take the pool away. I'm bored brainless here. You've taken everything else. My career, my house, my swim squad." She broke down and sobbed.

Gary rested an arm around her shoulders. "I'm sorry. I know it's been hard for you to give up your career. But it's not forever. Why don't you ask Damian about the supply list for teachers?"

She shook off his arm. "How nicely do you want me to ask Damian Howard? How high up the waiting list do you want me to go?" She looked him in the eye. Surely he knew about his head teacher's extracurricular antics. His face hardened, then he nodded. An unspoken understanding passed between them.

He pulled her towards him and she felt his lips on her hairline. "I shouldn't have said that about the pool. It's up to you."

She wanted to stay mad at him despite the warmth of his breath through her hair. She forced herself not to respond.

He held her at arm's length. His fingers played on her shoulders, soft and conciliatory. "I want you to be happy."

"I want that for both of us," she said. She kissed him.

She felt him relax, let out a sigh. He must be as relieved as she was that the squall had passed.

"I was going to tell you about something that you might like, but it can wait," he said.

"What? Tell me." She suddenly thought of half-term. Perhaps he was going to surprise her with a trip. She still hadn't mentioned her idea of visiting the German lakes, maybe he'd come up with the same thing.

But he looked away. He was still bloody doing it.

"Just tell me, Gary."

He sighed again but didn't look at her. "The Elementary School runs an after-school swim club. They need more volunteer teachers."

It wasn't what she was expecting, but it was still good news. "That's amazing. How do I sign up?"

"It's not coaching and the kids are beginners mostly."

It sounded like a lifeline. She'd be teaching again.

"So you're interested then? You'll give them a call? No backing out?"

"Why would I want to back out?"

He fetched his briefcase, handed her the school newsletter and studied her face.

She read the headline: *Swim Club Needs Helpers*. Below it was a colour photograph. She recognized the perfect chestnut hair before she read the caption: *Club Chair Louisa Howard*. She threw the newsletter at him.

Fiona

I offered to get the first round while Liz and Cheryl hunted down an empty table.

I hovered at the back of the bar scrum, reckoning on a fifteen-minute wait and wishing I had sharper elbows. When someone got served, a gap opened and the crowd regrouped. My arm bumped against the tall man next to me.

He smiled down. "Is it always like this?" he said.

"I've only been once before so I don't know."

"It's my first time," he said, taking a £20 note out of his pocket and waving it at the bar staff. He must have landed in this undergraduate watering hole by mistake. I concluded it would be his last visit too.

"Hello, can you serve me, please?" he called out when a harassed-looking barmaid came within range.

It was worth a try but all the staff were feigning deafness and not catching anyone's eye. But to my surprise the girl looked up and took the money from his outstretched hand.

He turned to me. "What's your order?" It was kind of him to save me queuing longer.

When the barmaid passed over the tray of drinks, she giggled and gave him a broad smile. He thanked her and refused to let me pay him back. "Where are you sitting?"

I pointed to where Cheryl and Liz had found the last free booth. When he put the drinks on our table, the girls shuffled along to make room for both of us. They must have thought I'd picked him up. I stayed standing and thanked him for the drinks. A blush grew on my neck and face. What must he think of three little girls assuming he'd be interested in one of them? But it was the second surprise of the evening: he sat down next to Cheryl and asked her name.

When I sat opposite him, he turned to me. "Where do you usually drink, then, if not here?"

"Union bar," I said quickly. I didn't want him to know this was a rare outing for me.

"I'm glad you came here tonight," he said.

I smiled and happily melted into my drink. He liked me, didn't he? I asked him his name.

He grinned. "You can call me Shep." But then he leant over to Liz and asked her about her course.

A bubble of disappointment rose and popped inside me but I made a show of flicking my hair behind my ear, telling myself there were plenty more postgraduates in the sea. He had to be a postgraduate; he was definitely older than us.

When Liz told him we were on the same course, he turned to me. "Have you done a sandwich year in France yet?"

I told him about Lyons, but it was like playing ping-pong. His attention moved back and forth between Liz and me. Then he looked at Cheryl, and she launched into a monologue about her set books. His eyes flicked to me. I waited. It was as if he had an invisible thread that could draw me wherever he wanted.

My patience was rewarded. "Do you miss Lyons?" he asked. When had any boy asked Liz or Cheryl an intelligent question like that? Shep was treating me like a grown-up.

I paused, deliberating on how to be intelligent back. "On the one hand, I miss the opportunity to speak French. But, on the other, it's time to finish my degree and go out into the wider world," I said, sounding like a GCSE essay.

"You're wise," he said, nodding. "You've got your head screwed on." He picked up his glass, and I admired his hands. He was the only drinker with well-manicured nails, and an ironed shirt. I asked him about his course.

His expression grew serious. "I'm not a student."

Had I blown it? Miskeyed the conversation? What would a grown-up do now? "What's your job?" I asked.

"Civil servant."

What now? Could I ask what that meant?

"My dad's in the civil service," Liz called down the table. "What branch are you?"

"I'm a shepherd," he said.

Liz laughed and made a joke about his name. As we listened to her account of her dad's admin job, Shep whispered to me: "I'll explain what I do later."

I blushed; there was going to be a later.

Two engineering students stopped at our table, and Liz and Cheryl went into all-out flirt mode. My eyes strayed to Shep. Every time one of the others spoke, he listened intently and nodded. He had the most beautiful eyes and he trained them on whoever was speaking. I sighed, feeling jealous, and tried to look away. But he caught me staring.

Eventually the girls went to the bar with the engineers. It was just Shep and me at the table.

"Was it hard to find a flat when you came back from France?" he asked.

"I'm in a student hall," I said and realized that made me sound like a baby who couldn't live on her own. "But it's Moser Hall. There are only third years on the first floor. And fourth years, like me."

"Let me get us another drink," he said. He found his way through the crowd to his friendly barmaid. Liz, Cheryl, and the boys were still queuing and looked peeved at his success. I gave them a thumbs up and we all laughed.

"Did you miss home when you were in Lyons?" he said when he returned with my wine.

"My father was ill. It was hard not being there."

His face was full of concern. "But things are fine now?"

I shrugged, blinking back tears. "I think so but you know how it is with cancer."

"You're a caring woman, Fiona." He rested his hand on mine.

I think I smiled. I meant to, but how was I supposed to function after he did that? Although a million watts of power surged through me, I didn't move my hand away. My blood thundered round my body, but I managed to sit still. Two grown-ups together in companionable silence. A couple.

He fetched out his phone. "I've got to read this."

I watched his face as he looked at the text. When his expression didn't change, it gave me hope that it wasn't important. But he put the phone away and said he'd been called into work. He gave a tight smile that showed how annoyed he was. "Will you be here next Friday?"

"I might be," I said. Grown-ups played it cool.

13

Helen expected to have trouble getting into the school campus out of hours, but Klaus, the security guard, opened the gate and waved her through from his sentry box. He must have recognized Gary's car. He didn't look surprised to see a woman driving it. Did he know Gary's wife was living here now? Probably. She stiffened and pressed the accelerator; the entire school knew her business.

She parked in the main car park and took the path round the science block. She knew where the pool was as she'd found it when she was looking for the library. But she would have located it anyway; the chlorine smell was a guiding beacon. It was a favourite smell. Home. She smiled and broke into a jog.

The door into the pool foyer was open. She stepped in and embraced the heat. There was no one about but she followed voices to a group changing room and went in.

"Come and sit anywhere, Helen. We're casual here," Louisa said, bestowing her with a smile that lengthened on the word "casual".

Helen waited for two young men to move along the bench to

make room for her. In pressed polo shirts and shorts, they resembled army physical training instructors, all cropped hair and muscles. The seat was lower than she judged so she made a crash landing and her handbag slammed into her hip. No one noticed because they were looking at Louisa.

"I'm sure you know everyone," Louisa said to her.

The only familiar face was Mel Mowar's. Mel a swimming teacher? She didn't see that one coming, but it fitted Mel's default position at Louisa's right-hand side.

Helen scanned the other faces, looking for identifying marks, a habit she picked up as a school teacher. To avoid the embarrassment of not recognizing a pupil or a parent in the street, she made sure their features were imprinted on her memory. It was going to be much harder to memorize this lot with no distinctive clothing style to go on. Louisa was the only one not in a white polo shirt. Hers was coral pink and it enhanced her skin tone.

Sweat pooled at Helen's armpits. Hoping there'd be a chance for a few lengths in the school pool after the meeting and before the lessons started, she'd put her swimsuit on underneath her tracksuit. The row with Gary had continued until they both lost interest and saw how stupid it was. As part of their passionate making up, she'd agreed to stay away from the open-air pool, so she was now in dire need of a substitute swim. It hadn't been a difficult compromise to make in the end because she was in no mood to face Sascha again. She couldn't care less about his feud with Louisa – if anything that lifted him higher in her estimations – but she'd trusted him and he'd taken her for a mug. She caved in about the after-school swim club too. Gary had her interests at heart and persuaded her to go whatever her view of the chairwoman.

"You need to put in your DTS claims to FD," Louisa was saying.

Helen took a deep breath. Acronyms, it was like being pelted by a typewriter. She felt like a complete outsider. It was another

Aldi moment – whenever she ventured out to shop in Dortmannhausen village, she felt an acute sense of foreignness. She'd only ever felt alien once before moving to Germany and that was on a student holiday in Sri Lanka where the people had stared and smiled, and some had asked to have their photo taken with her. It had been a good-natured curiosity and she went home feeling exotic and beautiful. But being foreign in Germany meant awkward supermarket visits where unsmiling cashiers scanned her shopping, rang up her bill and had her change ready before she'd even opened her purse. And now this meeting, on the supposedly home territory of Gary's school, was pocked with jargon she didn't understand.

"Let's move on to Item 4: Paired Teaching," Louisa said.

Helen checked her watch. Item 4, the bloody woman had started the meeting without her.

The bloody woman was still speaking. "Now this is a new initiative of mine. Darren. I assume you're working with John?"

The man next to Helen nodded.

"And I'm with Kate." Louisa paused, her gaze lingering on Helen.

Helen, partnerless, looked down, pulling her sleeves over her hands, feeling like a teenager picked on by the mean girl. Then a shoot of defiance grew in her. "Mel, have you got a partner yet?" she said, pushing a tone of confidence into her question which she didn't feel.

Mel flushed. "I …"

"Do you want to work with me?" Helen said before Louisa could intervene.

Mel smiled, blushing even redder. Helen smiled back, trying to hide the smugness of her victory over Louisa. This was more like her old self – assertive; inventive; no problem too large; no petty-minded, coral pink chairwoman too small.

But her triumph was short-lived. Louisa trumped her. "Mel's the changing room monitor. She's here to take the minutes." Mel picked up her pen obediently. "But you won't need a partner, Helen, while you're observing classes."

"Observing? I've got several years' experience. I don't think ..."

"Not here you haven't." Louisa tapped the edge of her papers against her knee to straighten them out.

"But you're desperate for teachers. I read the newsletter. Some of you are having to double up classes. What do the rest of you ...?" Helen's voice trailed off; no one was looking at her. She'd been the head coach of the most successful junior squad in the West Midlands but here in this stupid drain of a swimming pool, she was an invisible nobody in over-heavy sports kit. Roll on half-term; she was getting the hell out.

14

Thursday, 6 May

Helen stood on the doorstep to see Gary off to work. Her smile made her face ache; she was turning into a proper housewife. Gary's mobile rang on the hall table. The screen said: *Steve C calling*. She grabbed the phone and caught up with him by the car, but Gary cancelled the call.

"Not important then?" she asked.

"It's just some insurance guy who rings me now and again," he said, starting the engine. "I'm surprised he bothers; I never buy anything." He drove off, waving his arm out of the window.

Helen waved until he disappeared round the corner, and she thought it was strange that he'd added an insurance salesman to his list of contacts. But then he was a sociable man with twice as many Facebook friends as she had.

She darted away from the kitchen window when Louisa came across the road. She was carrying a file of papers. The woman lived her life in other people's houses. What was it this time: Parents' Association agendas for Audrey Garcia, the American teacher at number 3; spaniel-masking aromatherapy brochures for Karola Barton at number 1; or corrections to the swim club minutes for Mel at number 7?

She cursed herself for hiding – so what if Louisa saw her? She was in her own home. Louisa didn't control everything; the swim class last night proved that. Louisa had deposited her with the instructor called John, insisting that she couldn't possibly be let loose with a group of her own until she'd been "assessed". But John had different ideas and gave her five children out of his class of twelve to teach front crawl.

"You'll warm to Louisa in the end," he said.

"How long will that take?"

"Until the Christmas social. She holds it at her house. All the booze you can drink. Best club chair I've ever worked for."

The swimming class had been an excitable bunch of 7 year olds. She recognized one of them as the dark-haired boy from number 6, the house opposite hers. Afterwards his parents introduced themselves in the foyer.

"My name is Dimitris and my wife is Maria. I am an exchange teacher from Greece. I normally run the history department at a school in Athens."

Helen smiled. "You speak excellent English and I think your son must do too; he understood his swimming lesson."

"Alexandros learns quickly. Only my wife has no chance to learn."

"I'm sure she'll pick it up." An idea occurred to Helen. "I could help. I'm a teacher too but I'm not working at the moment."

"You would do that for Maria? I can pay you."

"I'm sure we can work something out."

Dimitris spoke rapidly to his wife. She beamed and took Helen's hand.

She'd driven home knowing she'd turned a corner in her frame of mind. The swimming lesson and the prospect of teaching English made her feel fulfilled. Her contentment lasted into the night as she made love with Gary.

She peered through her kitchen window again but could no longer see Louisa. She must have gone into Mel's. If the lessons with Maria worked out, she could offer something similar to local German people. She smiled as more warm feelings of usefulness came over her.

The doorbell had a way of shrieking whenever Louisa pressed it. Helen stood still. She'd ignore it, pretend to be out. But she was curious about the paperwork Louisa was carrying. A teeny bit of her ego wondered if the visit was to do with the swim club. John must have reported back how well the newcomer had done and Louisa was calling to offer her more classes. She answered the door.

"I hear you intend to teach English. Are you qualified?" Louisa said, stepping inside without a greeting.

"I was head of PE at my last school," Helen said and savoured the surprise on Louisa's face.

But it didn't last. "The Niers School is clamping down on people who set up businesses for which they aren't trained."

"It's hardly a business; I'm helping a neighbour." Helen balled her fists. If Louisa thought she was the job police, she could think again.

"Well, I've brought some brochures about TESOL courses anyway," Louisa said. "And while I'm here I can collect your balance."

"Balance?"

"The skiing trip payment. Surely Gary mentioned it? I organize a trip to Austria. It's an annual event during half-term."

The leaflets shook in Helen's hand. Half-term. Another prison door slammed shut behind her. But who the hell went skiing in May? Didn't people need snow or was one look from Louisa enough to freeze rain?

"First I've heard of it, and I don't remember Gary mentioning it last year so I don't think—"

"He excused himself last year to visit you."

Helen felt annoyed and proud at the same time. Annoyed with Louisa's insinuation that Gary needed permission to drop out, but proud that he had the balls to stand up to the Dickensweg mafia.

"In that case, I can't see him fancying it this year either," she said.

"Oh dear, have I ruined the surprise? He's already paid the deposit."

***

She knew she was thrashing, using far more energy than her progress through the water warranted, but there was rage in her limbs and she wanted it out. How could he think of booking a holiday without consulting her? Is that the way their marriage would roll: he made the decisions and she did as she was told? Well, he could forget it. She'd show him and start by returning to this pool despite her promise.

Half a dozen other swimmers were there, word having got round that the pool had opened for the season. Disapproving eyes bored into her as she caused the water to splash and chop. She smashed her wrist against the side, having misjudged her finish. She stood up as the pain throbbed through her arm, adding more fuel to her fury. She pushed off again, narrowly missing a woman who drifted over on her back. She managed a lopsided arm pull with her throbbing hand and speared the water with her good one.

It hadn't only been the ruddy ski trip that made her mad. Top honours had gone to the tiny white business card that slipped out of the teaching leaflets when she flung them across her hall. *Louisa Howard, RELATE Counsellor* and on the back she'd written: *Call me if you need to talk.*

She cleared her goggles but they were misted with tears. That poisonous woman, who tried to tell her what to wear, when to exercise, how to teach, was now saying her marriage was in trouble. How dare she when her own husband was unfaithful?

What could Louisa have seen to make her think it? The sleepless nights? The arguments? Louisa couldn't know about them. They were nothing. She and Gary were solid. She gripped the goggles with both hands and twisted them. The action hurt because of her bruised wrist but she kept on twisting, squeezing, wringing. If it meant losing the deposit, so what? No way were they spending half-term with Louisa as she scrutinized their marriage.

A figure dived in beside her, making her drop the goggles. Sascha. How dare he come near her? Another one she couldn't trust.

"Why did you lie to me?" she demanded when he resurfaced. "Why are you hounding my neighbours?" She rubbed her throbbing hand and fought off the urge to slap it against his face.

He ducked under to retrieve her goggles. When he came up she shouted, "Give me those."

The elderly swimmer glared at her and paddled away.

Sascha hooked the goggles round his finger. "Louisa Howard is a hard woman, isn't she?" He offered them to her but, as she took them, he snatched them back. "And her husband – what do you know about him?"

She tugged at the strap on the goggles with her good hand.

He tightened his grip and said: "He's dangerous." His wet eyelashes had clumped in peaks making his expression deranged.

The menace in his voice made her shudder. She tugged at her goggles, but he yanked them harder and pulled her towards him. She felt his breath on her shoulder. "You know what he's like, don't you?" he hissed.

He gave one last pull on the strap. She put out her hand as she fell forward. He put out his. They met palm to palm. The connection tingled through her arm, across her skin. The pain in her wrist intensified and she had to break away.

"Don't tell me what to think," she gasped. "Everyone here tells me what to think."

His eyes were everywhere except on her. Had he felt it too? Eventually he said: "But all people must control their thoughts and actions, *all* people, Helen."

She tried to summon the emotions that she knew she should feel – anger, indignation, even fear – but her head echoed with the sound of her name on his lips. She tingled again, not just her arm, all of her felt it. *Palm to Palm*. What should she do now? To leave would be sensible but why should she? She was fed up with being sensible. Sensible meant sitting through Ordeal by Coffee Morning, watching Louisa dismantle Mel bit by bit. Sensible meant letting the vile woman cross her threshold with her poisoned business card. Sensible meant listening to her instead of making up her own mind about Sascha.

"Would you like to train some lengths?" she heard herself ask.

He handed back her goggles and nodded.

15

The face staring back in the mirror had clown lips that bled into the surrounding flesh. Mel didn't know how long it had been since she'd last applied lipstick but it had been a while.

Chris had come into the bedroom while she was dozing after her heavy meal – an extra egg tonight, and the portion of chips seemed big. She was tired after picking up Murdo from school. It was nice to spend time with the youngest Howard boy while Toby and Leo were at their music lessons and their mother had a governors' meeting. She once heard another mother telling her child: "Murdo doesn't speak because he doesn't understand." But the woman was wrong. Murdo understood things very well.

When Louisa had returned home, she was still tense about the man in her front garden. Was it the same man who'd accosted her by Chris's car? Thank God he ran off. She never told Chris, although she knew she should have done. What if he was dangerous? At least three times he'd been loitering in the close. What if he broke into a house next or approached a child?

"Come on," Chris had said when he interrupted her nap. "It's time you and me made a night of it. There are some clothes on the chair, and I've seen the lovely Helen wearing this shade of lipstick so let's see what it does for you. The table's booked for eight."

Her heart pounded at the thought of going out. It was hard enough going to swim club every week. She could tell him she was a bit off colour. He'd believe her because she so often was ill: headaches, wheezing, palpitations, every cough and cold Louisa's boys brought home. But he'd already changed. The silk shirt looked new and expensive. She didn't want to let him down.

She slipped on the kaftan he'd left for her. The coarse cloth chafed her nipples. She would get sore again. It wasn't a colour she would have chosen. It even smelled yellow, sort of sickly, but at least it hid a lot of bulges. She was more conscious of her weight when they went out. The German waitresses would be goddesses, wearing crisp blouses and money bags strapped around their slender hips. She turned sideways to look in the mirror and blinked away tears. She looked pregnant.

***

"I thought we agreed you wouldn't go back." He'd been home for all of five minutes when he spotted her swimming things on the washing line. "Was he there?"

Palm to palm. Helen supressed an urge to lie. "Yes, I spoke to Sascha Jakobsen. Why shouldn't I?"

He shrugged and looked disappointed rather than angry. He seemed ready to drop the subject, but she was still boiling about the ski trip and Louisa's business card, and wanted a fight.

"He could be a terrorist, a bigamist or a serial killer for all I know, but maybe he had a reason to destroy Louisa Howard's garden. Maybe she sent him one of her RELATE cards." She gave a short bitter laugh. "That nearly had me reaching for the garden shears. Only it wasn't her wisteria I wanted to deadhead."

She sighed at the bemused expression on Gary's face. "Let me explain. She thinks our marriage is in trouble. In her expert

76

opinion we need counselling. So what are you waiting for? You better give her a call."

Gary opened his mouth but she continued, "Or maybe it's too late for that. Should we skip that neighbour and go direct to Karola Barton at number 1? I hear she's a trained lawyer." She started to sob.

Gary held out his arms and she collapsed into them. But she pulled away again.

"How could you book us a skiing holiday without even telling me? We really are in trouble, aren't we?"

He gasped, sounding close to tears himself. "Don't say that, don't ever say that. The holiday was meant to be fun, a chance to get out of here and see Austria. I thought you'd be pleased."

Helen was crying now, sobbing too much to speak.

"Our marriage is the most important thing in the world to me," he said, pulling her into him. "We don't have to go on the stupid holiday."

They held each other, silent except for her sighs. As she calmed, she considered her part in their marriage. In the month since she'd arrived, she'd done little but complain about being here. Was she meeting Gary halfway? He was doing his best, wasn't he? Maybe there was more she could do. Would it kill her to go on the holiday? Just because they were in the same resort, they wouldn't have to spend the entire week with Louisa. It might even give them more chance to be alone. No work, no Dickensweg, just romantic days in snowy mountains.

"Okay, let's go to Austria."

"Are you sure?" he said, tipping her chin upwards. His eyes watered, full of concern. He kissed her gently on the lips.

"*Jawohl.*" She tried out one of her few German words and smiled.

They held each other again, and laughed and kissed.

"Let's not cook tonight," he said eventually. "I know a brilliant restaurant, you'll love it."

***

"Luigi, my friend," a familiar, booming voice said, directing his salutation to a waiter with "Andreas" written on his name badge.

Helen threw down her napkin.

Gary finished his mouthful of bread and reached for her hand across the table. "I swear I didn't know he would be here. Do you want to go?"

"Our food's arrived now. Let's hope he doesn't see us."

Thank God for the low, whitewashed walls that curved round each booth. The tacky Mediterranean courtyard theme might save them. She peered through a trellis of fake ivy at Chris Mowar. He was still addressing the waiter.

"How's that beautiful wife of yours?" he asked him, shrugging off his leather coat to reveal a peacock blue shirt. He draped the coat over a startled waitress who'd come over to the entrance to answer the phone.

Andreas/Luigi's reply was inaudible.

"Divorced? I remember now. You did tell me. Anyway, my usual table."

The waitress came off the phone.

"Put it on a hanger, my darling," he said to her. "What's your name?"

The girl muttered to the carpet.

"Look at me, my darling, so I can see you properly."

Her face ablaze, she lifted her head.

"You've got good eyes. I could use you in my next film."

The waitress, a flattered smile playing on her mouth, slipped away.

When Mel came in, her anorak and mustard-coloured tunic were mottled with rain. She followed Chris as he strode across the restaurant.

Helen and Gary settled down to their meals, Helen praying they would finish and leave before Chris and Mel spotted them.

Gary took out his mobile. "Oh, by the way, I'm texting you my new number. I lost my old phone."

"But you had it this morning." Helen dabbed her mouth with her napkin. "I gave it to you when you got that call."

"I lost it at work so I had to nip out at lunchtime and get another."

"Did you check you hadn't left it in the car?" Helen said. It wasn't like Gary to splash out on things he didn't need.

"I looked in the car and everywhere at work. It's gone, okay."

"Okay," she said quietly. He was clearly annoyed with himself for losing it. "At least Steve C won't be able to bother you any more."

"What?" He stared at her.

"You know, the salesman who rang this morning. He won't have your number now."

He breathed out and laughed. "I hadn't even thought of that."

Helen laughed too, but not for long. "Now look who's walked in. Has the school got the franchise here or something?"

Damian Howard was on his mobile and Louisa stood, stony-faced, beside him. A beaming waiter, heading towards them, executed a neat U-turn when he realized they weren't ready.

Damian came off the phone and stepped towards Louisa but she turned her back on him and folded her arms. The waitress approached and offered to take their coats. She hovered, shifting her weight from one foot to the other, and watched Damian's hands ping-pong between his coat buttons and his wife's shoulders as he tried to reason with her. Eventually he handed over the coat.

Louisa yanked off her jacket and bombarded Damian with her reply. Neither Damian nor Louisa had booming voices like Chris Mowar so Helen couldn't hear what they were saying. Several times the waitress raised her arms to catch the jacket but Louisa held onto it, using it to punctuate her sentences.

Helen hunched over the menu as they went past the side of the booth. But Louisa was too busy laying into Damian to notice the other guests.

"Are you listening? She came home with wet hair today. What if she's meeting him? We're not safe with him prowling around," she said.

Indigestion burned in Helen's chest. There was no doubt that she and Sascha were the subjects of Louisa's grievance.

"Good evening, Chris, Mel," Damian called out, in a voice that Helen felt was designed to silence Louisa.

Chris shouted back. Louisa said nothing.

The next voice she heard was Damian's again. "We could get a takeaway."

"Do you want the Mowars to see us leave?" Louisa said.

Helen shot a look at Gary. The Howards had come to the booth behind them, obscured by a forest of greenery and plastic bougainvillea. Damian ordered the dish of the day, commenting on its reasonable price despite Louisa's protests that he could afford the whole menu.

"I'm a teacher with a house refurbished to the hilt and a large family to support," he said.

"Keep your voice down; Chris will hear you," Louisa whispered. Helen and Gary gave their full attention to their meals. "We haven't even checked whether it's organic. The cheaper options are full of additives. At least let me ask."

"You can't keep spending money like water," Damian said.

Helen chewed her pasta mechanically and kept her eyes on her plate. She sensed Gary doing the same.

"What do you mean?"

Even with background noise from other tables, Helen heard the uneasiness in Louisa's voice.

"We can afford it, can't we?"

Damian took a breath. "There'll be no holiday in the Far East this summer. If we start saving now, we can have a week at Center Parcs as well as the skiing trip."

"Are you serious?" she said. "Murdo has never been to Malaysia; we have to go."

"Murdo is five years old. His idea of a holiday is a bucket and spade and a raspberry ripple."

"You're on an expat head teacher's salary and you want our son to have an ice cream instead of a summer holiday."

"Isn't that what you did as a child? Remember that? Changing your name doesn't change—"

"Stop it. Someone might hear," Louisa hissed.

"Perhaps Murdo could go on the trips you do. Where've you been? Now, let me think: New York, Paris. Or Rome – that was a good one, you researched that one well."

"Don't mock me. How can you be so cruel? Just be quiet."

"You're the one raising your voice ... Hi, Chris, leaving, are you?" Damian changed his tone.

Through her hide, Helen saw Chris give Damian a thumbs up on his way to the exit, Mel by his side.

"Changed our minds. The little lady isn't feeling well," he said. He took Mel's hand and she smiled at him.

When they'd gone, Louisa started again. "You've never queried what I spent before so what's changed all of a sudden?"

Helen looked at Gary. Could they move without being noticed?

Damian said: "I don't want you spending so much time with Chris."

"What?" Louisa gasped. "You're the one who's ... Doesn't matter. What's Chris got to do with our finances?"

Helen twisted her fork so deeply into her pasta that it scratched glaze off the plate. She should speak to Gary. If they talked, the Howards would know they were there and moderate their conversation, but it was like driving past an accident on the motorway, she couldn't tear herself away.

"You're always round there," Damian said.

"I ... it's not what ..."

Helen had never heard Louisa lost for words but the woman was struggling.

"Chris … he asked me to keep an eye on Mel. She's manic depressive but in total denial."

"Manic depressive? Mel's just fat and miserable. You can't fix everyone in Dickensweg, however hard you try. Let Chris worry about his family. You need to concentrate on ours." He summoned the waitress and ordered a bottle of house red.

"I thought we were economizing," Louisa said.

Gary broke the silence that followed to whisper that they ought to go.

Helen shook her head. Too late now. Her food was tasting so good with its revealing accompaniment. Relate Counsellor heal thyself.

"And we can't be out too long," Louisa added. "The babysitter's only a kid."

"Shelly's 19, Louisa. Perfectly old enough," Damian replied.

Gary choked on his bread. He covered most of his face with his napkin until the coughing subsided. Helen tried to catch his eye but his gaze returned to his meal. She recalled Damian's hushed phone call outside the library. *Shelly, Sweetheart.* She felt sick. Was he having an affair with their babysitter? A girl half his age? And did Gary's coughing fit mean he knew?

"I'd rather go now, if you don't mind," Louisa said in a pained voice. Did she know too?

Damian sighed. "I'll cancel the wine."

A few minutes later, they came around the open side of the booth and saw Helen and Gary. The men shook hands. Louisa leant towards Helen for an air kiss. Helen was glad no contact was made; her cheeks were burning. Louisa's perfume was exquisite, as was her composure. She must have known their row had been overheard, but no fleck of colour beyond that of her expensive make-up invaded her face.

"We must do supper sometime. After Austria," she said, over-smiling as she swept to the exit.

Fiona

As we walked, my stride chased his. Even before we got to my room and saw the terrible thing that had happened, he took charge, the good and handsome shepherd. It was a chilly night, but I was glowing inside. Who wouldn't be when they had him there?

"Are you warm enough?" he asked.

"Yes, thanks," I replied and winced at my mistake. I should have said no. Then he'd have offered me his jacket or put his arm around me. But I blew it, missed my cue.

He did like me, didn't he? I couldn't have got it completely wrong. We'd bumped into each other three times at the pub. And it wasn't by chance, was it? He knew it would be full of students but kept coming back. I think it was to see me.

Should I invite him in for coffee? What state was my room in? The translation I'd been working on was out on the desk but all my clothes were put away and I'd tucked my Hello Kitty nightshirt under the pillow.

A couple of girls I didn't know were on the porch smoking. Shoulders hunched, it was colder than they must have thought when they nipped out without coats. Their eyes lingered on him. He smiled, and their faces lit up. He'd had the same effect on everyone at the pub.

"Do you want to …?" I asked.

"I'll see you to your door …"

We spoke at the same time, and I felt stupid. One girl smirked as she stood aside to let us enter.

My room was on the first floor. I clomped up the steps ahead of him. His feet were silent, the bare wood pliant for him. What should I say? Attempt the coffee offer again?

We stepped into my corridor and strains of "Santa Lucia" hit us.

"My neighbour's a music student," I told him.

He mimed along to the song. It made me laugh and I skipped ahead. But I halted outside my door and my skin prickled. Something wasn't right. The door was ajar and swung open when I touched it. My bookcase loomed in front of me, propped diagonally between the two opposite walls of the narrow entrance. The books were in a heap beneath it and there was a broken photo frame on top. Mum, Dad, and me at the Eiffel Tower when they'd visited me in France.

I felt my face blush and I damned my carelessness. Stupid, stupid timing. Not only had I forgotten to lock my room, I must have put the Larousse dictionary on the top shelf. Dad had told me not to.

I thought the top-heavy bookcase had toppled over. When it happened again all these years later I got it at once – I thought they had caught up with me – but in my student digs that night I simply bent down to pick up the photo and hoped he'd still come in despite the mess.

But Shep said: "Don't touch anything." He took my arm – finally – and pulled me back. "I need you to be strong, Fiona."

I followed his gaze beyond the bookcase. Duvet and pillows flung on the floor and my Hello Kitty nightie stretched across the wrenched-back anglepoise lamp, a bizarre clothes horse. Posters ripped off the wall. Kanye West grinned from the windowsill, the top of his head missing.

"I should have stopped this," he said, pulling out his mobile phone.

I didn't see how he could have done anything but I felt some comfort when he said it.

The drawers of my desk and bedside locker were overturned on the bed. Screwed up sheets of Le Figaro translation beside bracelets, knickers and Tampax.

My face burned, and his shepherd's arms caught me as I fell.

16

Friday, 28 May

Clutching her shopping bag like plundered booty, Helen strode through the copse along the back of the neighbourhood. She wondered why she hadn't used it before, it was far better than staying on *Lindenallee* with cyclists coming up behind and pinging their bells. She slipped the bag to her wrist and swung it around. Perhaps it was the day for doing things differently. Why shouldn't she? She wasn't one of Louisa Howard's sheep. She tapped the bag: her act of rebellion.

She'd been to the school second-hand shop, congratulating herself for picking a Friday when she knew it was Sabine, not Louisa, on duty. She bought a fluorescent pink puffa jacket and olive green salopettes. She had a perfectly good ski-suit in her wardrobe, but she would show Louisa and the rest of them her complete contempt for the communal skiing holiday by spending the week in mismatched scruffs.

Oh, yes, she was so over Louisa Howard. If that was even her name. That snipe she'd overheard Damian make in the restaurant about researching a trip to Rome had stayed in her mind. She always suspected something false about that woman, and wished she knew what Damian meant about changing her name. She gripped the bag again and thought about the tense conversation she'd witnessed a couple of weeks ago between Chris and Damian by Chris's car. Did Chris know Louisa's secret? Was that why he got away with giving Damian, his boss, the runaround? As far as Helen could see, he was always late to school and called the shots when the two men spoke. What the hell had Louisa done? Helen just hoped she would be able to keep her trap shut for the duration of the holiday. If Louisa annoyed her – *when* Louisa annoyed her – would she stop herself from mentioning the eavesdropped conversation?

She turned left when she thought she'd got to the top of Dickensweg. But there was a row of garages at the end of the street with *Ausländer Raus* daubed on every door. The graffiti looked freshly painted. Despite what Gary said, someone had a grudge that wasn't going away. It wasn't her cul-de-sac so she went back into the copse. Had she missed Dickensweg? A flutter of nervousness tickled her belly. She wasn't lost, was she? How could she be, she'd been going in a straight line. She carried on, telling herself she would retrace her steps if she didn't find the turning.

She jumped when a crow landed on a tree ahead of her. The branch bounced, and the bird flapped, bashing its wings against the leaves. Helen froze, sure there was a different sound coming from somewhere nearby. The bird flew off, and the tree became still. But the wood fell too silent. Had it been this quiet before she heard the crow? There must have been car noises or birdsong, now nothing.

Fear pressed her feet to the ground and she couldn't move. The sun had been casting a splintered light through the trees, but now went behind a cloud. The copse grew darker. She moved the bag to her chest and hugged its contents. How could she be so stupid, trapping herself in a shadowy woodland like this? It was all in her mind, but still her feet wouldn't move.

Through the trees she caught a glimpse of a child's buggy at the top of the next cul-de-sac. The pushchair looked like the one Polly Stephens had for her daughter. She crept forward and spotted the broken gate at number 4. She'd found Dickensweg. She gave a jubilant kick to a pile of discarded cigarette ends and laughed. What would Louisa say to whoever had up-ended a car ashtray in their bit of the copse?

A cold prickle crawled up her back. What if somebody regularly stood there on that spot? A silent smoker watching the cul-de-sac, observing their every move. Knowing who had children, who was out at work all day and who was home alone. The chill tingled through her body. Sascha smoked and the figure she saw on the Howards' fence during their dinner party had a cigarette. Was Sascha stalking them? Is that why he attacked their garden? He wasn't safe.

The sun came out again and warmed her. She told herself that she was thinking nonsense.

She checked her watch. She could still fit in a swim if she wanted. And why shouldn't she want to go swimming? Sascha was fine with her, a gentleman. They hadn't touched again, not even when they passed the floats between them. Just that once. Palms, fingers, fingertips. He must have seen his effect on her through the thin material of her swimsuit. Was that why he looked away? To stop his own reaction?

She came out of the woods and saw Mel at an upstairs window. She was staring at the top of the road even though there was no sign of life at old Manfred's house, or at the Bartons'.

Mel disappeared from the window. Helen decided to invite her round for coffee, right now. After her scare in the woods, she would enjoy the company. And it was an excuse to put off the holiday packing, and the swim. *Palm to palm.* Maybe it was best to leave the swim for another day.

She saw a flash of colour appear at the end of the street. If the sun hadn't glinted on the paintwork she wouldn't have seen the open-top sports car, crawling along. It was Chris's car, strangely quiet. He usually drove at an ear-splitting roar.

Helen mentally postponed the coffee invitation and jogged into the woods out of sight to wait until he'd gone in. Chris pulled up outside his house, climbed out and was about to knock on his door but changed his mind, went back to the car and drove off at full throttle, the engine noise reverberating against the windows of the houses.

Mel came out and looked up the street after the noise, but the sports car had gone. A twig snapped when Helen shifted her weight. Mel walked towards the woods smiling, but froze when she saw Helen. She turned, lunged for her door and closed it behind her. Helen decided it was the wrong time to offer coffee.

17

"We don't have to ski in a pack, do we?" Helen said.

"This is the third year I've been on holiday with them," Gary said. He parked near the chairlift where the Howards and Mowars were waiting. "It was always fun before."

Before what? He must mean before her. Life was fun before her. She stayed in the car while he unclipped his skis from the roof. She willed him to get back in so they could have it out, but he was oblivious to her sit-in protest. By the time she gave up and left the car, he was chatting happily with the neighbours.

"Poor Helen," Louisa said by way of greeting, "if only I'd known, I could have lent you some of our skis. We're bound to have an old pair in the attic. And a ski suit."

Helen smiled tightly. She'd chosen to rebel with her tatty outfit so why did Louisa's comment still irk?

Louisa, Damian and their three boys were dressed in identical red and black ski suits. Helen was certain their provenance wasn't the second-hand shop, although she reckoned they'd end up there when Louisa cast them off in favour of next season's look.

"I hope you don't have to queue for long," Louisa said, looking at the snaking line of beginners, waiting outside the kit shop to have their feet clamped into skis. Children were variously rolling in the snow, chucking snowballs, or crying, having lost interest in the giant Pingu the Penguin whose job it was to distract them from the wait.

"I'd love to stay with you but I need to keep an eye on Damian. Now that our boys are such excellent skiers, he insists they go off-piste and you know how dangerous that can be."

"Of course, stick close to them. I wouldn't want them falling into a ravine without you," Helen said.

Louisa, not sure whether to smile or glare, managed both before she swished expertly over to the chairlift.

With Louisa airborne, Helen fought hard to shake off an image of gusts of wind and crashing cable cars. She turned to Mel, the only other member of their party left behind to queue for skis.

"Is it your first time?" she asked. Mel's ski suit was so tight that there must have been a risk of cutting off the circulation.

Mel shook her head. "Chris thinks it's better if I hire. I lost both poles last year when the paramedics carried me down on their ski-stretcher."

Helen wasn't sure what shocked her more: what Mel had said or that her nervousness had made her unusually talkative.

Helen shivered. It was supposed to be blazing hot on the ski slopes. Never mind broken ankles and dislocated knees, it was blistering sunburn you had to watch out for. So how could she explain the dank duvet of mist that had wrapped itself around the entire resort and was sucking the last ounce of warmth out of her bones? As a PE teacher she loved all sports, but she couldn't be bothered to spend today freezing off her backside in this clown suit.

"Fancy a *Glühwein*? There must be a café round here."

"If we leave the queue now, we might never get to the front," Mel said.

"How about *Bratwurst* as well?"

Mel gave a tiny smile and nodded. They followed the sounds of trilling Tyrolean music and found a café above the ski hire shop.

"So, two mulled wines?"

Mel shook her head.

Helen tried to remember whether she'd seen her drinking alcohol at Louisa's dinner party. She wasn't sure. "Hot chocolate?"

This time Mel nodded.

Helen gave the order to the waiter and turned to Mel, ready to settle in for a chat. But Mel was staring at the table. Helen pulled off her hat and neck warmer, wondering what hook she could use to drag Mel into a conversation.

There was a blast of cold air as a group of skiers entered.

"Chilly, isn't it," she tried.

Mel looked up but said nothing. She was still wearing a white bobble hat. And knitted mittens – if she ever made it onto the slopes they'd get soaked through in seconds.

"How did you end up on a stretcher?"

Mel's eyes watered. She dragged her hat lower over her ears.

Helen had judged the question would get her attention but hadn't intended to upset her. "You don't have to tell me …"

The drinks arrived with towers of whipped cream encased in marshmallows. Mel took off her gloves, reached for the sugar bowl and added four sachets.

"You have a sweet tooth," Helen laughed.

Mel's hand was reaching for a fifth but she snatched it away. "Sorry … it's what I'm used to." She stirred her chocolate – round and round – like winding a clock. "I got dizzy," she said and it took a moment for Helen to realize she was talking about the stretcher incident.

"Did you bang your head? We should wear helmets like the Howard boys."

"I wasn't concussed; I just hadn't eaten."

Helen waited but nothing more came. She looked at her watch.

Acres of time stretched before her. She summoned the waiter and ordered *Bratwurst* and two mulled wines.

When the drink was set in front of Mel, she didn't protest as Helen had expected. She added four sachets of sugar. When it had cooled she drank it straight down. Pink circles appeared on her cheeks and she smiled.

Helen ordered another round. When it arrived, she pushed the sugar towards Mel. She was confident she'd warmed her up enough to chat. "What did you do before you moved to Germany?" she asked.

"Not much. Telesales."

No wonder the woman seemed so low. "How long did you do that for? It must be quite demoralizing when people hang up on you."

Mel shrugged and stared into her hot wine.

Helen found the silence unnerving and had to fill it. "I taught PE at a school in Shrewsbury. I have a house there. I got it before the house prices took off …"

Mel closed her eyes.

"Mel?"

Maybe the second wine hadn't been a good idea; Mel had dozed off. Helen looked at her watch again.

***

"You've been in here all day drinking *Glühwein*, haven't you?" Gary said, grinning, when he and the others piled in.

Helen, who'd played her way through every game on her mobile phone while Mel slept, was thrilled to have company and forgot they'd parted in a sulk. She laughed. "We had hot chocolate as well."

Mel woke up and giggled.

"You're both very flushed," Gary said.

"We're not the only ones." The earlier mist had burnt off so that the face of every skier who came into the café glowed red from the sun's glare.

"Pot and kettle," Mel said and burst out laughing.

Chris placed his hands on her shoulders. "I think my wife had better come on the ski lift with me from now on. That way she won't get led astray."

For a moment Helen thought he was angry but he smiled and she decided it was the sunburn. Chris's face was red-raw and would be on fire tomorrow. Helen glanced at the others. Louisa had sprouted a few more freckles but she'd obviously used a top quality sunscreen to protect her skin and applied the same to the boys. Mother and sons sported a gentle tan. Naturally swarthy, Damian had darkened by a good couple of tones and when he took off his sunglasses had white eye sockets beneath. Helen sniggered and to her surprise found that Louisa was laughing too.

"You're a panda, darling," she said.

They ordered beer and chips, and Louisa said she'd like a glass of water.

Gary sat down next to Helen, wrapping his arm around her, and the Howards found space further up the table. In her continued spirit of reconciliation, Helen leaned into Gary's arm and asked him how the skiing had gone.

"Superb. We raced around the lower pistes. Young Toby is a great skier. Anyone would think he'd been born in skis."

"But Louisa's glad he wasn't," Chris said and everyone laughed, including Louisa.

The foaming beers and the chips arrived and were seized upon by the entire party, except Louisa who sipped her water. For the first time since she'd met her Dickensweg neighbours, Helen felt warm and part of the happy chatter.

"*Lutscher für die jungen Männer,*" the waiter said, presenting the three boys with lollies as he brought the bill.

"I see they let anyone into Austria these days."

Helen thought it was the waiter making a joke. But a chill went through the others and they stopped talking to stare at the person who'd spoken. Helen looked up into the sneering face of Sascha Jakobsen. Her happy haze of *Glühwein* and beer evaporated and she froze too.

Louisa found her voice first. "What the hell are you doing here?"

"Visiting my neighbours," he said.

"We're not your neighbours. If you've followed us, we'll have you arrested for stalking," Louisa said.

"The Austrians are my neighbours. And I had no need to follow you. I knew you were here."

"How the hell …?" Damian shouted, his eyes wide with alarm. He stopped when he saw his wife staring at Helen.

Louisa's ice-cold, accusing eyes were not the only ones fixed on her. Chris and Gary were looking and even Murdo was gazing in her direction.

"It wasn't me," she said, all feelings of conviviality and inclusion swept aside.

"Whose side are you on?" Louisa said.

"I didn't discuss this holiday with anyone. Gary, say something," she pleaded.

"I'm sure Helen didn't mean for this to happen," he said.

"You could have said if you didn't want to come. There is no need to ruin it for the rest of us," Louisa said.

"I expected better of you," Chris said, tutting at Helen.

"It wasn't Helen." The sound of Sascha's voice silenced everyone. "She didn't tell me."

"Who told you?" Louisa said. "I demand to know."

Sascha shook his head. But an involuntary glance in Mel's direction did his talking for him.

"Mel?" Louisa said. "This man is a stalker." She waved her arm towards Sascha. "Why on earth would you tell him we were coming here?"

"I wasn't …" Mel flushed a darker red than any of the sunscorched skiers. "He spoke to me in our street, but I didn't …" Beads of sweat formed on her brow.

"You could have walked away. Or were you too slow?"

"I'm sorry," she sobbed and dashed to the ladies' toilets.

Sascha clapped his hands. "What a caring community you have. The first sign of trouble you chase off the weakest member like a pack of dogs."

"Leave us," Louisa hissed.

Sascha stared at her. He cocked his head to the side as if to appraise her but found her wanting. He turned his attention to Damian, holding his gaze until Damian looked away. "I can wait," he said and strode out of the restaurant.

"We'll have to move to another resort," Louisa said.

"It's May. This is the only ski centre high enough for snow," Chris said. "Why should we go? If we split up he can't follow us all."

"It's only me he wants to stalk," Louisa said.

"You're surely not going to let a runt like that get to you," Chris said.

Louisa seemed to take in his words and she sipped her water, calming down. The men returned to the dregs of their beers, and the boys sucked the last of the candy off their lolly sticks. Helen said she'd go and check on Mel.

"Good idea, Helen," Chris said. "Get the snitch before her sobbing floods the place." His booming laughter followed her as she crossed the room.

***

In the toilets, Mel's body was shaking with the after-sobs of someone who had been crying heavily.

"No one blames you," Helen said without conviction because she knew everyone did. Even the woman's husband had called her a snitch.

"I can't get anything right," Mel cried, rubbing her nose with a sodden lump of toilet paper.

Helen softened her voice. "That man duped me, too. I drove him into our street. Louisa nearly laid an egg when she saw him near her garden."

Through her sobs, Mel coughed out a laugh.

"She could have hatched it and taught it to play the cello," Helen said.

Mel, chuckling more than she was crying, blew her nose. Soon they were both laughing and Helen had tears in her eyes. She fetched more loo paper and gave some to Mel who said she was ready to go in again.

***

When Helen led her back to the others, the mood was sombre. Only Chris, face the colour of ripened beetroot, seemed cheerful. He was explaining movie cameras in a loud voice – ostensibly to Toby but probably for the benefit of the waiters in the by now quiet restaurant. Toby seemed vaguely interested but at the same time distracted by his mother who was staring a hole into the cork tablemat in front of her. Damian was halfway through another beer and seemed determined to greet the bottom of the *Stein* sometime soon.

Gary suggested they order more food.

"And more anaesthetic," Damian said and lifted his *Stein*.

Helen found menus on another table and shared them out. Toby dropped any pretence of listening to Chris and seized a menu. Leo tried to prise his older brother's fingers off the laminated pages so that they could share.

Damian looked up. "You boys are having mini pizzas. And the adults can have the *Tageskarte*. It will save time."

"And money," Chris smirked.

"But the main dish is goulash. It's bound to be white rice," Louisa said.

97

"We can order extra chips," Gary suggested.

"We just had chips," she snapped. Sascha's visit had clearly fixed her mood.

The atmosphere relaxed when the pea soup starter arrived, but just when Helen thought the day could be salvaged, she glanced out of the window and spotted Sascha returning. She excused herself, went downstairs and met him outside.

"Why did you come here?" she asked, cold without her coat and hugging herself. "What do you want from us?"

"I'm waiting for justice." His expression was serious and he moved towards the entrance.

She called after him, "Please don't go in and ruin our meal."

His eyes narrowed. "You told me once not to tell you what to think but now you tell me what to do." He put his hand on the door. There was still time to stop him if she could work out how.

"How did you make Mel tell you we would be here?"

"The Howards are cruel as dogs." He pushed the door. Helen grabbed it. He didn't resist her, and she found herself touching his hand. *Palm to palm.* She let go, expecting him to go in but he didn't move and asked her: "Why do you care?"

"Mel's caught in the crossfire between you and the Howards. Let her eat her meal in peace."

He hesitated as if her words might be getting through to him. He narrowed his eyes again. "It's always the innocent who suffer. But someone pays in the end." He strode away.

As she climbed the stairs back to the café, she overheard the neighbours.

"Helen's too headstrong," Chris said.

"Mel wouldn't have got in this mess if it wasn't for her," Louisa said.

"Thick as thieves," Damian said.

When Helen approached the table, they fell silent.

***

Helen challenged Gary when they got back to their hotel room. "I heard what you were saying, you know."

"I didn't say anything."

"That's the point. Not one single word in my defence."

"We all saw you talking to him," Gary said, throwing his T-shirt on the floor. His neck was pasty in contrast to his pink face.

"What's it to you? For some reason he has a grudge against Louisa. Why do you have to get involved? Or do you know what's made him come all this way to stalk her?"

He looked away, avoiding her glare. "Of course, I don't know. But he must be unhinged, can't you see that? You could be …" His voice trailed off. "Forget it."

"What? Say it."

Gary sighed, still not catching her eye. "You could be leading him on."

Her hands trembled as she unbuttoned her clothes, raging at his accusation, but angrier still that there might be truth in it. *Palm to palm.* "To set the record straight, I persuaded Sascha to leave. I wish I hadn't bothered."

She slipped into bed and switched off her lamp. When Gary got in, they turned their backs towards each other, a cold trench of no man's land between them. For all the arguing, she sensed that they were still in the calm before the storm.

She woke at 2 a.m. when Gary went to the bathroom. He spent an age in there. It was their second night in the ski resort but the change of scene hadn't cured his night-time restlessness.

18

Monday, 31 May

The hotel restaurant was busy the next morning, so breakfast was a noisy affair that Helen welcomed as it disguised the rifts in their group. She barely spoke to Gary, Louisa barely spoke to anyone and no one spoke to Mel. When they sat down with their ham and rolls from the buffet, Chris made an announcement.

"As you can see, I had a touch too much sun yesterday." He jutted out his raw-coloured chin and soaked up their attention. "So to avoid damaging my youthful good looks permanently, I'm heading back north this morning."

"That's a shame," Damian said. His face was neutral, but Helen had the oddest feeling he sounded pleased. Or was she projecting onto Damian her own gleeful relief at Chris's proposed departure?

"Don't be silly, Chris, I have plenty of spare sunblock. The same brand the Royals take to Klosters," Louisa said.

Chris shook his head. "What I'd really like you to do for me is look after Mel."

"I'm not coming with you?" Mel asked, her voice becoming a squeak.

Chris raised his hand to show he hadn't finished speaking. "And at the end of the week you can give her a lift back."

"I'm afraid we can't help on that score. The dog cage is still in the boot. We can't transport your wife in that," Damian said. The men and Louisa laughed. Mel peered desolately into her orange juice.

"We'll take you home," Helen said.

The laughter stopped dead.

"Generous offer," Chris said, "but are we safe putting both our double agents in the same car?"

Mel's shoulders trembled.

Chris rested his hand on her arm. "I was only joking," he said softly. He stroked her hair and she leant on his shoulder. Helen hadn't thought him capable of such tenderness.

He pulled away from Mel. "Bye all, and make sure you behave yourselves." His eyes lingered on Damian as he spoke. Damian's suntanned face went a shade darker.

Chris gave a smirk and left without another word to the wife he'd been comforting a moment earlier.

"Perhaps we could all stay together on the nursery slopes this morning," Helen said. "The boys can show us their slalom racing."

Gary declared his support for Helen's idea. He squeezed her hand. Was it a step towards an apology for not defending her the night before? She'd need more than that. She retrieved her hand.

***

The slalom races started off well despite Louisa's attempts to instil competitive spirit into Murdo. "Stop eating the snow, poppet, and bend your knees. Don't let the others lap you."

"Leave him. He's enjoying himself," Damian said.

Toby won everything: short and long slaloms, and a race with mini hills to vault. He was set to try a jump over a bigger hill until Louisa forbade him lest he injure his cello hands. He threw himself angrily into the snow so Louisa organized a race for Leo and Murdo without him. Leo won it but Louisa was ecstatic for Murdo. "You were second, my little man. What a clever boy you are. Murdo's the champion," she chanted.

"Well done, Leo," Damian called.

The final race was to be a combination of slalom and jumps. On Damian's insistence, Louisa allowed Toby to join in as long as he was careful. The three boys hunched forward ready for Louisa's order to start. A figure skied across their course and sprayed the adult spectators with loose snow as he stopped dead.

"*Guten Morgen Zusammen. Bin ich spät dran?*" Sascha Jakobsen raised his ski mask. "Good morning everyone. Am I late?"

Louisa gasped and slid backwards on her skis.

"Get lost," Damian said, pulling Louisa towards him in a protective gesture. He clenched his fists and his thick ski mittens resembled boxing gloves.

Sascha skied up to Toby. "Is this the start line?"

"Keep away from my children," Damian yelled.

The shout acted like a slap across the face. Sascha stopped smiling and skied down to Damian. "I would never hurt a child."

To Helen's surprise, the anger faded from Damian's face and he looked unsure of himself.

"Let's start the race," Gary said with surprising enthusiasm. He didn't catch Helen's eye. She had the feeling that his jolly intervention was to rescue Damian from something she didn't understand.

Sascha skied back to the children. There was a look of mirth in his eyes. He'd found another way to antagonize the Howards: through their children. It was a low blow. Helen shook her head, slowly, to show her contempt, but he didn't respond.

"Are you ready?" he said to the children. "*Auf die Plätze, fertig, los.*" He set off down the course. Murdo followed him but Toby and Leo looked to their parents.

Louisa shouted: "Murdo, come to Mummy. We're going home." She threw down her ski sticks. "We're all going home."

Toby and Leo burst into tears.

***

The neighbours met in the hotel car park an hour later and loaded their cars, the silence broken only by the children's sniffs and sobs.

Damian suggested they drive back in convoy but Helen persuaded him that it might be easier if they went their separate ways. She had frightening recollections of the trip down the A8 Autobahn when Gary had dodged HGVs with his foot to the floor attempting to keep up with boy racers Damian and Chris.

Mel climbed into the back of Gary's car. Helen noticed that she ran her hands underneath the seats and along the seatbelt strap and buckle before she fastened it. A bit OCD as well, then.

Whenever Helen tried to make conversation, she'd nod or shake her head. She spoke once, to ask why they'd stopped, when Gary turned off his engine at the border into Germany.

"Traffic jam. We might have to show our passports."

Through the wing mirror, Helen could see her fumbling with her handbag. She clutched her passport.

"We're moving again." Gary started the engine.

They had a couple of stops at motorway service stations on the eight-hour journey. Mel followed Helen to the toilets. Helen tried a quip about Damian's reckless driving making Louisa lay another egg, but couldn't rekindle the intimacy of the joke they'd shared in Austria. Mel stared at the floor and said nothing. It was like having a sulky child in tow. By the time they drove into *Lindenallee*, she'd been asleep for a good two hours.

"What's going on?" Helen asked. They were in a queue of at least fifteen cars. Ahead they could see temporary traffic lights and the swirling blue of a stationary police van. Mel stirred in the back but remained asleep. After a while, the car at the front of the queue moved on.

"They're letting us through one at a time," Gary said.

They watched as the driver on the opposite side of the road got out to open his bonnet and boot. A police officer peered in.

"I wonder what's happened," Helen said.

"We'll find out in a minute. There's an officer coming down the line to speak to the drivers."

Another car was let through before the German policeman reached Gary's window. Gary wound it down.

"Good evening, sir. Where are you going to?" the officer said in English, presumably having noticed the England footie badge on their windscreen. Gary replied in German. The officer smiled in relief and launched into a speech which Helen couldn't understand.

When the officer moved on, Gary explained: "There's been a bomb scare at the school. They're searching all the cars leaving the neighbourhood."

Mel was wheezing heavily on the back seat.

"Do you need to get out?" Helen said.

Mel shook her head.

"You'll be home in five minutes, back with Chris. You can have a lie-down."

When they reached the lights, another police officer waved them straight through.

19

"I've made you some toast," Gary whispered.

Helen yawned. "Thanks, but I was planning on sleeping through breakfast today."

"Louisa's called a meeting to discuss yesterday."

Helen sat up in bed. "Don't tell me that woman runs the local police force while she's waiting for her jam to set?"

"Not the bomb scare. She wants to talk about the stalker. She's invited the whole street."

"Why does she have to involve the neighbours in her quarrel? It's got nothing to do with us."

Gary sighed. "Don't start, Helen. Let's pull together and support her. She'd do the same for you." He left the bedroom before she could continue the argument.

***

"Gary, nice to see you," Louisa said, answering the door, "both," she added belatedly.

Napoleon padded into the hall and came straight to Helen.

105

She rubbed his belly as he wagged his tail in ecstasy. Given the choice, she would have stayed with the dog, but she followed Louisa and Gary into the lounge.

There were strains of violin and cello scales coming from behind the closed music room door, and Murdo was occupied with Lego on the lounge floor. Whatever power Louisa thought she wielded over the street, it wasn't evident here; she hadn't drummed up a quorum. She explained that the Bartons from number 1 were at work. As the school's PR manager, Geoff Barton had been called in to deal with press enquiries about the bomb scare, and his wife, Karola, a native German speaker, was helping him. The geography teacher from number 4 had gone on a half-term holiday with his girlfriend. The Garcias at number 3 and the Stephens at number 8 were also away. There'd been no reply from the Greek household. Louisa offered no explanation for her husband, Damian's, absence. Helen wondered if he was showing Shelly Sweetheart their holiday snaps.

"But Manfred's here." Louisa turned to the old man standing by the patio doors. "I'll get you some tea, Manfred." She formed her hands into a cup and saucer and mimed having a drink.

Chris, who'd been pretending to film Murdo with a camera he'd made out of the Lego, said: "Mel and I would like coffee." His face was still pink and his forehead was flaking. Mel sat beside him on the sofa.

From the kitchen, Louisa produced a tray laden with cafetière, teapot and cups and instructed Gary and Helen to help themselves. She stood in the middle of the room and clapped her hands. "I've called you here to discuss what's to be done about the stalker. The man is so fixated, he hounded us into another country."

Helen looked at the others, but they were listening and nodding. Was no one ever going to challenge Louisa's word? Sascha had interrupted their holiday but he wasn't responsible for them being in Austria, for leaving Germany. How much longer could Helen live in the same pen with these sheep bleating after Louisa? She stayed silent, but the effort of suppressing her annoyance left fingernail marks in her palms.

"As you know, he destroyed our garden last year, and now he's back," Louisa continued. "He inveigled his way onto my property by duping a naive newcomer – I'm sure you won't mind me saying that, Helen – by tricking her into thinking he worked at the school. Goodness knows what damage he would have caused if I hadn't chased him away."

Helen poured herself a coffee, trying hard to hold the jug steady as she trembled with fury. Her recollection was that Sascha had been outside the garden with the naive newcomer when Louisa had come out of the house screeching.

Louisa went on: "He knows when we're at home, when we go out, what cars we drive, where our children play. None of us is safe."

Mel's cup slipped, and she spilt coffee on her skirt.

"Go and splash cold water on yourself and give me that before you spill more," Louisa said. She took Mel's cup from her as she left the room "Not only did he trick Helen – who was new and could be forgiven to some extent – he also manipulated Mel into telling him where we were going this week. Goodness only knows what pressure he brought to bear on the poor thing."

Helen swallowed a sneer. So Mel's a poor thing now, is she? A definite improvement on the slow person that Louisa judged her to be in Austria.

Mel re-entered the room with a big wet patch across her skirt and took her place beside Chris.

Louisa was in full flow. "He's almost certainly mentally ill. He must be on drugs, or a dealer."

Chris took Mel's hand. "If you ask me," he said, "this stalker character is capable of anything. I wouldn't put it past him to be behind the bomb scare."

"How could he have done it? He was with us in Austria."

"He wasn't *with* us, Helen. Get that notion right out of your head," Louisa said.

"He could have made the call from Austria having planted the fake device on Saturday before he left here," Chris said.

"You mean someone made a fake bomb? It wasn't just a kid making a crank call?" Gary said.

"Klaus, the security guard, told me someone rigged a box of wires to vibrate in a bin outside the refectory," Chris said, standing up and taking the floor. "It wasn't a kid at all. The hoax call was made in English to the guards' office by a man with a German accent."

"Anyone can put on a German accent," Helen said. She looked at Chris, running his hand through his hair. And anyone could quit their holiday with sunburn, drive like the wind from Austria and rig up a toy bomb – especially a wannabe moviemaker with a secret project, who loved to push people's buttons.

20

Helen was used to waking up without Gary's warmth beside her; it was weeks since he'd slept through the night. His nocturnal tapping on the games controller was so much the norm that she no longer got up to check on him. But tonight, the coldness went beyond physical discomfort and seeped through to her core. Did all marriages go cold? Was it inevitable that something or someone would spread ice over a once hot union? Louisa Howard? Sascha Jakobsen? Or had the chill set in the minute she chose husband above career? Whatever the catalyst, she worried that they might become a mismatched pair of skaters, sliding towards each other and dodging apart before impact. The thaw was on its way; the ice would shatter, and they would slip through the cracks.

Despite her inner cold, she was sweating. She went to the bathroom and closed the door, not wanting Gary to hear her. This action pricked at her heart. There had been a time not that long ago, if one had heard the other, they would have taken them back to bed and made love. Neither seemed willing to initiate much anymore.

The cold flannel made her flinch when she pushed it under

her arms. She could hear sloshing sounds next door. One of the Mowars was awake. She realized that she hadn't seen Mel for days. Was she away?

She went back to bed. When light glowed peach through the school-issue floral curtains, she decided to get up and go for a run along the river. She found Gary asleep in front of a paused computer game, one of his arms stretched across his body, cupping the side of the chair. He'd get a bad back but she couldn't face waking him and having to talk. She laid a blanket over him and went downstairs.

***

She set off for her run. Not that she cared, but there was no chance of bumping into Louisa as she'd gone to America for a shopping trip with some girlfriends. Helen loved Louisa's girl-friends. It was the third time they'd lured her away. She thought of the comment about Louisa's trips that she'd overheard Damian make in the restaurant. Was he jealous? She didn't have him down as the possessive type, but who knew what happened behind the gleaming shutters of Number Ten?

She ran round a pile of dog turd, still soft but there was no sign of the culprit. Louisa once suspected dog walkers of letting their pets do it on her lawn. The problem disappeared after she put out chilli-laced dog food. Helen had felt a moment of unity with her neighbour.

A cat was toying with a dead sparrow. When it saw her, it stalked off with some of the entrails in its jaws. It was the first cat she'd seen for months. Her neighbours were dog people. For a delicious moment she thought of getting a cat but she preferred dogs too.

The day was heating up. Helen tied her fleece around her hips. There was something magical about being outside on a summer's morning while others slept on. As she ran along *Lindenallee* all her knotted thoughts from the previous night untied. But a figure came round the side of a row of garages and she felt a jolt of fear. She ran on, intending to sprint past, until she saw who it was.

"Oh Manfred, I thought I was the only person up this early."

"I'm sorry if I disturb. I think you like the roads for yourself alone."

"I'm pleased to see you. Good morning." She held out her hand, adopting the formal German greeting. As he took it, the holdall in his other hand chinked.

"Have you been shopping?" she asked.

"A walk. I think even German shops don't open at this time."

She blushed and hoped he hadn't thought she was being nosy. A crow flew over and provided a welcome subject change. "Those birds give me the creeps. I see them all the time round here."

"*Er ist kein Kranich. Schade.*"

"I don't …"

"Shame it isn't a crane. I always hope I will see a crane. *Kranich ist Heimat.*"

"*Heimat* means home, doesn't it?"

He nodded. "*Schlesien*. Silesia. We had so many *Kraniche* there. But never here. *Schade.*"

He sighed, and she sensed the need to change topic again.

"I see there's more graffiti."

She had his attention.

"The school fence is also broken and a street sign no longer stands up," he said.

"The vandalism has got worse even in the few months I've lived here and then we had the bomb scare," she said.

"I read in the *Tageblatt* that the police know the call was from the telephone box near the school."

"They should be able to get fingerprints. No one uses it now we have mobiles."

Manfred shook his head. "I have myself used that phone."

111

"It was probably teenagers on a half-term rampage."

"What do you think is the motive?" His eyes fixed on her, waiting for an answer.

"Nothing to do, I suppose. Their Xboxes must be broken."

"Perhaps the person has a message?" he asked, his eyes still on her.

"Maybe. I hope the police put a stop to it before someone gets hurt."

He lifted his bag and changed his grip on the handle. "*Die Rache wilder Sieger.*"

"I don't …"

"Victors and spoils," he said and walked on.

***

It was bedlam in the girls' changing room when Helen went to teach her lesson that evening. The high-pitched squeals of long-haired girls being forced into tight, tugging swim caps were deafening. Helen felt a grudging respect for Louisa. Without her forthright stewardship, the place was in chaos.

She was relieved to see things running smoothly poolside. The five children whom John had allocated to her on her first night had become her group. She picked Alexandros, the son of her Greek neighbours, to demonstrate the symmetry of breaststroke kick to the others.

***

The changing room was even worse afterwards as mothers struggled to peel tired and crabby children out of their wet swimsuits and locate errant knickers and socks. It dawned on Helen what the problem was. Parents didn't usually come into the area because the children got dressed by themselves under the supervision of the changing room monitor, Mel. It wasn't Louisa who held the place together, it was Mel. Helen tried asking the mums where she was but they shook their heads. A few volunteered the fact that Louisa was in New York until Saturday but no one knew about Mel.

***

Chris was polishing his car when she got back. Curiosity got the better of her and she stopped to ask him why Mel had missed swim club.

"Lanzarote," he said. "I've sent her on a convalescence trip after the ski debacle."

His smug voice ground through her and she wished she hadn't asked. She fought to get out her key.

"She's lucky to have you," she said, not bothering to hide her sarcasm.

"Aren't you all," he called after her.

She slammed the door.

21

Sunday, 19 December

Detectives Zanders and Simons – who've been on the murder case from the beginning; no doubt because of their excellent English – place a transparent evidence bag in front of her.

"Do you recognize this, Mrs Taylor?"

Helen hesitates. It looks like one of her green teardrop earrings. Where did they find it? Is it best to deny it's hers? She feels dizzy and wishes now that she'd tried the breakfast they put in her cell.

"Answer the question, please, Mrs Taylor."

Helen looks at her lawyer. Karola nods.

"I have a pair like that," Helen says. Should she mention she hasn't worn them for months? She crosses her legs; she's starting to need the loo.

Before she can speak again, Zanders says: "Thank you, Mrs Taylor, that's all for now."

***

When they get back to the cell, Karola Barton sits down on the bed and smooths the seam of her trousers. Helen paces the floor, still holding her head, trying to make sense of what happened in the interview room.

"Were the earrings a present from Sascha Jakobsen?" Karola asks suddenly.

Helen stops pacing. "Of course not; he never gave me anything." She can feel the colour rising in her face. She must look as if she's lying. "I bought them years ago."

"So why didn't you answer the detective's question straight-away? Your body language seemed evasive."

Helen folds her arms and wonders how Karola is reading the gesture. Does she learn that stuff as a lawyer or a dog breeder? What would she have made of her body language outside Number Ten that night? What's the predicted stance of someone after they've … The blood-cherry cheesecake comes into Helen's mind and the topping cascades down the leg of the breakfast bar. It seeps into her dress – the special dress she's worn that night – and under the sole of her boot. She stomps cherry footprints across Louisa's pristine floor. There's blood everywhere but she can't shake it off.

She sways in the cell. Karola takes her arm and leads her to the bed before she falls.

When she's recovered, she presses her about the earring.

"I think I lost it in the burglary. There was such a mess. In all the houses, not just mine." She hopes that talking about the incident that took place on a balmy summer's day will stop her fast-forwarding to what happened two weeks ago. "Gary dealt with the scenes of crime people. He was dependable in a crisis." Her throat grows hard; she still can't cry.

"So at no time did Sascha Jakobsen have your earring?"

"Of course, he had it. He stole it." She stands up, fights off her dizziness. "Everyone knows he committed the burglaries. He did everything. The vandalism, the burglary, poor Murdo, everything. You were there, don't you remember?"

Karola smooths her trousers again. "I recall you defending Jakobsen at the time, protesting his innocence."

"I know different now," Helen whispers. "I wish I'd never met him."

22

Thursday, 1 July

As Helen, trowel in hand, came round the side of the house, she noticed Damian on the front doorstep of Number Ten. The rest of the Howard clan were in their back garden, the children out-squealing the Stephens's pair on the trampoline. No doubt Louisa was regaling Polly with her New York trip over a glass of Chardonnay.

Helen fetched a watering can and filled it. But despite taking her time, Damian was still there when she returned to the front, now on his mobile by his car. He seemed to be giggling. "Yeah, Sweetheart ... I'll call you back." He saw Helen and slipped the phone into his pocket. He opened the boot, got out a bottle of wine and returned to sit on the step. He unscrewed the lid and poured red wine into an empty glass beside him. Some dribbled on the step. Helen decided it wasn't his first glass of the evening. He caught her looking, so she waved. She wondered if it was the same Sweetheart he'd phoned outside the library. Shelly the 19-year-old, or had he moved on?

He headed towards her, unsteady on his feet. His eyes were on her legs; she was wearing shorts. She cursed herself for waving.

But he shifted his gaze beyond her to a figure in the road. Mel Mowar was dragging a suitcase. She shuffled a couple of paces and stopped to get a better grip.

He went to help her but, even relieved of her heavy luggage, she still shuffled. Shadows under her eyes, greasy hair, shrieking body odour.

"Good holiday?" Damian asked.

"The flight back was delayed for hours, but glorious weather, breathtaking volcanoes," she replied. After she'd fumbled for her house key, she took the case from him and closed the door behind her.

"That's the trouble with airports. You need another holiday to get over them."

Before Helen could react to Damian's joke, his face changed. Louisa was walking towards them. Helen mentally trawled her list of excuses for not attending whatever invitation his wife was about to deliver.

But she had something else on her mind.

"Is Murdo with you?" she asked, striding up to Damian, her back towards Helen.

"He's on the trampoline, isn't he?"

"We thought he came round the front. You must have seen him."

"Has he gone inside the house?" Helen said.

Louisa turned round. "I've looked under the beds, in the wardrobes, in the airing cupboard, the cellar, even inside the washing machine. He's not there." Her face was paler than Helen had ever seen it.

"Has he gone to play with Polly's children?" Damian asked. Helen could tell he was doing his best not to slur his words.

"Polly's two are with Leo and Toby."

"He won't have gone far. What about the Garcias? Is he with them?" Damian said.

Louisa darted away to knock on the door of number 3. When Audrey Garcia answered, she shook her head.

"Oh Christ," Damian said under his breath. He shifted his weight from foot to foot, watching his wife run to number 1.

The Barton couple came outside but Helen couldn't hear the exchange above the dogs in their garden. Louisa belted across the road to Manfred's. She hammered on the door and shouted through the letterbox. When no one answered, she ran to number 4 and hammered there. No reply. She had no luck at number 6, the Greek house, either. When she turned round, her expression was bleak.

"Don't get upset, darling. He'll be back in no time," Damian said, opening his arms to her.

She stepped past him and rang Chris and Mel's doorbell. Chris answered.

Both Bartons came out with their dogs on leads. Polly Stephens brought all the children out of the Howards' back garden and walked over to Audrey Garcia, who'd stayed in the street. Toby and Leo Howard wore pained expressions. When they saw their mother's face, their eyes started to water.

Damian ruffled their hair. "Cheer up, chaps. Your brother won't be far away. He'll be back."

"Stop saying that. He's not a fecking boomerang. How do you know he'll be back?" Louisa snapped.

Helen had never heard Louisa swear. Damian's mouth was wide open. Husband and wife stared at each other. Louisa started to shake.

Helen thought she should say something but didn't know what.

"We need to search all the places Murdo might have gone, get knocking on doors," Chris said.

Through sobs Louisa told them Murdo liked the playground. "And the computer games at Spiel World but that's five miles away and I never let him play on them."

Chris told Damian to check the playground and said he and Mel would take the neighbouring streets.

"What can I do?" Helen asked. There was a pause before Chris replied. The hesitation was fleeting, but it was there. Even in this crisis, he revelled in it. He dispatched her with Damian.

"I can't stay here and do nothing," Louisa sobbed, rubbing her hands through her hair and leaving it untidy.

"You're here for when your son comes back," Chris told her.

"But what if …?"

Chris squeezed her shoulder. "I'll find him. I promise."

Helen hurried up the road after Damian. He seemed determined and aimless at the same time. Helen sensed Chris's gesture had rattled him. He wanted to be the one to find his son, but he had to find the playground first and neither of them had a bloody clue where it was. She struggled to keep up. Nothing had happened to Murdo. He would come home and go straight to his Lego with no inkling of the anxiety he'd caused his parents. But why the hell hadn't anyone brought him back already? What if a car …? What if someone …? No, this was a respectable neighbourhood. A close community. Safe as houses.

They followed a bilingual sign *Spielplatz/Playground*. It led to a copse at the end of a cul-de-sac. The playground was in a clearing. It looked like Armageddon. A dozen empty pizza boxes dumped in the sandpit; swing seats chucked onto the frame so that they couldn't be reached; soft-play paving slabs ripped up. Three boys of about ten years old were examining the slide.

"There's glass round the bottom and someone's poured cola down it. Sir," one said. He was English, obviously a pupil at the Elementary School. He must have recognized Damian as head of the senior school and stuck on the "Sir" as an afterthought.

"There were German cuss words on the roundabout last week," another added. His accent was American.

Damian kicked the base of the slide. "Why the hell does Louisa bring my children to a place like this? We've got a perfectly good climbing frame and trampoline. God knows they cost enough."

Helen smiled apologetically at the boys, but they ran off. Damian climbed over the playground fence and stumbled into the undergrowth. Helen went after him. Nettles stung her shins. Her T-shirt clung to her back. Evening sun shone through the gaps in the canopy onto weeds and shrubs, intensifying their summer smell. It was still light but would be dark in an hour. A shiver went through her. They hadn't brought torches.

Something moved at the base of a tree ahead of them. They stopped.

"Murdo?" Damian called. No answer.

She tried. "Murdo? Murdo?"

"Murdo, where the hell are you!" Damian shouted.

A squirrel scuttled up the trunk, and Damian blinked away a tear.

He walked ahead, his long legs increasing the gap between him and Helen. She stumbled over tree roots and snagged her hair on twigs in his wake. When he accidently pinged a branch into her thigh, she cried out.

He didn't hear her and marched on. "This is my fault, my penance for what I did, what I still do …" He seemed to remember Helen's presence and checked his words. "Louisa will lose all reason if … She'll wrap Toby and Leo so tight in cotton wool they'll stop breathing."

"I'm sure it won't come to …"

They emerged from the wood into a street Helen didn't know. They stood together, looking at the unfamiliar houses. Could a 5-year-old roam this far on his own?

"He's my boy too. I'm not an ostrich like Louisa. I've seen people look away. I've sat opposite his teacher at parents' evening with Child Psych hanging unsaid between us. I should know, I've dealt with enough deluded parents in my time. But he's perfect. My Murdo. Perfect."

Helen nodded but didn't know what to say. There was a crack in Damian's voice; she wasn't sure how much longer he'd hold it together. How long had they been looking? Half an hour? Damn Chris Mowar for granting Damian and Louisa bit parts in the hunt for their own child. They were wasting precious time. They should call the police.

She took a breath. "Shouldn't we …?"

"I swear I'll be a better father to him after this." He strode on, wiping away a tear. "And a better husband. I won't ever do it again. No more …"

His mobile rang. He yanked it out of his shorts. "Have you got him?" His shoulders sagged. "Don't cry, darling. I'll phone Chris. Maybe one of the others …" His jaw tightened. "I see, you phoned him first … Look, we're running around like headless chickens. It's time to tell the police. I'm coming back … You're where? … Of course I don't blame you … The stables was a good idea, worth a try … Go back home and I'll meet you there." He broke into a run.

23

When Helen and Damian arrived back, Louisa was pacing the drive, still dragging her hands through her hair. It hung down, greasy and unkempt, a stark contrast to her usual grooming. Sabine, the school nurse, stood watching her.

A police car pulled up, and a young female officer climbed out. Louisa rushed over to her. The woman shook her head and said something in German.

Sabine stepped forward. "The police called me; I'm here to translate. The officer wants us to go inside."

"He's not in there. She needs to be out searching," Louisa cried. "Why doesn't she bang on doors, ask one of the windae-hingers. Some auld bag must have seen him." Her mouth had curled into an ugly snarl. There was no sign of the polished chair of the Parents' Association.

"Steady on, darling." Damian moved to stand behind her and placed his hands on her shoulders. But she shook him off.

Sabine hesitated, unsure how to translate Louisa's outburst. She decided not to bother. "The officer will take some details. Let me make us all a cup of tea."

"Tea?" Louisa said it as if she'd never heard the word before.

"I could make it," Helen said. "Sabine can help with the interview."

Louisa glared at her, but nodded as the fight went out of her and she swallowed a sob. Rivulets of mascara leaked down her face. Sabine spoke to the officer, and they all went inside.

Helen tried to hide her shock at the state of the Howards' hall. Drawers pulled open, contents strewn across the floor, potpourri littered on the hall table. Evidence of the panic that had consumed Louisa.

"Shall we do this in the lounge," Sabine said, eying the debris.

Louisa let out a small "oh" when she saw the sofa cushions dumped on the lounge floor but tidied them up without another word. Damian righted the overturned coffee table. The police officer said her name was Wolters.

The Howards' kitchen was in its usual pristine order. Helen found Polish pottery mugs and a matching teapot in a cupboard, and was relieved to see a box of PG Tips next to the kettle; she didn't fancy messing about with Louisa's posh tea leaves. She winced, ashamed of herself for criticizing Louisa when her son was missing.

When she brought the tea tray in, Wolters was questioning Louisa and Damian about Murdo's routines, and Sabine was translating.

"Do you have a recent photograph?"

Helen shivered; it had got as far as the photograph. You saw photos of children in newspapers – happy, smiling faces – when they'd been … when … But they were distant, unknown children. Murdo was real to her. He was the boy on the tambourine who had charmed her by saying "Noh Noh".

"His school photograph is in the dining room," Louisa said. "He's got baked-bean stains on his chin. I told the school they should have organized the photographer for before lunch." Her back stiffened and she started to rock. "So much evil. But, not on my wee man, it cannae happen to him."

124

She leaned towards Wolters, invading her space. "You find him, you hear me. There are bad people who'd …" Damian took her hand and her voice tailed off.

"I'll get the photo," Helen said, hoping to avoid seeing Louisa cry.

When she opened the sliding doors to the dining room, she found chairs tossed on their sides. Something crunched under her feet. The glass-fronted dresser had been smashed, and a shard of glass used to etch scratches into the table. Random gashes, not words. But the message was clear: someone had trashed the room.

She gasped, and Louisa came over to her.

"Oh God," she said and clutched her chest. It was obvious she was seeing the chaos for the first time and it wasn't the result of her frantic search. This was a calculated attack.

Helen balled her fists. "Bastards."

Louisa fell against Damian, her body quivering. Neither of them spoke.

The doorbell rang.

"I'll go. Don't touch anything," Sabine said, suddenly sounding on firmer ground translating a burglary rather than a missing person's enquiry.

Helen heard Manfred's voice. "Good evening. I have here the son of Mr and Mrs—" They all flew into the hall. Louisa pushed Sabine and Wolters aside to scoop up Murdo. Her sobs rocked her body and his. Murdo wiped her snot and tears from his face.

Wolters led Manfred and Damian into the lounge. She left Louisa at the foot of the stairs with Murdo on her lap, arms clamped tight around him, still rocking and sobbing.

Manfred explained: "I came home and I saw him over my fence in the next garden. It was a game, I think."

Damian offered him his hand. The old man took it and waited until Damian, tears streaming down his face, was ready to release it.

Wolters cleared her throat and spoke to Sabine. She translated.

"She says she'll have to talk to Murdo, but it looks as if he was playing the whole time."

Helen went to the door when the bell rang again. A white-faced Polly Stephens stood on the doorstep. She saw Louisa with Murdo on the stairs. "You've found him. Thank God. I came home to check in case he was hiding there, but … Our house has been broken into. There's mess everywhere."

24

Friday, 2 July

The pool was packed with occasional swimmers attracted by the warm weather but no Sascha. The shallow end was standing room only so Helen confined herself to the deeper water. But it was like swimming in glue; too cloying to allow her limbs to move. And her mind stayed on the burglary. How could she swim with that violation pressing on her?

The forensic team had caused as much chaos as the thieves. They hadn't let them tidy their ransacked belongings until they'd dusted every surface with their sticky powder. There were distressed heaps of socks, pants, and tights in the bedroom. Helen nudged the clothing apart with her foot and pincered each piece into a bin bag with the tip of her thumb and forefinger. She wanted to chuck the whole lot out; it all felt tainted to her. But Gary persuaded her to run it through the washing machine. Thank God for Gary; she would have caved in without him. She found one of her earrings on the floor but couldn't find the matching one. She didn't mention it to Wolters as she thought the woman would never leave. And it hardly seemed important.

The forensics team had taken longer at their house than the

others because they found a partial print and a speck of blood on the back doorframe. The burglars had got into each house the same way: by smashing the glass in the back door and turning the key that was in the lock inside. People thought that it was safe to leave keys like that in this neighbourhood. As well as Helen's home, the intruders had trashed the Howards', the Stephens's, and the Mowars'. But nothing had been stolen. Helen couldn't help feeling that simple theft would have been preferable to the wanton destruction they'd suffered.

She cut short her swim and drove home. When she parked, Chris Mowar marched out of his house and asked if she'd seen his DVDs. She composed her face, banishing every trace of glee. "Did they steal your documentary project?"

"Just some background recordings. They're meaningless to anyone but the producer," he said, a vein pulsing in his neck.

"What did the police say?"

"They'll hardly be interested."

Helen stared at him. "You haven't told them?" So even he must have realized how worthless his Mr Big-I-Am films were. They would inevitably get dumped by the thieves. They wouldn't give a monkey's, any more than she did. "How is Mel taking the burglary?"

"She's in bed. It's shaken her up. Louisa is with her now."

"I'm sure that's a comfort to her."

Chris missed her sarcasm and went back to his important topic. "Can you check your garden in case the burglar lobbed them over the fence?"

"The police were pretty thorough so I don't think—"

"Just check, will you?"

She went indoors, unsure whether she acknowledged his order. It didn't matter; she'd no intention of looking, no intention of doing anything neighbourly ever again.

25

Monday, 5 July

Louisa was knocking at number 2, with Napoleon beside her on a lead, when Helen tried to hurry past.

"You haven't seen Manfred, have you?"

"Perhaps he's gone out," Helen said, squatting down to pat the dog.

"Manfred, can you hear me?" Louisa called through his letterbox. She turned to Helen, an anxious look in her eyes. "You read about the elderly collapsing in their own home and not being found for days."

"You don't know he's in there."

Napoleon placed his paw on her shin when she stopped stroking him. She took the hint and rubbed his chest. He was a soppy old thing. She was glad he'd been shut in the garden when the burglar broke into Number Ten. There was no telling what might have happened. He was no guard dog.

"I'll set up a rota," Louisa carried on. "We can take it in turns to look in on Manfred, discreetly of course. He's bound to have his pride."

"Bound to," Helen said and wondered if she could walk on without appearing impolite.

"Bad luck is supposed to come in threes. First Murdo, then the burglaries. Surely number three can't be Manfred?"

Helen looked at the dog and rolled her eyes. Was he saner than his mistress? She decided she preferred Louisa's hysteria when it was delivered in dialect. In hindsight it was almost amusing to think how her middle-class veneer had crumbed in front of the policewoman. Almost. Her precious Murdo had been lost. That kind of trauma would make anyone regress. But Helen couldn't help wondering what else she was hiding under her top-wife façade.

"I'm being silly," Louisa said in her fully restored and modulated voice. "Things like that don't happen in this neighbourhood."

As if to confirm her optimism, Manfred opened the door. The old man's face was drawn and his eyes were rheumy.

"Thank heavens," Louisa said, adopting a slower way of speaking. "Damian and I would like you to join us for dinner tonight. To thank you properly for finding Murdo. Shall we say seven thirty?" Invitation delivered, she stepped down from his doorstep.

"*Danke, nein.* I don't need to have food. That I know the boy is safe is a thank you."

"But you must, we insist."

"No."

Louisa's face was a picture, clearly unused to such a blunt refusal. "Well, come so that we can ask you how you found Murdo. We knew the geography chap at number 4 was off on a field trip, but we looked over into his garden. The gate was swinging open. I'm sure Murdo wasn't in that garden then."

"But that is where I found him," Manfred said. "It stays a mystery, I think."

Polly Stephens came towards them from number 8.

"I'm telling Manfred about the supper tonight. You and Jerome will be there, won't you?" Louisa called. "And you, Helen, of course."

Was it Helen's imagination or had Louisa lowered the pitch of her voice when extending the invitation to her?

"That's sweet of you," Polly said, coming over, "but don't you have enough on? Our place is still a mess, isn't yours?"

"You'll have to put up with glass missing from the dresser and a cloth to cover the scratches on the table, but we'll cope. It's nothing compared to what we could have lost." She sighed.

Helen sighed too. Despite what she thought of her, Louisa loved Murdo fiercely. His safe return was all that mattered about that awful evening.

"It's the nerve of a complete stranger I can't get over. In broad daylight breaking into four houses on one street," Polly said.

"*If* it was a stranger," Louisa said.

Helen had been aware of Manfred retreating into his house, but now he stared at them.

"You don't think it was a stranger?" Polly asked.

"Do you remember that man who vandalized my garden?"

"Surely you don't think it was him?"

"Why not? He's been stalking us for months; he even followed us to Austria."

Helen felt an angry cough in her throat. "But how could he have known that Murdo would go missing and that we'd all go off to look for him? Isn't that too much of a coincidence?"

They stared at her. Had she raised her voice in defence of a man who'd stalked them?

"There, Helen, is the damning evidence. He must have taken Murdo to get us out of the street. The more I think about it, the more it makes sense. I want to tell the police but Damian says we have no proof."

Helen suppressed another cough. At least one Howard was talking sense.

"I think your husband is right," Manfred said. "It is not my affair, but you cannot accuse a man without *Beweis* … proof."

"Do you know him?" Louisa asked. Helen heard the allegation in her voice.

He shook his head. "But your husband has a good advice." He retreated inside.

Louisa stared at the closing door. Her face had grown a shade pinker.

Polly looked from Helen to Louisa. "How are you both coping after the break-ins?" she asked. "Chris Mowar is going around like a bear with a sore head, and I haven't seen Mel, have you?"

"You know what Mel's like. She's taken it badly," Louisa said, recovering quickly from Manfred's snub. "Chris is at his wits' end. He's managed to get some medication from the doctor but she's scarcely been out of bed."

"Our girls keep checking their toys in case he stole something. We don't think he did, but downstairs was ransacked. I hope they forget about it soon," Polly said.

"That stalker has a lot to answer for." Louisa glared at Helen, leaving her in no doubt she held her responsible for the stalker's reappearance in their street.

26

Friday, 16 July

"Bloody typical," Helen mouthed as she climbed down the metal steps she was forced to use. The pool was too packed to slip in off the side, let alone dive.

She set off doggy paddle and stop-started around bombing kids, petting couples, and the elderly regulars. After the stifling heat of the car she should have found it refreshing, but the usual bite of cold water was more like a lethargic slap. The weather beamed summer heat over the *Freibad*, but for Helen the day had begun as lukewarm sludge and descended into stolid fug.

She'd swallowed her pride and joined the school library on her way to the pool. She wanted to pick up a couple of textbooks for her lessons with Maria. They were both finding grammar a bit of a trial.

"I see English isn't as straightforward as you thought, Helen," a voice behind her said as she'd waited for the library assistant to stamp her books. It was Louisa, smug and spouting the grain of truth that made Helen dig her nails into her palms.

And she was there. Again. In the same square metre of space as Helen. If Helen went to the school shop, it would be Louisa's day behind the counter. If she went to the swim club, Louisa would lord it over her as the chairwoman. They couldn't even go for a meal without Louisa and half the street piling in. And now, on the day Helen had picked to visit the library, Louisa was stocking up on Shakespeare for her gifted children.

Helen reached the far end of the pool and stopped to look around. Whatever course she'd managed to plough was obliterated by more splashing bodies. Could she be bothered to swim back? She might as well pack it in and go home. She was about to climb out when a swim float appeared in front of her face.

"I've asked the *Bademeister* to put in a rope for us." Sascha squatted on the poolside.

The smog in her head lifted and she grabbed the float. The day finally smiled as the pool attendant ushered the leisure swimmers to the side, put in a lane rope and added a *Training* sign at both ends. The pool was her escape – away from the fakery and arrogance of Dickensweg. Was Sascha dangerous? Not to her.

Helen and Sascha, the only serious swimmers, had the lane to themselves. They set off side by side at speed, but not racing, their bodies flat and streamlined to the water. Helen breathed on alternate sides, so did Sascha. At every sixth arm-pull their heads turned towards each other as they inhaled.

At first she balanced her energy throughout her body and pictured him next to her doing the same. Eyes forward and down, spines relaxed and tilting to the hips, stomachs taut to support their lower backs. But after two lengths, her only thought was for the synchronicity of their sixth arm-pull. Her right elbow, then her shoulder came out of the water in time with his left. Her neck was smooth to the turn of her head and she stretched her mouth up to take it above the water. Through the mist in her goggles she saw his mouth do the same. She wanted to raise her head for a clearer view of him but knew her feet would sink and break the spell.

Almost touching, their palms turned to each other so that

their thumbs could re-enter the water first. They swept their arms – her right, his left – through the water towards the centre of their torsos and out to their thighs, charting a perfect hour-glass shape between them.

Their wrists clashed, sending searing pain up her forearm, but she didn't lose the rhythm or pull apart. Neither did he. Instinctively they slowed their pace and the touching increased. Elbows, wrists, ankles, hips. Sometimes hurting, sometimes not. That sixth beat was everything.

They reached the end and made a turn. She curled into a tuck, bending her knees. As she threw her legs over her pelvis and planted her feet on the wall, she was aware of him doing the same. She power-pushed away and stretched out her body, baring it to the water below her. She kicked harder and pulled faster. Swimming back up the length, her left arm matched his right. The waves from her movements rippled into his and rocked the lane. Was it a race now? Not with each other, not exactly. And yet more was at stake than in any competitive swim. She no longer imagined his movements beside her; she knew they were part of hers: every kick, every sweep, every explosive exhalation into the water.

Eventually they stopped. They stood in the shallow end, mouths wide and panting for air. They took off their goggles but looked at their hands on the rail, not daring to catch each other's eye.

Sascha pushed against the wall and sprang catlike from the water. Helen hauled herself out on her belly and twisted into a sitting position, feeling spent, sated. She pulled off her swimming hat. He drew her to her feet. She was aware of the beating sun on her hair and neck but the heat didn't start there, it radiated out of the hand he was holding.

"Let's stay for a while," he said and walked across the grass. She followed, still gripping his hand.

Without speaking, they lay on their backs, eyes closed against the sun's glare. Blades of grass pricked her naked arms and thighs.

This was the freedom she'd been denied for months. He'd let go of her hand but now stretched his fingertips to hers. He pressed their palms together and she felt the muscle memory of their previous palm to palm encounter, the one she'd relived every day since.

Sascha leant towards her. "Shall we take your car? I know a place."

Mute, Helen sat up and nodded. Obedience and freewill were one. There wasn't a choice to make. This decision had been made months ago.

But as they headed towards the changing rooms, Sascha said: "Later you can drop me in Dickensweg."

She stopped walking. *Dickensweg*. He'd screamed a safe word – a hated word – that shattered her stupid fantasy. The coercive stalker didn't want her; he wanted the information she had on her neighbours.

She bolted to the changing room, feeling every speck of grass and soil and grit that stuck to her back and legs. Her badge of shame. Without brushing off the dirt, she threw her shorts and T-shirt over her damp swimsuit, chased her trembling feet into her sandals and dashed to her car.

***

She drove through the village and headed south onto the A61. At the first service station, she pulled into the car park and burst into tears. What had she been thinking? How could she do that to Gary? She'd never go to the *Freibad* again. Thursday couldn't come soon enough. It was the end of term, and she and Gary were spending the whole summer in Shrewsbury. That was what she needed, to get back to the real world, away from this stifling expat enclave that turned her crazy.

With the windows wide open she headed home, letting the wind buffet the cabin fever out of her.

When she turned into Dickensweg, Chris was polishing his car as Damian walked out of Number Ten with his mobile in his hand. Chris turned towards the engine noise to wave at her. She groaned. He carried on watching her car so she pulled up short, in front of Manfred's house. She pretended to get a text message and made a theatrical display of taking her phone out of her bag. It was a delaying tactic until she'd psyched herself up to run the gauntlet of Chris's sarky comments and Damian's letching. They'd see she'd been crying and offer two unwelcome brands of comfort.

"Escaped again, have you?" Chris called.

For a second Helen thought he was talking to her, but he was aiming his sarcasm at Damian.

Damian dropped his phone. He picked it up and walked out of his drive, his eyes on Chris. That was all Helen needed: both men standing by Chris's car as she went to her front door. But Damian turned left along the path into the copse. She felt a pang of guilt for calling him a letch. He'd been more attentive to Louisa since they nearly lost Murdo. He'd washed Louisa's Landcruiser yesterday and he'd taken to watering their lawn most evenings.

She was about to get out of the car – at least, with Damian gone, Chris wouldn't have an audience to show off to – but she heard shouting from the copse. Sascha strolled out, smoking a cigarette. Of course, he'd found his way here ahead of her; he didn't need a lift from her despite what he'd said.

Helen's insides lurched. Had he come for her? Or Gary? Was he going to tell him what she'd done?

Damian rushed out of the copse behind him. "What the hell are you doing here?"

Sascha took a drag of his cigarette. Helen couldn't hear what he said. *Please God, don't let him mention me*, she prayed.

"Don't lie," Damian said.

Sascha blew a smoke ring and said something else that Helen couldn't hear.

"I'm calling the police." Damian marched towards his house.

But Sascha followed, shouting: "We both know you won't do that, don't we?" He sounded calculating. Helen trembled; he'd manipulated her too. Thank God she'd bolted when she did.

Damian stopped walking. Clearly there was something in Sascha's veiled threat.

Chris Mowar leant against his car and folded his arms. "Aren't you going to answer him?" he said.

"He stole from you, too," Damian shouted. "Don't you care?"

"Did you steal my DVDs?" Chris said, suddenly angry, striding over.

Sascha didn't reply.

Damian shouted: "If I catch you near my family, I'll kill you."

Helen could hear her heartbeat. Would Gary threaten the same thing when he found out how close Sascha had come to her?

Sascha leapt towards the men. "I told you I would never harm a child."

Chris let out a laugh. "Just ignore him, Damian. I doubt he knows what family means."

Even before Chris had finished speaking, Sascha's fist connected with his jaw and Chris stumbled to the ground.

"I know family," Sascha snarled and stalked into the copse.

Helen let out a gasp. Now what was she supposed to do?

For once she was grateful to her nemesis. Louisa rushed out of her house.

"What happened? Are you hurt?" She examined Chris's bloodied lip and led both men indoors.

Helen got out of the car and scurried indoors. Was Sascha still watching? She had a knot in her belly that said he was.

27

They laid the blanket by the drystone wall, out of the breeze. Helen's calves still prickled from the gorse on the climb up Lyth Hill and her arms and face were now absorbing the burn of the sun. She knelt forward and kissed Gary.

They released each other when two teenage boys came into view.

"Lovely day," Gary said.

The boys sniggered and ran on.

Helen fetched the champagne out of the rucksack. Gary opened it, bursting the cork into the air. The boys, who'd stopped in the next field to unfurl a kite, cheered.

Helen held out her glass. Gary filled it to overflowing. He brought her hand to his mouth and licked the froth off her fingers.

There was another cheer when the boys' kite took off, some kind of superhero, an upstart against the sky. In the distance behind it, miles away, was the grey-green crag of the Long Mynd.

Helen scanned left to the Wrekin, its pointed summit obscured by wispy white clouds. It looked like Mount Fuji. It was hard to believe they were only three miles from Shrewsbury.

She squeezed Gary's arm. "I can see the whole world from here."

Gary tilted his head, his eyes on the bodice of her summer dress. "It's a great view."

She play-slapped him and chimed her glass with his. "Here's to the best teacher," she said and pulled him towards her for another kiss. They'd phoned Damian the previous day to get the international GCSE German results. This was their celebration. She took a sip. It danced into her head, tickling the roof of her mouth.

There was another whoop from the boys as the kite ducked and weaved in the wind.

Birdsong carried from the trees behind the wall.

"A wood warbler," Gary said.

She laughed. "Since when did you become an expert?"

"I've always appreciated nature." His gaze was lopsided again.

A thought she'd forgotten came back to her. "What do you know about Silesia?"

"What?"

"Something Manfred Scholz said. He mentioned cranes in Silesia."

Gary sat up, resting his arms on his bent knees. "Millions of German Silesians lost their homeland at the end of the war. I expect he was a refugee. Next term I'll ask him to talk to the students about it." He dropped down onto his elbow and caressed her thigh through her dress.

Helen stayed sitting up. *Next term* – one more weekend before they had to catch the ferry back to Germany. Back to Louisa Howard, Chris Mowar, and Sascha Jakobsen. Her body tensed under Gary's caress. No, not Sascha, not back to him. The pool would be closed by the time they returned. No access to dangerous waters. She looked at her husband. There wouldn't be another swim.

"What are you thinking?" he asked.

"Nothing." She calculated the days until the school Christmas holidays and their next escape to Shropshire. She'd never longed for winter so much in her life.

A wispy seed ball floated close to her and got caught in her hair. She brushed at it, but Gary picked it off and blew it back into the air. His large, gentle palm stayed upwards for a moment. She admired the deep lifeline across it. She smoothed out the blanket and lay down on her elbow, mirroring him. She felt his eyes all over her.

"That colour suits you," he said. He leant towards her. "There's a bird hide across there, secluded. How about it?"

She scanned the horizon. The boys had gone beyond the brow of the hill, their bobbing kite still visible. She could no longer hear their excited commentary.

"But …"

He breathed kisses on her collarbone.

She scooped up the blanket and took his hand.

28

Saturday, 27 November

Helen gripped Gary's hand as they headed towards the wooden huts that glowed with Christmas lights. She could see their painted stall signs, although she didn't have a clue what they meant.

"I hardly recognize it as Dortmannhausen," she said, feeling disoriented.

"That's why we waited until it got dark – to get the atmosphere," Gary said. He led her past a crêpe stall that smelled of cinnamon and Nutella.

The mention of the darkness unsettled her. She hadn't felt right since they returned from their summer break. The sense that someone might be watching crept up on her. She scanned the market, but saw no one looking in her direction, just people enjoying themselves. Nearby a small boy was playing a violin. Gary tossed a euro coin into his open music case. Further on a jazz band supplanted the child's hesitant strains. Helen felt a hot blast from the two big heaters on the musicians' stage. She and Gary watched for a few minutes, absorbing the welcome warmth, as well as their high-tempo rendition of "Santa Claus is Coming to Town".

Her stomach rumbled when they came to a man spit-roasting knuckles of pork that wouldn't have looked out of place in a cave painting. Ahead, people of all ages were gliding across a temporary ice rink.

Helen spotted Chris Mowar with Louisa Howard at a *Glühwein* kiosk. They had their backs to her but she recognized Chris by the huge Cossack-style hat that he'd taken to wearing. It made his head look even bigger than usual. Louisa was hiding her trim figure in a shabby ski suit that was several sizes too big. Helen remembered the conversation she'd overheard in the restaurant months ago and guessed Louisa was doing her best to economize.

She took Gary's hand and tugged him in the opposite direction but, too late, he saw them. She put on her bravest smile and suppressed the *expletive* that came to her lips as he led her over to say hello.

But when the woman turned round, it wasn't Louisa; it was Mel. According to the occasional public announcements that Louisa made, Mel was bedridden and not eating. Well, she got the not eating bit right – although Mel was cocooned in the shapeless ski suit, she must have lost two stone. She had her grubby white bobble hat pulled low over her head, but there was no disguising her serious cheekbones.

Chris made a show of buying them all mugs of *Glühwein*. "I asked for a shot of amaretto in yours, Helen, because you like a kick in everything."

Gary squeezed her hand: *don't rise to the bait*. She squeezed back: *I won't*. But Chris stopped teasing to read a text message. He looked up from his phone. "Damian says they'll meet us after the boys have been on the big wheel."

"They must love it here," Helen said. "I expect Louisa can't get them off the rink."

Mel shook her head. "She won't let the boys go skating in case they slice off a finger. They're all promising musicians, she says."

Was there a smirk in her voice? Her extended stay in bed had done her good.

Eventually Gary released Helen from Chris's anecdotes and said they'd catch them later. They swept into the throng of the market. Helen stayed clamped to Gary's arm. She couldn't shake off the feeling that someone in the crowd was watching.

Later they bumped into Mel again, this time without Chris. "Shall we get something to eat?" she asked. Whatever had caused the dramatic weight loss hadn't killed her appetite.

Gary led them through the stalls and ordered chips at a catering trailer. He also bought *Backfisch*, oblongs of battered fish with chunks of white bread. As they ate at a customer table, two teenage saxophonists serenaded them with a decipherable attempt at "Silent Night".

After he tipped the musicians, he and Mel went to look for drinks. Helen wandered about on her own, unnerved and feeling heady with the scents of two huts selling perfumed candles.

***

The lights from inside the church illuminated its one stained glass window – of Saint Boniface, wearing what looked like Marigold gloves – but failed to throw much light beyond the nearest stalls. Helen headed towards the flaming torchlight further on and came to a makeshift stable housing two sheep and a donkey. Life-size models of Mary and Joseph knelt over an empty manger, awaiting the arrival of the *Christkind* on Christmas Day. Recorded organ music from a loudspeaker completed the effect. She'd never seen a living nativity before and couldn't imagine UK councils allowing beacons of naked flame outside a stable.

Sascha Jakobsen appeared next to her. The sounds of the market blurred into the background behind the noise of alarm in her head. She hadn't seen him since that stupid day in July, but the same feelings of fear and anger and craving thundered through her. She wanted to flee, but stood her ground, gripping the top of the stable gate. Why run when he knew where she lived? He could catch her any time he wanted.

"Was it cold by the river this morning?" he asked.

"You were there, in the copse; you followed me?" A tremor went through her.

Sascha shook his head. "I've seen you often enough to know where you go. Sometimes you run, but not when there is ice on the ground."

"You're stalking me?" Oh God, he'd seen all her comings and goings. Her walks to the school library, her jogs around the neighbourhood, her visits to Maria for English lessons. She'd dismissed Louisa's paranoia, but she was right. None of them were safe. She'd have to tell Gary everything despite what it would do to their marriage. She blinked away tears.

Sascha's jaw tightened. "It's not all about you, Helen," he said. "I wait and I watch, but it's not about you."

Helen's eyes pricked with more tears. Why did she care about the coldness in his voice? There was nothing between them, never had been.

He placed his hands next to hers on the gate. They'd been side by side on the pool rail at the end of their last swim. She flushed at the memory of how her body had kicked and pulled and pulsed in time with his. She looked around to see if anyone was watching them.

"Your husband is listening to the jazz band with the fat woman who is no longer fat."

Sascha was stalking them all.

"Stay away from us or I'll call the police."

"*Gratuliere!*" Sascha clapped his hands. "Finally you sound like Howard's wife."

"Get lost, Sascha," she shouted. "I'm nothing like Louisa." A woman looking at the nativity scene turned to stare. Helen lowered her voice. "Leave me alone, I don't want you near me."

Sascha's eyes narrowed and he snarled: "Are you sure about that?" He stole away into the crowd.

Helen stood for several minutes, listening to the munching of the animals at their hay nets. She tried to let the gentle sound relax her, but her whole body was shaking.

The organ CD finished.

"You can't cherry-pick the easy parts." A loud English voice filled the gap left by the music. Chris Bloody Mowar again. Idiot. Just because he was speaking English, it didn't mean the locals couldn't hear him. Gary said all Brits were guilty of it; they never learnt to keep their voices down when they went out. She flushed, praying Chris hadn't heard her with Sascha.

"It ends now," another strident voice said. Louisa. They must be on the other side of the stable.

"I'll try to protect you, but I can't guarantee …" Chris's voice trailed off.

"Are you threatening me?" Louisa sounded nervous. "The whole thing is laughable."

"You should know where your loyalties lie."

"This has to stop. I should have stopped it long ago. I don't want to do this anymore."

Helen pulled into the shadows of the church as Louisa emerged from behind the stable and hurried away. When she was sure Chris wouldn't follow, Helen moved back into the main market. She found Gary and Mel listening to the jazz band as Sascha said she would. She couldn't look either of them in the eye.

They browsed the stalls for another hour but the magic had gone. Sascha had killed it. And Louisa, Mrs Perfect Wife and Mother, the Relate counsellor who poked her nose into Helen's marriage, was the one having an affair. She was a fake with her homebaking and piano soirees, and aromatherapy balls.

When they bumped into the Howards, Louisa was hanging onto Damian's arm like a love-struck teenager. Even he looked suspicious when she laughed hysterically at one of his jokes. The guilty madam had the brass neck to offer Mel a lift home when Chris texted to say he wanted to stay on.

Helen suggested Toby ride back with them so there'd be more space in the Howards' car for Mel.

"Did you enjoy yourself tonight?" she asked him when they set off.

"Yeah."

"Do you think your mum enjoyed it?"

"'Spose." He yawned and closed his eyes.

Helen stopped digging. Louisa and Chris deserved each other. She looked at Gary. And she deserved her husband, not Sascha. Never.

Fiona

My stomach lurched every time I moved up the queue. I wanted to get it over with, get the hell out, but I had to wait for the only payphone on campus to become free. Shep had taken my mobile to get me an untraceable SIM card and hadn't brought it back yet.

The man in front of me was in his early twenties, a couple of years older than me. He had black curly hair and a couple of flecks of skin on the shoulders of his heavy coat. He stepped forward and picked up the phone. My heart dropped down my insides. My turn next. Too soon. I wasn't ready. I turned to let the girl behind me go first, but she stepped out of the queue to talk with a friend walking past. No one else was waiting.

The man raised his voice and laughed. He didn't sound English. God, no, was he with the Syndicate? Should I run? Scream? My heart banged against my ribcage but I made myself stand still. Stay calm, don't draw attention. One more day and I'd be away and safe. My best chance of keeping alive until then meant waiting behind a man who could kill me. As long as he didn't turn round, as long as he didn't catch my eye. After tomorrow I'd have control. One more day.

As I stood there hiding in plain sight, the unfamiliar lilt and jolt of his voice became reassuring. He sounded Eastern European. From

Poland or Hungary. A postgraduate, not a killer. But when he hung up and walked away, my heart raced again. I couldn't put it off any longer. Lives were at stake. I dialled.

"Hi, Mum, it's me," I said, forcing bright and happy into my voice and thanking God it wasn't Dad who'd picked up.

"Fiona, love. We've been trying your mobile but it won't ring."

"I ... I switch it off when I'm studying."

"Have you done that Molière essay you told us about?"

Tears pricked. The Molière essay was last month. I got another First for it, but it hardly mattered now. "Still working on it," I said. "But the thing is – and I want you to be happy for me. The thing is ... I've been offered a job as a trainee journalist on a regional newspaper in France but I have to start straightaway."

The silence on the line lengthened. Was my excitement an octave too high to be convincing?

"Where in France?" Mum asked eventually.

"Er ... Marseilles."

"But you did your sandwich year in Lyons. How do they know about you in Marseilles?"

Oh God, nothing got past her. "They heard ... I mean, I applied. Lyons gave me a reference."

"But you were a language assistant at a school. What kind of reference could they give for a post as a trainee journalist?"

"How good my French is, maybe?" I winced.

"But is it good enough to land a job that's rarer than hen's teeth? I didn't know you wanted to be a journalist. Did you know, Paul?"

"Let me speak to her." Dad's voice in the background. Then clearer: "Fiona, love, are you in some kind of trouble?"

He sounded so tired. I nearly cracked then, gave it up. But I remembered what was at stake. I had to protect them.

"Everything's fine, Dad. It's a great job. You don't know how lucky I am."

"There isn't some bloke putting you up to this?"

My breath caught in my throat.

149

"It's Mum here again. We'll come over at the weekend and talk about it."

"No! I've got … coursework to do. I'll be flat out."

"Why are you doing coursework if you're leaving university?" Mum asked.

"I want to … well … I need to practise …" I looked around the empty foyer. "I've got to go; there's a queue of people waiting for the phone."

"Switch your mobile on and we'll ring you back."

"It's in my room." I swallowed down a sigh. "Be happy for me."

"Phone us tomorrow to discuss this properly"

"Tomorrow …" Tears splashed down my face. "I love you both." I hung up the phone and sobbed.

29

Wednesday, 1 December

Helen and Gary stood shivering with half a dozen others on Louisa's front path. Helen clutched her tureen of chicken korma, trying to absorb its heat. She would rather have been anywhere else, but Louisa had lobbed a "do pop over if you're free" missile out of her Landcruiser window as she swept past that morning. Gary had taken it as a royal command.

"Have you brought cash for the drinks," Polly Stephens whispered to her husband, Jerome.

John, one of the swim teachers, was standing behind her. "It's always been free before. You can't blame her though. There must have been forty-odd people here last year," he said.

Louisa opened the door wide, welcomed them to the swim club social and gave them instructions. "Put your food in the kitchen. Hand your coats to Mel. Damian will serve your drinks, and the prices are labelled."

By the time Helen shuffled through the hall, Mel was behind the pile of coats. Helen kept her jacket on. In the kitchen she stacked up plates of nibbles to make space for her pot of curry. She stopped to exchange pleasantries with Dimitris, their Greek neighbour, and to listen while his wife, Maria, practised her English.

She squeezed her way through to the music room in search of space. Toby and Leo were hard at it on the cello and violin, and Murdo was bashing his tambourine whenever the mood took him. She couldn't hear them above the hubbub of the drinkers who spilled into the room. Poor kids, wouldn't they rather be on their Xboxes?

She went back to the dining room and found Gary. He was leaning against a sideboard. It was a cheap, veneered one these days. She recalled the mess that greeted them the night they'd been searching for Murdo. Why hadn't the Howards used the insurance money to buy a new glass-fronted cabinet?

"Has everyone got a drink?" Louisa asked, coming over to where the tide of guests had swept Helen and Gary to Jerome and Polly Stephens and their girls. Louisa air-kissed them all and explained that there would be mulled wine in the garden. "Although I think it will have to be later than planned because it's snowing a bit. Damian's set up some lights and I've laid out a winter wonderland trail for the children." She squatted down to Freya Stephens. "You'll get a bag of fairy dust to sprinkle in your garden to show Santa the way." She stood up again. "We've put up two gazebos so that the little ones can make glitter cards out there without getting snowed on. We're not charging for those. As the chairperson, it's my gift. I thought they could ..."

Helen's attention switched from Louisa to Mel who was chatting with the Barton couple from number 1. Having shed the baggy ski suit she wore at the Christmas market, she'd dressed her newly svelte finger in a black polo jumper and skinny jeans. And, as if that wasn't enough, the transformation above the neck was spectacular. Mel's greasy auburn hair was now a spiky peroxide crop. Her usually dull and bloated face was glowing.

Helen wasn't the only one who'd noticed. "Wow," Jerome Stephens said.

"You're married to me, remember?" Polly laughed.

"Am I?"

"I wonder what her secret is," Polly said.

"Chris asked me to help," Louisa said, bringing the conversation round to her. "You could say I nursed her back to health. I took her to my salon for the hair-do – a decent stylist can work wonders with the most unpromising head – and I lent her those old clothes; they're a wee bit big for me."

She must be seething to see her cast-offs worn so well. Did it explain the argument Helen had overheard at the Christmas market? Did Louisa break off her affair with Chris because he was in love with his wife again?

She couldn't resist a dig. "Chris is a lucky man."

It hit the mark. Louisa said: "By the way, Helen, thanks for the chicken curry. Two other guests had the same idea. We're awash with the stuff." She walked over to Mel, said something to her and they left the room together.

Helen went with Polly to say hello to Karola and Geoff Barton.

"It's nice to chat," Karola said. "We often see you in the street but daren't stop because the dogs jump up and not everyone likes that."

"I wouldn't mind," Helen said. "Speaking of dogs, I haven't seen Napoleon yet. Is he hiding?"

"Louisa had to shut him in one of the bedrooms for Mel's benefit."

"That was considerate of her," Helen said, remembering the dinner party when Louisa let the dog gnaw his bone by Mel's feet.

"Mel insisted on it. And to think she used to be such a little mouse."

"Where is Mel, by the way? I saw her go off with Louisa."

"Louisa wanted her to check the ingredients on a torte she brought in case it contained gelatine."

Helen bristled. Couldn't Louisa read the blasted packet herself?

153

Eventually Mel came back with a glass of wine. Helen toyed with complimenting her on her appearance but didn't want to say anything that might make her uncomfortable.

Polly Stephens didn't share her dilemma. "You look gorgeous tonight. I think my husband fancies you."

Helen held her breath, expecting Mel to gasp and sweat, but she smiled and accepted the compliment with grace.

Conversation in the group was smooth. Polly explained about their planned Christmas break to Center Parcs with the Garcia family. Karola and Geoff Barton said they were staying at home because Geoff had a new school prospectus to write. Mel sipped her wine and smiled.

Louisa cut in next to her. "Just to let you know, Mel, the wine is €1.75, not €1.50, so I've put the extra 25 cents in for you."

Mel blushed. "I'm so sorry ... I ... I'll get more money from Chris."

"No need to be petty, Mel. It's sorted now," Louisa said and turned to face the rest of the room. She tapped a fork against her glass. When she had everyone's attention, she said: "It's lovely to have so many swim club members and other friends here ..."

There were replies of "Nice to be here," and "Thanks a lot," before everyone returned to their conversations. But Louisa hadn't finished and tapped the glass again.

"If you'd like to go through to the garden. The snow is easing off now. There are activities free of charge for the children, and mulled wine for €1. Serve yourself and put the money in the box."

Helen smiled to herself as the €1.75 wine queue dispersed in the direction of the patio door. School teachers knew a bargain when they heard one. She stayed with Mel and the Bartons. Mel was becoming chatty and asked Geoff about his PR job at school.

"Sorry to interrupt," Louisa said, coming between Mel and Geoff. "Mel, can you show me how to warm shop-bought choco buns. I'm afraid I only know about home-made pastry."

Mel followed her to the kitchen again. Helen rolled her eyes.

There was a blast of cold air as people with steaming styrofoam cups opened the patio door and stepped back into the house. They stamped the cold out of their feet and cupped their mulled wine in two hands. From nowhere Louisa fetched towels for her guests to dry the glistening snowflakes from their hair and shoulders. She looked down at her doormat, sodden with slush, and said she'd get more towels.

Gary came in with two cups and handed one to Helen. The noise levels were higher than ever as people swapped stories of previous ordeals in blizzards to rival their snowy adventure in the Howards' back garden. Helen squeezed Gary's cold hand. Except for Louisa's sniping at Mel, it was turning into a fun evening.

Chris barged into the circle to ask where Mel was. "One of you must have seen her," he said.

Helen told him to try the kitchen.

"Obviously I checked there first."

"What about the garden?" another woman suggested.

"Will you help me look?" Chris said, turning to Gary.

He followed Chris through the patio door. It was like watching Mel follow Louisa. His acquiescence irritated the hell out of Helen. She went after them.

It was freezing outside. Helen hugged herself. Fairy lights twinkled on the climbing frame and on two canvas gazeboes. The guests had trampled across the snowy grass to get to the urn of mulled wine that steamed in front of the summer house. The lawn looked like the top of a large, thinly iced wedding cake on which a rugby match had taken place.

A few children stood at the table under one of the gazebos, attempting to make glitter pictures, but their numb little fingers struggled to hold the glue sticks. The Howards' lawn would be all shades of silver, gold, and sparkling pink when the snow melted.

There was no sign of Mel but she saw that Gary and Chris were standing by Damian, their silhouettes lit up against the lanterns on the summer house. They held steaming cups and seemed to be about to head into the hut to sit down. It looked as if their search for Mel had become less pressing once they had inhaled the *Glühwein* fumes.

Sascha Jakobsen shot out of the summer house, catching his head on a string of bells and setting off a peal of Christmas chimes. He sidestepped Damian and the others, and upset a table, sending empty foam cups skittering into the snow. He scrambled over the back fence and left the men to shout and swear after him.

They fell silent when Mel also emerged from the summer house.

"You!" Louisa screeched from the patio.

"I didn't know he was in there," Mel said. "I went in for a sit down."

"Why didn't you come out again and phone the police?"

Mel's shoulders slouched and she lowered her head.

"You're even more pathetic than you used to be!" Louisa went back into the house.

Before Helen's eyes, Mel reverted to her old self: her confidence vanished. The young face with killer cheekbones grew old, grey, and gaunt.

Helen stormed inside in a rage, her hands trembling, and found Louisa asking Karola Barton about how to get a restraining order in Germany while topping up her glass.

"Make sure you pay the full amount for that wine, Karola, or Louisa will chase you for the rest. She'll tell you it's petty but she'll still ask you. Isn't that right, Louisa? Or is it only Mel that you choose to humiliate at every opportunity?"

"Helen, what's got into you?" Louisa said.

"Mel was happy tonight, but you made it your business to squash her flat."

"I have a right to be angry." She clutched the wine bottle, like an official holding a clipboard.

"You heard what she said: he was already in the summer house."

"She should have come straight back out. He destroyed my garden and ransacked my house."

"You have no proof he burgled our houses."

"I welcomed you into this cul-de-sac and invited you into my home. You have a warped sense of loyalty." She turned away, her point made, her opponent dismissed.

Helen wasn't having it. "You didn't welcome me, you hounded me until I submitted to your so-called hospitality. But it's only ever about showing off and lording it over everyone else."

"Steady on, Helen," Gary said, appearing beside her.

She ignored him. "The other neighbours might put up with it but I've had enough. I'm not one of the herd, never have been. I go my own way."

Louisa came towards her. "Then I suggest you go your own way out of my house. We don't want you here."

"*We* – does that mean you're speaking for everyone?" She waved her arms around. Most of the guests were giving their wine beakers close scrutiny. Jerome Stephens was admiring the carpet. "Don't set yourself up as a matriarch, Louisa, you might find you're not up to the job."

"Helen, that's enough," Gary shouted.

She looked into his horrified face and then ran to the front door. She expected him to come after her but he didn't.

30

Thursday, 2 December

Gary got changed in their bedroom. At least he hadn't moved out completely even though he'd spent the previous night in the spare room. The relief on seeing him adjusting his tie in their mirror softened her resolve. She could do what he asked: go to Louisa's dinner party and apologize. But the guilt she was feeling about making a scene in front of the neighbours took second place to the fury that he hadn't defended her.

She put the argument out of her mind and sat down.

"You can't go in jeans," he said.

She took a deep breath and prepared for the fight to start again. "Why can't I fake a headache like Mel?"

Gary eyed her in the mirror. "You think Mel's faking? Last night set her back to how she was after the burglary. Chris says she's on sedatives."

"That wasn't my fault. I could have throttled Louisa."

"I noticed. And so did half the school."

"Someone had to stick up for Mel. Louisa pokes holes in everyone."

"Louisa's nothing like that. I don't understand you sometimes."

"It's odd that she's throwing a dinner party, the day after the swim club party, when her own husband has gone to a head teachers' conference. And why has she invited Creepy Chris when his wife is ill in bed? There's something not right about any of them."

"Why do you look for a conspiracy in everything? Our neighbours are perfectly normal people. You haven't known Louisa as long as I have, and she's very kind." He took her arm. "Please get ready, love. The fact is you've never given her a chance, just like you've never given this place a chance."

Helen shook herself free. "I'm here, aren't I?"

"Sometimes I wonder why." He looked at his watch. "I'm going over. You can catch me up."

"Run along then," she shouted after him. "Mustn't keep Lady Louisa waiting."

***

After an hour of stewing over the row and knowing she couldn't leave it unresolved, Helen decided to join Gary at the Howards'. She slipped on her cotton dress and teamed it with tights and boots. It was a peace offering. Special memories of the summer: the picnic on Lyth Hill. To make it right again, she'd play-act the perfect dinner guest. In her blush pink dress.

It had snowed so heavily since Gary headed over that the street looked like a freshly made bed. Snow clogged the soles of her boots, making her slip. She wrapped her arms – as good as naked in the thin sleeves – around her body and hunched her shoulders, trying to protect her bare neck from the chill.

The Howards' porch roof provided a temporary refuge but, when no one let her in, she cursed herself for not putting a coat on. She tried the door handle but it was locked. The upper windows were in darkness but light shone behind the closed blinds downstairs. She banged on the kitchen window, sure they'd be able to hear her from the dining room. Why didn't one of them break away from Louisa's organic beef Wellington and let her in? Couldn't Gary guess it was her outside, freezing her earlobes?

"Sod it." Her voice cracked through the air and bounced off the house.

The side gate wouldn't budge. Bloody typical; the one night they locked it. They never locked it, not even after Murdo went walkabout. She shook the wrought-iron railings in frustration and the gate moved a fraction, causing the security light to come on. It wasn't locked; thick snow had wedged it shut. She shoved it back and forth and managed to open it about three inches but the compacted snow meant it wouldn't yield further.

Why was she even bothering? She should go home, back into the warm. But if she didn't resolve the row with Gary, the atmosphere at home would turn glacial. She had to make amends with Louisa to have any chance of getting her marriage on track.

She waved her hand to bring the light back on. Children's spades were propped by the back door. The Howard boys must have been using them to build snowmen and, like the tidy children they were, leant them against the wall when they'd finished. She squeezed her arm through the railings and her long swimmer's fingers reached a handle.

She was sweating by the time she'd shifted enough snow to open the gate a few more inches, but her hands and feet were blocks of ice. Her dress hooked itself on the gate catch as she pressed through the gap, but her hands were too numb to release it. She felt it rip.

She banged on the back door with the spade. No response. She formed her hands as far into fists as her numbed nerves would allow and hammered on the glass. As she fell against the door, her arm caught on the handle. To her surprise, the door wasn't locked and opened into the warmth of Louisa's laundry room. She stepped inside and let her dead hands and feet soak up the biting, pricking heat.

"Sorry I'm late," she called as she closed the door and breathed in the smells of cooking. Entering Louisa's kitchen usually meant assault by lemon freshness, but approaching it now from the laundry room it smelled like raw meat.

A stack of used plates at the sink might explain the odour, or the old pans on the turned-off hob. Louisa was at the breakfast bar. Helen smiled to herself. She'd caught top wife bent over, struggling to get her icing perfect. Cherry topping spilled over the edge of the gateau, dripping onto the floor.

"Hello," Helen said, "that looks tricky."

Louisa didn't turn round.

"Do you need any help?" she asked, coming up closer. Her breath stuck in her throat. Louisa's face was pressed into a cheese-cake with cherry sauce spattered on the back of her crisp white collar. Asleep? She gave her shoulder a nudge. Louisa's body shifted, but her head didn't. Helen recoiled; it wasn't cherry sauce but the frayed edges of a bib of blood.

Something warm and sticky touched Helen's knee. Blood seeped into her dress where she'd leant against one of the stool legs. Her boot nudged into a pool of it and she left a bloodied print on a fresh part of the floor.

She coughed up bile. Her heartbeat jerked and jolted in its own panicked rhythm, but she forced back control of her breathing. *Deep breath.* Gary and Chris must be in the dining room. *Deep breath.* They would know what to do.

Someone came in here and did this. But not through the gate because it was stuck. Over the back fence. Like Sascha Jakobsen the night before. But, no, a complete stranger did this, a mad man roaming the streets and knifing women in their kitchens.

The hall smelled metallic and fleshy. Napoleon lay on his side, paws outstretched. His guts spilled through his downy belly fur which was mottled black and red. Her breathing lost it then. It pummelled her body, shallow and rapid.

"Gary," she gasped.

Silence. Don't be stupid. She put her hands on her knees, panting, thinking. Gary and Chris must have gone to get more beer from the late-night store. That's why the lunatic struck when he did. But he's gone now. Her breathing calmed enough to let her step around the dog and push open the dining room door.

Gary was slumped over the table with his face turned away from her. She saw the tuft of hair on his neck where he'd missed shaving for a couple of days. She'd meant to tell him. A bloody patch oozed below his left shoulder blade. She let out a breath, perhaps he wasn't dead. But when she moved round, she saw his open, empty eyes. The room whirled. Sweat burst out of her. She gripped the table edge.

Trembling, she bent to look underneath in search of another corpse but there was nothing there except Gary's crossed ankles and a discarded napkin. If Chris wasn't dead, he must have … He'd flipped. That craziness behind his eyes was always there.

The music room door was open. *Get the hell out! Move!* But her legs wouldn't take her. She listened hard but heard no sound except her own short breaths. She stepped towards the door and saw Chris lying on the floor.

She could only see his legs, twisted at an odd angle. Toby's cello lay on its side in a pool of blood. There were splashes all over its varnished body and the sound holes were gunged up. The strings had been cut and had pinged apart, coiling themselves into the blood pool. The neck was snapped and it looked like a wounded animal drinking at a water hole of its own fluids.

Poor Toby, how could someone do this to a child's cello? *Oh God, the kids.* Upstairs, asleep, or … She stubbed her toe on something heavy. When she saw what it was, her bladder gave way. Warm pee ran down her thighs and soaked into her tights. She ran through the house, retching. She'd tripped over Chris's severed head.

From the foot of the stairs she could see Gary's body at the dining table. She wanted to fall on the bottom step and weep but she had to check on the children first. She reached the top but had no notion of where she found the strength to make the climb. Outside the first door on the landing she halted. The fear of what she might find hit her. Her body stiffened; some things should remain unseen. But what if they were hurt, still alive? She held her breath as she opened the door and switched on the light, bracing herself for new carnage.

The mound in the bed moved and Murdo sat up. "Heh," he said sleepily and rubbed his eyes in the harsh glare. She'd forgotten how it felt to meet a living, breathing human being. The shock made her heartbeat rocket. The colour drained from Murdo's face as he made out her blood-soaked dress.

"It's okay. I spilled some wine. Go back to sleep," she whispered. Her voice sounded splintered.

He lay down, and she waited until he'd closed his eyes. She grabbed a chair from his room, switched off the light and closed the door. She wedged the chair under Murdo's door handle. She couldn't do anything about Louisa, or the dog, or the severed … or Gary – but she could stop these children from going downstairs.

There was another chair on the landing. She wedged it under the next door. She'd never been upstairs in Louisa's house before and had no idea if one of the other boys was asleep inside. She couldn't open any more doors to check in case she disturbed them. If she acted quickly they could sleep on until she fetched help.

Three times, she told herself afterwards, three times she went downstairs into the dining room. Three times she walked past her dead husband. Three times she carried one of Louisa's heavy dining chairs upstairs to wedge it under the remaining doors on the landing. When she tried to prop up the last one, the door crept open. She held her breath but gasped with relief when it turned out to be the empty bathroom, still smelling jasmine-fresh.

Now get out, get help. She threw herself down the stairs and out of the front door. She heaved up her guts on the snowy lawn, aware of the cold air assaulting her. She felt faintness coming on and wanted to curl up in the snow until the nightmare ended. But the children. She sprinted to the street and collided with Manfred Scholz. She clung to him and didn't let go.

31

Gisela Jakobsen lolled against the residents' mailboxes in the foyer. She wasn't sure it was her own apartment building but at this time of night she didn't give a damn. *Es ist mir völlig Wurscht. Ich will pennen* (I want a kip). She sank to the floor ready to sleep. She thought of the angry man's voice on the intercom as he let her in. Too tired to stand outside and fumble with her door key while a polar wind snatched at her backside, she'd pressed the buzzer to every apartment. The man who answered said he'd set his dog on her.

She hauled herself to her feet and put her hands out to stop the foyer from spinning. *Wo wohne ich?* She laughed out loud as she wondered where the hell she lived. She caught sight of a fern wreath on the door in the corner. It was a Christmas present from one of the neighbours. The Saviour's birth. She hadn't bothered to tell the silly woman they didn't decorate anymore.

She staggered over to her front door. Purse, fags and other entrails fell out of her handbag when she unzipped it. Her head thumped as she squatted down to retrieve her bunch of keys. *Scheiße*, how was she supposed to know which stupid key to use? She'd sleep on it. She closed her eyes.

***

She came to with her face pressed against the Christmas wreath. She pulled away and rubbed her dimpled skin. How long had she blacked out for? She blinked hard, trying to kick-start her brain but she couldn't remember how she'd got back to her flat. It was the second part of the evening that had gone missing.

She knew she'd been thrown out of *Gasthaus Holtmühle* because the landlord had called her *besoffen* (plastered). He ordered her a taxi to take her home but she told the driver to take her to another bar. She accused him of clocking up an extortionate fare so he pulled up outside a bar near the international school and ordered her out of his taxi. She screamed at him that she wasn't drinking with no British lowlifes but he drove off. Had she gone into the bar? She had no memory of what the hell she did until she found herself drinking *schnapps* in Dortmannhausen Christmas market at midnight.

She selected a key at random and stabbed at the door lock. *Verdammt, zu klein* (too small). She switched to a bigger key but couldn't get within five centimetres of the lock because of the tremor in her hand. She slid down to the floor. It was pointless knocking; Sascha wouldn't hear her. She doubted he was even there. He'd set out about seven with a grim look on his face. It frightened her when he set his jaw like that, spoiling for a fight.

She found herself on her feet again. This time the key hit the target and the door let her in. She felt her way through the darkness to her bedroom. *Ich muß mal* (I need a wee). But when she reached the bathroom, she heard running water and saw the light on under the door. What was Sascha doing in there at this time of night? She tried to see the hands on her watch but the darkness and the drink stopped her focusing. Why couldn't he wait until morning before taking a shower?

32

"I think you need hospital. Perhaps I fetch your husband?" Manfred said.

Helen gripped him tighter, feeling dazed. "Phone the police." The effort to speak exhausted her and she didn't reply when he asked her what had happened.

He stepped back and tried to give her his coat but she refused it. "I'm covered in blood." She wrapped her arms around herself and shivered.

"We can call from my house."

Manfred's hall was barren – a worn carpet and a telephone resting on an upturned vegetable crate – but after Number Ten, it was the cosiest place on Earth. She sat at the foot of the stairs while he made the call and talked to the operator in German. He sounded calm and authoritative. Afterwards she asked him what he had said.

"That perhaps an accident has occurred at Dickensweg, number 10. They will send a policeman to check."

"Did you tell them about the boys?"

Manfred looked baffled.

"Police sirens will wake them up. We have to go back. They mustn't see the bodies."

Manfred narrowed his eyes as if weighing up how to respond. "If you won't take my coat, you must have my hat and scarf."

He lifted his felt hat from his head and put it on hers. It was warm from his body heat. When he put his scarf around her shoulders, it smelled of tobacco. In normal circumstances such intimate contact with her elderly neighbour would have repulsed her, now it was the nearest thing to fatherly love.

As they reached the Howards' garden path, a police vehicle pulled up behind them. Two young men got out and adjusted their caps.

Manfred approached them and spoke in German. He pointed at Helen. In the light from the street lamps, Helen saw both officers alter their posture. They'd seen her dress.

One said something to the other and went to the front door. He was moving in and out of focus as if Helen were watching him from the end of a long telescope. He disappeared inside. A million miles away she heard Manfred give his name and address to the other officer. The policeman moved on to her and spoke in English. On autopilot she gave her date of birth. A buzzing noise rushed through her head.

"Catch her," she heard him say and in the next moment she was in the passenger seat of the police car wrapped in a foil blanket. The officer squatted in front of her, the bottom of his jacket trailing in the snow. There were traces of acne at his temples. She wondered if he was old enough for this. He asked her to describe what happened. She rambled about children's spades and cherry sauce.

She looked up at Number Ten and stopped speaking. Snowy roof, climbing trellises around the door, Christmas lanterns in the window. "Chocolate box," she mouthed. The only sign of any disturbance was a dark patch on the snow-covered path where she'd vomited.

"You were telling me what happened in the kitchen," the man

prompted but, before she could reply, his colleague reappeared at the Howards' door.

He shouted something and stood there for a moment, taking deep, steadying breaths, before going back in.

The other officer abandoned his questioning and spoke to Manfred. Apparently following his instructions, Manfred helped Helen out of the car while the policeman got on his radio.

More German police cars arrived and a civilian van. For a while, Helen and Manfred waited there, ignored, while officers set up floodlights and taped a police cordon around the house. Others donned plastic coveralls and entered through the front door. A female officer stepped out of the house and under the police tape. She was small but with an air of command about her. She strode over to them and spoke to Manfred. Then she talked into her radio.

A few minutes later another female officer came out carrying Murdo. Leo walked between her and Toby, holding their hands. They were wearing wellington boots and coats but Helen could see their pyjama trousers too.

"The officer asked if they can shelter at my house for a moment," Manfred explained.

The boys and the policewoman trudged through the snow, following Manfred to his house. Their faces looked bewildered but not unhappy. Helen's throat knotted: when those poor boys find out what's happened ... She turned away so that the floodlights wouldn't pick out the vivid pattern on her dress, made up of their mother's blood. She pulled the foil blanket tighter and found herself looking up at house number 8. Jerome Stephens was standing at an upstairs window staring down at her.

The first female officer, the small, confident one, brought a tall man in jeans and a thick anorak over to her. She introduced him as Detective Zanders of the *Kriminalpolizei* and she said her name was Simons. "Mrs Taylor, we will interview you formally in due course, but are you well enough to answer a few questions now?"

Helen nodded but they'd already fetched out their notebooks; it had been a statement of their intent, not a request.

"Were you a guest at the house?" Zanders asked.

"I should have been but I was late."

"Who let you in?"

"No one. I went around the back. It was unlocked."

"Through the kitchen?"

She nodded and swallowed hard.

Simons took over the questioning. "Where was the woman when you entered?"

"Where she is now."

"Tell us exactly where that was, please, Mrs Taylor."

"In the cheesecake." She suppressed an urge to laugh. How long before hysteria got her?

Her two interrogators looked at each other. Simons said: "You're saying she was dead when you found her? Did you try to revive her?"

Her legs were aching now. She was tired of standing and wanted to get back in the police car. "I could see she was dead. If you mean: how did I get the bloodstains, I brushed against blood on the stool. It was hard not to."

"What did you do after you realized the woman was dead, Mrs Taylor?"

"I went to tell Gary, my husband."

"You left the house immediately?"

"No, Gary is at the dining table. I went to tell him, but he wasn't much help." She heard a harsh, ugly sound and realized it was her own bitter laughter. The officers made notes on their pads. The harder she laughed, the more they wrote. Between her wild giggles, she heard a car door slam and running footsteps approach. She carried on shrieking and only stopped when someone shouted: "What the hell's going on, Helen?" Hearing someone call her by her Christian name for the first time in a hundred years, she shut up and turned around to reply. But the newcomer backed away from her. Helen, stinking of sweat and piss and blood, was facing Damian Howard.

PART TWO

33

Gisela hated Aldi even though it was the cheapest place for *Sekt* and spirits. She always got the same woman at the checkout who peered at her down her spectacles and said: "*Schon wieder?*" Gisela would glare back. *Why shouldn't I be here again already? If I don't buy booze, you're out of a job.*

She preferred to take the car to the Lidl on the ring road but her head was hammering and she was seeing double so driving was out of the question. She had no option but to walk to Aldi. She'd wanted to stay in bed but sleep had deserted her when a streak of winter sun had bounced off the snow and in through the gap in her blinds. Her mouth felt like the bottom of a birdcage and she needed a drink. She'd made contact with a pair of jeans and a sweatshirt from the pile on the floor and pulled them on – slowly because every movement sent a jangling pain through her head.

Outside the apartment block she wheezed and coughed, the contrast with the centrally heated flat sending shockwaves through her lungs. She went back indoors to get her coat from the bedroom but she saw Sascha's jacket hanging in the hall and grabbed it instead. He wouldn't need it; as far as she knew, he was still in bed, more dead than she was.

She picked her way along the pavement. Law-abiding owners had cleared the snow from the front of their properties but it had fallen again, making the surfaces treacherous. When she turned the corner, she felt the full blast of the December air. She ducked back against the wall and put her hands in the jacket pockets, looking for Sascha's Marlboros. They weren't there but she touched a tiny object inside. Key ring? Jewellery? She took it out. An earring. It was a dainty piece – tiny emerald stones and one larger teardrop that would dangle as the wearer moved her head. *Has Sascha got a girlfriend? The swimmer he mentioned months ago?* She stuffed the earring back in the pocket.

Two elderly women with as much fur on their upper lips as on their collars, walked past her. "*Besoffen,*" one said.

"If you're going to call me drunk at least whisper, you deaf bats," Gisela called after them.

Their backs jerked upright. They tried to hurry away but had to make do with an affronted shuffle to avoid falling in the snow.

***

In Aldi people cluttered up the aisles. They must be buying cheap booze before hitting the *Weihnachtsmarkt.* She had to abandon her trolley to get round them.

"*Mindestens vier Tote,*" she heard one man say. (At least four dead.)

She squeezed through a group of women to get two bottles of *Sekt.* One was asking, "*Wer tötet einen Hund?*" (Who kills a dog?)

The queue at the checkout wasn't moving. The normally deadpan features of the shop assistant she loathed were animated as she talked to the customers around her. She had bright teeth. All those years of clamping her *Maul* shut must have kept them nice.

She shifted her weight from foot to foot, balancing the *Sekt* bottles in each hand. Hot air blasted out of wall heaters and she wished she had a spare hand to undo Sascha's jacket. She pushed to the front. "*Feiern Sie, oder?*" She asked the till operator if they were having a party.

Instead of her usual withering gaze, the woman smiled. Those white teeth again. "*Haben Sie schon gehört?* Have you heard? It's been on the news and one of our customers drove past and saw the roadblock. There's been an attack near the international school."

Sascha. Gisela's hand went to her throat.

"Police have been drafted in from all over," the woman was saying.

Not Sascha. Police drafted in must mean a terrorist attack.

"Where was the bomb?" Gisela asked. It was idle curiosity now. She didn't care if the whole damn school had gone up in flames.

"Was it a bomb?" the man next to her said. "I heard it was a gun."

"You're both wrong," the assistant said. "The latest radio report said they are still searching for the weapon, probably a knife."

Knife.

The woman continued her broadcast. "Stabbed an entire family. British."

Gisela bolted to the exit, desperate for cold air. Damian Howard was a teacher. Mareike's letter said it. And Sascha called his wife a stupid goat with expensive taste. The emerald earring burned in her pocket, Sascha's pocket. Hotter and hotter.

"You haven't paid for those," the woman called. Gisela put the two bottles down in the bag-pack area but one slid off the ledge. It smacked onto the floor and shattered. She stepped over the sweet liquid and broken glass, and ran.

"*Das geht aber nicht!*" the woman shouted indignantly after the closing door. "You can't do that."

Gisela fell on the slippery pavement. Her hands stung and a

wet patch at her knee turned red. She moved on, wishing she'd hung onto the *Sekt*.

***

She found Sascha standing in the lounge, smoking and wearing nothing but the housecoat that had belonged to his father before he walked out on them. Sascha had asked her to mend the pocket but she never had.

"I've been looking for that," he snapped when he saw her in his jacket.

"Why? Are you going out?"

He ignored her, taking the jacket. She trembled in case he felt inside it. Was the earring in the wrong pocket? He caught her looking at him.

"*Na und?*" she said. She would bluff her way out of it.

But he turned away without challenging her. She could let him go to his room, to his separate life. Never knowing, ignoring her nagging doubt. But she'd been knocking around hell for the past two years. Could another truth make it worse? She followed him into the hallway.

"Why were you taking a shower in the middle of the night?"

He dragged on his cigarette. "I didn't."

"I heard you when I came in."

He dragged again then tucked his hair behind his ear. He used to do that as a kid, giving himself time to think, the precursor to a lie. "But you didn't go out, Mama."

Wie bitte? (Pardon?) A lie about his own whereabouts *schon gut* (fair enough), but she hadn't expected one about hers.

She said: "I was out all evening and came home late. I heard the shower."

He placed his hands on her shoulders – gentle, fatherly. "Mama, please try to remember. You stayed at home last night."

Gott im Himmel, was I that far gone? She'd had the odd

blackout, now and then, for the last few months but she always recalled fragments. Last night was no different. Like crochet – holes in places, other parts firmly joined. *Schnäpse* at the Weihnachtsmarkt; more *Schnäpse* at Konys Bar; a car smelling of dirty leather and sweat; a bloke shouting; stupid keys not working; Christmas wreath; the sound of running, splashing water.

"You took a shower. I heard you. I'm sure of it."

"That was earlier, Mama. Remember?"

When was it? *Um wieviel Uhr*? What did her watch say? She scoured her memory. Her wrist came into focus, then the dial but not the figures. Try as she might they would not come. "Around two in the morning?"

It came out as a guess and he knew it. "Mama, Mama, Mama. We were both asleep by two. I made you hot chocolate at eleven but you were too tired to drink it so I sat on your bed and drank it myself. Remember?"

"*Ich* …?" So many holes, wool unravelling. How had she got this bad?

He led her to the sofa in the lounge. "Take a nap. It might come back to you after a sleep. We spent the whole evening together."

Together. The wool yanked tight. They never spent time together. She could have been semi-comatose but if they had spent even half an hour together, she would have remembered.

"What did we do all evening?" she asked.

He took another drag of cigarette and tucked away his hair again. "We watched TV."

"What did we watch?"

"I don't know … some stupid celebrity thing …" Drag, tuck. "Thomas Gottschalk, I expect."

"Are you sure it wasn't *Tatort*?"

"I don't think … yes … *Das stimmt*." He looked sure of himself now. "That's right. You're starting to remember. That's right, we watched *Tatort* together, a good old police story."

She was shaking and couldn't stop. *Lie down on the sofa, drop it. He said you were together so you must have been.* But she couldn't let it go.

"I remember now," she said. "It was an episode I hadn't seen before."

"*Okay, gut.* Sleep well, Mama." A dispatch.

But she wasn't about to be dismissed. "It was set in an international school. Everyone got stabbed. Isn't that right?"

His eyes shot away from her and he swallowed as if trying to suppress something that was rolling up from his gut.

"Isn't that what you saw last night?" she asked.

His shoulders sank and he gulped – a last, defeated attempt to contain his panic. But what she dreaded burst out of him: "You've got to help me." He knelt in front of her.

Hold him and say everything will be fine. Stroke his wiry hair. Kiss his head. Breathe in his fear and take it away. Eine gute Mama. A good mama.

He stood up, bearing over her. "I just need you to say I was home with you last night."

He brought up his hand to his cigarette. She flinched.

"Don't you see?" he said. "If they find out about Mareike, it will lead to me."

Her crocheted thoughts vied for attention. Wool tugged, knotted, snapped. *Sascha, Mareike, Sekt.*

Heilige Maria, Mutter Gottes. "What have you done?" she whispered.

He sank to the floor and clasped her knees, making her graze sting. "I was at the *Freibad.*"

She struggled to get her breath. "That pool has been locked up for months. You're lying."

He let go of her legs, shoving them away, and strode out of the lounge. Gisela heard his bedroom door slam.

34

Helen went in the police car. It took ages but felt like moments. A long way and no distance at all. A police station but more like a doctor's surgery. Chair, computer, couch. In front of a latex-gloved female doctor, she scraped off the torn dress, wet with her urine and Louisa's blood. Then the rest – boots, tights, underwear. What did nakedness matter? What she'd seen had stripped her bare from the inside out.

There had been swabs from her fingernails and from the rusty stains on her wrist. She was given a tracksuit and a blanket for the journey home. Later a black-haired policeman had taken her fingerprints. She could see his grey roots when he leant over the paperwork. Sabine was there throughout, in her nurse's uniform. On her "side" she supposed. She was too knackered to thank her.

An English-speaking police officer stayed in the house with her overnight. "Until the school's welfare lady can get your family out here." The woman, whose thick, smiley lips made her face look wrong for her job, went upstairs and removed Gary's razor and spare blades from the bathroom. Until that moment Helen hadn't thought of slitting her wrists. But, as she stood in the shower trying to wash away stink and sweat and slaughter, she cursed the woman for denying her an escape route from the hellish images in her head, from the knowledge that Gary was gone and that she was alone.

Helen brought a duvet downstairs and wrapped herself up on the sofa, too exhausted, too blunted to sleep. She and the woman, *Call me Jutta*, didn't talk. They'd have time to get acquainted in the coming days because there was no way Helen was letting anyone interrupt her parents' cruise. And her brother would be of more use to her in Shrewsbury, negotiating with her new tenants to get her house back. She crushed the quilt in her fists. After months of longing to return to England, this bloodbath would get her there.

After an age of pointless wakefulness, she went upstairs. Jutta followed and watched over her shoulder as she switched on the computer and Googled: "Death Germany what to do."

"I can help you with that," Jutta said. Her voice sounded concerned but the damn mouth still smiled.

"I'll manage."

But all the best websites were in German. Even with Google Translate and Gary's Langenscheidt dictionary she couldn't understand them. She was glad of the distraction when Zanders and Simons arrived to question her, but soon wished they'd get lost and leave her to her … what? Grief? Could she call it that? But wasn't grief intense, passionate, demanding? She was too empty for that.

They took up position in the two armchairs in the lounge. A pair of uneven German bookends: the petite uniformed woman and the lanky, leather-jacketed man. Simons asked if she'd slept. Helen nodded. Zanders got down to business.

"What time did your husband go to the party?" he asked.

"About seven thirty."

"What time did you go there?"

She crossed her legs. "Just before nine."

He wrote something and took ages over it. How long could it take to jot down a couple of numbers? Eventually he asked, "Why were you so late?"

"I … I wasn't going to go, but I changed my mind." Her throat constricted. "I didn't want to let Gary down."

"A glass of water?"

She shook her head. "I'm fine." What a stupid thing to say. She'd never be fine again.

Zanders was at his notepad, slow and precise. His eyes concentrated on his writing but Helen figured his mind was planning his next move.

"Did you and your husband often disagree over dinner invitations?"

"It hadn't happened before." She pulled her sleeves over her wrists.

The officers exchanged a glance. Zanders unbuttoned his jacket. Jutta had turned up the heating but Helen didn't feel any warmer, doubted she ever would.

Simons said: "Our liaison officer noticed that your spare bedroom has been occupied. Do you have a house guest?"

Thanks, Jutta. She trawled her mind for a plausible lie and came up with a partial one. "The night before last, Gary couldn't sleep and didn't want to disturb me." She looked at the detective's brown eyes determined to hold his gaze. He mustn't see her wavering. She didn't want this stranger dwelling on their sleeping arrangements. It made no difference where they slept; Gary was still dead.

Zanders surprised her by breaking eye contact first. He changed the subject. "Who else did Mrs Howard invite to dinner last night?"

"Only the Mowars, but Gary told me that Mel, that's Mrs Mowar, wouldn't be going because she was ill." A thought occurred to her. "Has anyone told her? I must go to her." She stood up and stepped towards the door.

"Please sit down, Mrs Taylor. The lady next door was admitted to hospital early this morning."

"What? Oh God, is it like the burglaries? Several houses. I

hadn't even thought of that. Who else did he attack?" She sank back onto the sofa.

"As far as we know the incident was confined to number 10 Dickensweg," Simons said. "Unfortunately Mrs Mowar saw the police activity through an upstairs window and came outside as the stretchers were being removed. The duty doctor admitted her to hospital as a precaution. I understand she suffers with her nerves. Why wasn't Mr Howard at the dinner party?"

Helen, fighting the image of Gary's body being carried out through the bitter night into a mortuary van, took a moment to register the question. She explained that Damian had left that morning for a head teachers' conference in London. Only then did it strike her as odd that he'd got back on the same night.

Zanders moved on. "So as far as you know, the intention of the dinner party was for Mrs Howard to entertain Mr Mowar and your husband without Mr Howard, Mrs Mowar or yourself being present?"

"Yes ... No. I was supposed to be there too." The word "entertain" sounded sordid. Zanders had made up his mind what sort of woman Louisa was. In different circumstances Helen would have delighted in his misconception. But not now.

"If you're trying to make out they were involved in an orgy, you're way off track. Our neighbours are perfectly normal people." She heard Gary's voice in her head; "perfectly normal people" was how he'd described the neighbours in their last row.

The detectives ignored her outburst. "What about Mrs Howard and Mr Mowar? How was their relationship?"

She hesitated. Louisa and Chris at the Christmas market. She should mention the conversation she overheard. Zanders was writing in his notebook again. There was something prissy about the way he held his pen. She felt a sudden allegiance to her dead neighbours that she'd never felt during their lifetimes. She resolved to keep quiet.

"Mrs Taylor, if you know something, it might help us find out your husband's killer."

At the mention of Gary, her fledgling loyalty vanished. The neighbours were bit parts in the scene in her head. Only Gary mattered.

"A few days ago I heard Louisa and Chris arguing. Louisa seemed to be backing out of something. I thought at the time she was ending an affair but it was probably nothing."

"Did you discuss what you heard with anyone: Mrs Mowar, for example?"

"I wouldn't want to upset her, and I didn't even know for sure what it meant. You said yourself she suffers from nerves."

"Did the Mowars have a happy marriage?"

Her mind went to Louisa and her bloody Relate business card. "I ... how should I know? Marriage is no one's business but the two people in it."

Zanders pointed at the wall behind him. "I think you hear perhaps shouting from the house next door?"

There'd never been raised voices, but she thought she heard sobbing once. "I never heard shouting," she said.

"And Mr Howard also loved his wife?"

Helen thought of Damian looking too long at other women across a cocktail party. His near admission of infidelity when Murdo was missing. His phone calls to Sweetheart. What should she say?

"Of course." Now was not the time to throw him under the bus. He, she, and Mel were the only passengers. They would need each other.

"And you got on with all of them except Mrs Howard?"

"Yes ... no. I liked Louisa too." Her cheeks grew hot as the officers scrutinized her. "Everyone did. I wouldn't be surprised if she isn't up for a posthumous award. Sorry, that was a tactless comment." She looked at the floor.

"But understandable. A lot of people use humour to cope with shock," Simons said. Sympathy dispatched, she returned to probing. "Is there anyone at all who might have a grudge against her, no matter how trivial?"

Sascha Jakobsen, shouted a voice inside her. He stalked the Howards, dogged them, attacked their property. *Don't get involved*, shouted another. If she told them about his feud with the Howards, the police might find out what happened between her and Sascha. What if they mentioned it to Gary's parents? Time to let it go. Enough damage done.

"No one," she said. She traced the seam on her joggers with her finger, looking away from Simons's sceptical eyes. "Surely you should be after someone unconnected to us? The culprit must be a nutcase on a killing spree."

"It is possible that these murders were random, but in my experience most victims of this kind know their killer. There's a connection. It's our job to find it," Zanders said.

Her throat went dry, desert-parched. She needed that glass of water now.

35

More bloody questions, she thought, when the doorbell went again. But Jutta led Damian Howard into the lounge before making herself scarce in the kitchen. He sat in a chair – Gary's chair – and caressed the leather arms. The laughter lines at his mouth had become more deeply etched.

"Have you been outside?" he asked. "I had to run a gauntlet of paparazzi. There must be a dozen. Cameras, microphones. Such ghouls."

Helen hugged her elbows, imagining the scene outside her front door. She felt besieged.

Damian took a breath. "I came to thank you for what you did: barricading the bedroom doors so the boys wouldn't see. Louisa trained them as babies to sleep through the night. The hours they used to scream, it ripped me in half hearing it. I wanted to go to them but she said we had to stick to the rules. Children needed consistency: 'Once in bed, you stay there.' God, she was a good mother. I see that now. If they'd come downstairs last night and seen …" He swallowed.

"Where are the boys?"

"With an emergency foster family. The parents of one of my sixth formers, so it will be all round school by tomorrow."

She was surprised at his naivety. What did he think the reporters were outside for? It was headline news.

"Do the boys know what's happened?" she asked.

"Sabine told them that a bad person killed Louisa and the dog. I was there when she broke it to them. I was supposed to do it, but I couldn't find the words." His voice tailed off and he rubbed his nose. "Leo burst into tears and hugged me but I'm sure he was crying for Napoleon more than for his mother. Murdo said, 'Mummy'. Louisa's been trying for years to get him to say a proper word. And finally he says one and it's her name but she's not around to hear it." He swallowed again.

"Toby didn't react at first, then he asked if he could have his cello to practise. How could I tell him the bastard who murdered his mother had mutilated his cello too? I said I'd borrow one from the school music department because the police wouldn't let me back into the house to get his. He told me to make sure I borrowed a half size one because he's got his Grade Four exam on Tuesday. I didn't even know that." He rubbed his eyes. "I expect that Louisa must have told me, but I never took much notice when she went on about Toby's music. She had him down as a virtuoso. I wanted him to be normal. I suppose she's won that argument in the end. Anyone whose first thought is cello practice after they've been told their mother is dead, must be a prodigy. And after this he'll never be a normal child again."

She put her hand on his. "With the right support, I'm sure the boys will get through this."

He didn't seem to hear her. "Yesterday I was an average Joe in an average family. Husband, wife, three children and a dog. Now we're a freak show. Louisa would hate this. Reputation and respect were what mattered to her. This humiliation would have killed her." He guffawed at his poor joke and balled his fist under her hand. "I keep asking myself why on earth anyone would do this to my family."

"And mine." She withdrew her hand.

He carried on speaking as if he'd forgotten she was there. "Sometimes it's hard for a man like me to be a husband. Louisa chose our friends, remodelled our house, and produced our children at pre-planned two-year intervals. Even when Murdo turned out to be not quite the child she'd ordered she threw her energies into making him special." He wiped away a tear with his fingertip. He remembered Helen was there and looked at her helplessly. "I wouldn't wish this on my worst enemy, never mind my own sons. I adore them."

"I know you do," Helen said, touching his hand again. She understood him as he must understand her. Apart from Mel, who else could know what they were going through?

"Louisa wanted to cling onto her perfect world at all costs. She turned a blind eye to my … stupidity for years and lately she'd started to rein in her spending." He looked down at Helen's hand on his and then up at her face.

She retrieved her hand. "Have the police interviewed you yet?" she asked.

"I've got round two later. They're meeting me at the Holiday Inn, where I'm staying. They don't know when I can have the house again but it will be a cold day in hell before I let my kids move back in there. I'll ask the school bursar to re-house us."

"You won't return to England?"

He shook his head. "My parents will offer to put us up but it wouldn't work. My job is here and I need the money – even with Chris gone."

"Chris?"

Damian coloured and changed the subject. "Have the police spoken to you?"

"They were here just now. They think the killer is someone connected to our families or to school."

"That's complete crap. Who do they suspect: you or me? Or do they think newly slimmed down Mel nipped across the road with a carving knife? Or one of Louisa's aromatherapy mums

189

lost the plot? Maybe Polly Stephens bludgeoned them with her baby monitor?"

"Mel's in hospital. All the police are saying is that she's comfortable. I hope they'll let me visit her tomorrow."

"I'm bound to be chief suspect; they'll dig around, find out about my dodgy marriage and my dodgy alibi. I'll fit the frame nicely."

"Alibi?"

He rubbed his neck. "I wasn't at the head teachers' conference. I'd arranged to …" His neck needed another rub. "To do something else."

With Sweetheart? It all became clear. Damian's regular conferences in the UK were covers for him to meet Shelly the babysitter or some other girl. Were Louisa's New York trips with her friends a cover story for her own infidelity? Were the Howards as bad as each other? And now one of them was dead.

"Why don't you tell the police where you were?" she asked.

Damian pulled at his collar. "I wasn't … she … left early. I stayed in a hotel room alone. No witnesses. I'll call her later, see if I can persuade her to say I was with her."

Should he be telling her this while Jutta was out of earshot in the kitchen? Did it make her an accessory? Only if he'd committed a crime.

"Don't look at me like that, Helen, it wasn't me," he snapped. "The most likely culprit is that stalker."

She voiced the argument she'd been rehearsing in her head, the one she'd been trying to ignore. "Why would Sascha Jakobsen go from gate-crashing your party to mass murder overnight?"

"He's been building up to this for months. He trashed our garden, stalked us, burgled our houses and now this. He was fixated on destroying us and, boy, did he get his way."

"We can't be sure he committed the burglaries."

Damian's skin reddened and he balled his fists. "Of course it

190

was him. He's demented. If the German police don't nail him, I will."

"How do you know Sascha? Why does he hate you?"

He shrugged his shoulders, looking away. "He's just a local nutter. I didn't even know his name until you told me." He stood up. "I'd better get to the hotel."

He opened the front door and turned back to her. "Steer clear of him. He did this, I'm sure of it."

"But why would Sascha kill Gary? He didn't have anything against him." Of course he didn't. He wasn't jealous of Gary; he used her to antagonize the Howards. But that was all, wasn't it? He didn't want her for himself, did he? Was she the reason Gary was murdered?

"Maybe Gary got caught in the crossfire," Damian said. "Or what if all your cosy little swims wound him up? In his tiny, depraved mind he hated all of us. It could have been you that sent him over the edge."

She flopped onto the sofa after he'd gone, grabbed a cushion to her chest, and then hurled it onto the floor. Sascha had said Damian was dangerous; was it the other way around? He'd snarled at her at the Christmas market and admitted he'd stalked them all. Should she have listened when the others said Sascha was a threat? Did she bring this hell down on them?

The phone in the hall rang. She went to it expecting to speak to her brother.

"Is that Helen?"

She sighed, recognizing the voice. "Hello, Jean." Gary's mother.

"We were wondering when the police are going to release … Gary. For the funeral."

Helen heard her swallow a sob.

"They haven't said," she replied. Should she mention the post-mortem?

"We've spoken to the vicar but we can't do anything until we know," Jean said.

191

A bubble of indignation rose in Helen's chest. Didn't she get a say in her husband's funeral? But she said: "I'm sorry."

"Well, I won't keep you. I'm sure you must have lots to do – with the police and everything. You will tell us when they release … him, won't you?"

She went back to the sofa, picked up the cushion and curled her body into it. Hearing the suspicion in Jean's voice made her almost ready to cry.

Fiona

Missing student Fiona Connors has finally contacted her parents. Paul Connors (59) confirmed to the *Herald* that he and his wife Cathy (51) received a brief phone call from Fiona late on Monday night.

"It was definitely Fiona although she sounded tired," said Mr Connors. "She told me she was enjoying a new life in France and that we mustn't worry."

The 21-year-old disappeared from her halls of residence at Southampton University in December. She called her parents the previous week to say that she had been offered a trainee journalist post in Marseilles but they hadn't heard from her since. Extensive police enquiries at several French newspaper offices failed to establish her whereabouts.

Mr Connors said he was relieved to know Fiona was safe, but urged her to ring again. Anyone with information about Fiona can contact our news desk.

A police spokesman confirmed that they were no longer pursuing the matter as it's clear that the final year French and

193

Business undergraduate left of her own accord. "We have no concerns for her welfare at this time."

(*Regional Herald,* 16 April)

36

Saturday, 4 December

The sound of computer keys clicking in the spare room drew Helen from her sleep.

Gary. She leapt out of bed, her foot catching in the bottom of the bedclothes. She stumbled but kept moving, on her knees by the time she reached the spare room. When she saw inside the dark empty space she fell on her belly.

In the next moment the light was on and Jutta was standing over her. "Mrs Taylor?"

"I thought I heard … It was a dream."

She went back to her room and climbed into bed. It hit her: she'd never hear the keys clicking in the spare room again. The loneliness crashed in on her and she came close to calling Jutta back upstairs.

She dreamt again. Bloodstained cello, computer keys, Napoleon's innards, bloodberry cheesecake.

***

When she got up later, Jutta had gone off duty. Her replacement was a bear of a man whose neck overhung his collar.

"I'm Meyer, Timo. I'm here until four, or later if Jutta can't get back through the snow."

Helen took his outstretched hand but was too knackered and headachy to speak to him.

Timo told her Simons would be round later. "Can I make you some ham and eggs? Or something else?"

Helen shook her head. How long would it be before Simons got fed up of making house calls and summoned her to the police station for questioning?

"Is there anywhere you need to go? The roads aren't fit for driving but we could walk to Aldi if you need groceries. There's been an explosion in the Ruhr so the journalists and TV people have left the street. You're lucky; you won't get followed if you step out," Timo said.

Yeah, so lucky. She said she'd like to visit Mel in hospital. The effort of speaking intensified her headache.

Timo walked to the patio window. The bottom of the garden was scarcely visible through the deluge of falling snow. "It's a good ten miles drive to the hospital and in this weather … I'll have to clear it with Simons." He put on his coat and with some reluctance stepped out into the garden.

The blast of air made Helen shiver. She pushed the door to and watched him wade his way over what had once been the lawn, his mobile to his ear. He walked back in, depositing snowy footprints on the carpet.

"Sorry about that," he said. He lumbered down on one knee, scooped up the snow with his bare hands and chucked it back into the garden. Helen blinked away a memory – the last time she'd seen Louisa alive she was getting towels to mop snow off her doormat. When Timo tried to undo his coat, he couldn't get his fingers to work so he shoved his hands in his pockets to warm them up.

"I'm afraid Simons can't permit you to visit Mrs Mowar at the moment."

"What on earth does that mean?"

"Routine procedure until the detectives have finished questioning you and Mrs Mowar."

Helen stared at him. The police thought they'd done it together. She and Mel must have burst into Number Ten, stabbed their husbands to death and taken out Louisa too.

"Can you at least tell me how Mel is?"

Timo hesitated, picking his words. "She's in a stable condition."

God, her head hurt. They must think Mel was in danger, that Helen had killed her own husband, two of her neighbours, and now she was after Mel. She seethed but made a superhuman effort not to show it.

She switched on the television and stared her way through back-to-back reruns of *Frasier*, the audience's laughter drilling more pain into her skull. Timo watched with her, snorting whenever he understood a gag in the rapid-fire American English.

***

She was still angry when Simons arrived with more questions. "Can't you check your DNA database or something? The psycho that did this must have been arrested before. You don't go from a law-abiding citizen to a homicidal maniac overnight."

"Mrs Taylor, we believe that the victims knew the killer."

Helen's stomach knotted. Gary's crossed ankles, relaxed below the table. He hadn't known what hit him.

"You keep saying that but I can't see how," she said. "Even if someone loathed Louisa enough to kill her, or someone had a grudge against Chris, no one I know hated all three of them."

Simons fetched out her notebook. She had tidy fingernails, clipped short, free of polish, and with a white half-moon showing in every nail bed.

"Mrs Taylor, I'd like you to think carefully. Did you move Chris Mowar's body?" she asked.

The thought of it made her squirm. "I tripped over his ... head," she whispered. "I didn't see it." And she tried not to see it again in her memory. Rocking on its back after she kicked it. Unstaring, staring eyes.

"Did you pick it up?" Simons asked.

"Of course not. It was disgusting."

Bile burned in her throat but she banished the image of a madman swinging Chris's head triumphantly around the room. Simons must have seen the nausea in her face. She reassured her they were doing everything they could to apprehend the killer.

It dawned on Helen that her tone was different today. Despite Timo's caution, Simons was treating her as the bereaved widow and not as a suspect. Something had got her off the hook.

"Have you made an arrest?" she asked.

"We have someone in for questioning, but it's early days yet. We have to work on the forensic evidence. The weather hasn't helped. We don't know how the killer approached the house. It could have been over the back fence, from the path at the side, or from across the street. Apart from Jerome Stephens at number 8, who arrived home at seven thirty and noticed Chris Mowar enter number 10, no witnesses saw anyone in the street. There was a snow blizzard between seven thirty and nine. The only footprints near the house were yours, Manfred Scholz's, and those of the police team that turned up afterwards. Any earlier footprints were covered by fresh snow."

Helen looked out at the garden. The deep troughs that Timo's boots had made were partially filled in again. Another hour and they'd be gone too.

Simons stood up to leave.

"Can't you tell me who you've arrested?" she asked but dreaded the answer. What if it was someone she knew? Sascha? A neighbour? Someone who worked in school?

"We will let you know if we charge someone." Simons put

away the notebook in her pocket and fastened the button with her neat fingers.

Helen asked when Gary – Gary's body – could go home; the limbo was destroying his parents.

"We've drafted in a specialist multiple victim unit from the city." Simons walked to the door. "We hope to release the bodies soon and let you travel to the UK for your husband's funeral. We'd like the families of the victims to stay here for the moment, but we'll keep you informed."

***

Helen wasn't sleepy but bed was the only place to get away from Timo's bonhomie. She lay down and thought about what Simons had said. "Families of the victims" meant herself, Mel, and Damian.

Families, spouses, suspects.

The police were stuck on the idea of the killer being close to home. Could Mel or Damian have done it? Was Damian the one being interrogated? They must have found out he hadn't been to the teachers' conference, and that he had a motive, of sorts. Get rid of Louisa and ride off into the sunset with Shelly Sweetheart. Or he could have found out about Louisa and Chris. Maybe he thought it was fine for him to cheat on his wife but not the other way round. Did he sneak into the house and slit her throat while she prepared dessert for her guests? Helen put the pillow over her head but it didn't block out the kaleidoscope of redandwhite whipped cream.

Mel then? Was that why Timo wouldn't let Helen visit? Mel wasn't in the hospital but in a police cell. Simons wanted to know if Helen had ever heard fighting through the house wall. Was there domestic violence? Had one slap too many from Chris set Mel on a course of revenge? But wouldn't she have reached for the carving knife in her own kitchen instead of attacking him in someone else's; and why kill Gary and Louisa?

The phone rang downstairs. "Who's calling, please?" Timo said then changed his tone. "Hello, Mrs Taylor, I'm sorry for your loss … I'll see if she's awake."

He lumbered up the stairs and knocked. Helen didn't move. He went downstairs again and told Gary's mother that she was asleep.

She escaped hearing the agony and doubt in her mother-in-law's voice. Was Jean right to be suspicious of her? You read about people having psychotic episodes with no memory of what they'd done afterwards. She was the one who found the bodies, got blood all over her. And the children – was barricading them in their rooms the work of a rational person? She threw her legs out of bed. No way. It was crazy thinking. She couldn't rip open a dog's belly. Sweet old Napoleon. *Christ.* Why was her first thought the dog? What about Gary and the other human victims? Didn't she care about them?

37

As Helen left the house, Polly Stephens rushed out. "I'm so sorry about this. Freya won it in the school raffle. We put it up for her." She gave an embarrassed nod towards the giant inflatable reindeer in her front garden.

Helen hadn't even noticed. Her eyes strayed to Number Ten. Louisa's handmade festive wreath was still on the door but the police had turned off the lanterns in the window. It was a house adorned in police incident tape. Christmas had no place there. Without looking back at Polly, she climbed into the police car.

Jutta drove her up the *Bundesstraße* to the hospital. The glare bounced off the piled up snow on the roadside. Helen pulled down the visor and wished she'd brought her sunglasses. But it wasn't just the weather giving her a migraine, it was the news that the suspect in for questioning had been Sascha Jakobsen. When Jutta told her, she felt like she'd been stabbed. It was a jabbing, puncturing blow of betrayal. Sascha. She'd trusted him despite everything everyone had said. But then Jutta explained they had let him go again when he provided an alibi. She wondered whether Jutta was breaching police code by telling her. They still hadn't arrested anyone but Helen felt they no longer regarded her as a serious suspect. Why else were they allowing her to visit Mel?

She wasn't sure what she expected but it wasn't to find Mel in bed with a saline drip in her hand. The glow in her that had turned the heads of Jerome Stephens and others at the swim club party had burnt out. The killer cheekbones were now skeletal. She pushed herself up on her pillows.

"How are you?" Helen asked – stupidly. She was the only woman on the planet who already knew the answer.

"They're worried about a vitamin deficiency and think I haven't been eating properly for a long time."

Helen looked away. The sudden weight loss couldn't have helped.

"No need to be embarrassed, Helen. I know I was the size of a baby hippo. I envied you and Louisa in your Lycra sports kit."

Helen had never, at all the coffee mornings and dinner parties, heard Mel talk about herself. It must be what trauma did: grabbed you, shook you, and when it dumped you down, all your hidden parts spilled out. She wondered about inviting her to go running, a way to keep the weight off and still eat well, but she hesitated. She ran alone to escape. She needed that solace now more than ever.

Mel rested her hand on hers. Her fingertips were stone-cold despite the tropical heat of the ward. "You'll get through this. We both will."

Helen hadn't thought of Mel as a woman of resolve – that accolade went to Louisa – but, despite the dark circles under them, there was a determined look in her eyes.

Mel asked whether she had heard from the police.

Helen told her Sascha Jakobsen had been in for questioning but released without charge.

"Why?" Mel asked.

"I couldn't believe they bothered with him. I think Damian put the boot in."

"I mean why did they let him go?"

"He's moody and unpredictable, but no one could take him for a killer," Helen said.

"What makes you so sure? You weren't here when Louisa's garden got wrecked last year. That was violent. And the way he stalked us, even to Austria. That's not normal."

"But …" Helen didn't know what to say. She was about to protest but didn't want to lose the new openness between them. She told her it didn't matter what they thought because Sascha had an alibi. "Apparently he was at home with his mother all Thursday evening."

Mel shrugs. "A mother would say anything for her son, wouldn't she?"

Helen's head started aching again. She changed the subject. "Have you got family coming over?"

"Not yet. Later, maybe."

Helen waited for Mel to ask her about her family. When the question didn't come, she explained that she'd asked her brother to sort out her house in Shrewsbury.

"How soon will you leave?" Mel asked, pushing herself upright against the pillows.

"Not until the police say it's okay."

"I don't want you to go."

Helen felt touched. "I expect I'll still be here at Christmas. I'm too dazed to think about packing up right now. I can't plan anything. When I close my eyes I see …" She swallowed hard.

"Sometimes I think about Chris and I'm overwhelmed with guilt," Mel said.

"Guilt?"

Mel stared ahead of her. She seemed to be replaying something in her mind. "Our last words before he left for the dinner party were angry. I was in bed and he came in, accusing me of taking the DVDs that were stolen in July. He cared more about his film than he did about me."

"Gary and I bickered that evening too but I know he loved me. I'm sure Chris loved you."

Helen watched tears well in Mel's eyes.

***

Helen pretended to doze on the journey back. She suspected Jutta's questions about how Mel was feeling were a police ploy to learn more about both women.

Mel had looked ill, frail, tearful, and yet there was certainty in the way she'd condemned Sascha. Did she know something about him? Helen had seen them talking once by Chris's car. She'd glimpsed them from her upstairs window. Was he threatening her? If Mel had spoken up, could she have prevented the murders? But Sascha had been with his mother, hadn't he?

"Do you get on well with Mrs Mowar?" Jutta asked.

Helen kept her eyes closed and didn't answer.

38

Damian was at the door.

"What time is it?" Helen asked.

"I'm sorry, were you asleep? It's about nine. Where's your policewoman?"

"I was catnapping. It's all I can manage. Jutta left yesterday."

"So you're in the house on your own?"

"My brother's coming out," she lied, unsure where Damian's question was leading. "Besides, Mel will be out of hospital soon and she might move in here for a few days," she added. Her belly felt uncomfortable – was it because of this second lie or the notion of living with Mel?

"Well, if you need any company before that, let me know. The Holiday Inn isn't bad, but I could do without businessmen and their drinking games right now. Look, can I come in so you don't catch a chill?"

The first time she met Louisa was on this same doorstep and Louisa had said something similar. At least Damian posed it as a question whereas Louisa had invited herself in. Helen had felt exposed, wearing nothing but her short towelling dressing gown.

Since the murders she'd been going to bed in Gary's old tracksuit but now, facing Damian, she felt as naked as the day she met Louisa. She went upstairs to get dressed.

"You don't have to put your clothes on for my benefit," Damian called after her.

Her cheeks burned as she locked herself in the bathroom to dress.

He was gazing out of the patio window when she came back down. His mood had changed. "I hope Dickensweg disappears in a white cocoon that freezes us all to death," he said.

Helen wasn't sure he realized she was there. She offered to make him a coffee but he ignored the question. "It's Toby's cello exam today. I went round to the foster house this morning to wish him luck and give the boys a lift to school. He had his music books out on the kitchen table and he was practising on an imaginary cello between mouthfuls of Coco Pops. It was like looking at my son and not my son at the same time. The last-minute revision had Louisa's influence stamped right through it, but tucking into sugary cereal – Louisa would never have allowed that.

"He looked so happy there. The foster mother sat next to him sipping her tea while her husband stacked the dishwasher. Murdo and Leo were watching the Disney Channel. It was the picture of domestic bliss. When I wished Toby luck in the exam, he said, 'Proper practice makes luck irrelevant'. That was pure Louisa; but then he refused to come in the car with me because the foster family's boy had offered to cycle with him, taking the hired cello on his back. He rejected me, Helen, my own son. Can you believe it?"

"He's a young lad who's been through something unspeakable and who's been given some attention by an older teenager. He probably looks up to him. Most boys would at that age."

"Leo and Murdo didn't want to know me either. They gave me a hug but didn't take their eyes off the TV screen, not for a single second."

She sighed and hoped he'd stop the self-pity; she wanted to be left alone to wallow in her own. "All parents despair of tearing their children away from Disney. It's normal," she said.

"But they're not normal, are they? Their mother's been murdered, had her throat cut. Violated in her own home. In their home, while they were sleeping. The place where they should feel safe."

When he rubbed his eyes, his hand trembled. She led him to the sofa and sat down beside him. There was no option but to listen.

"We're not a family without her. I used to fantasize about becoming one of those weekend dads with the best of both worlds: fatherly and footloose at the same time. Taking them to Kids Planet and McDonald's and then handing them back to Louisa to grapple them into bed when they were too full of cola to shut their eyes. But it's not like that, Helen. I'm not their dad anymore. I'm a shadow to them, a hazy memory of a different life." He burst into angry tears.

His open grief bemused her. If only her own could work like that. She wanted it to harrow through her, to penetrate the deadness in her body. She told him: "It's only been a few days. None of us know who we are anymore." She made to move away but he moved with her and rested his head on her shoulder. The intimacy of the gesture kicked her. It was the first physical contact she'd had since Gary. But this man repulsed her. He smelled of yesterday's shirt.

He lifted his head. "I'll kill Jakobsen. I'll find out where he lives and I'll take a knife to him like he did to Louisa." His eyes bulged with anger and his face was red. There was no trace of the debonair neighbour she'd lived opposite for the past eight months.

"But Sascha didn't do it. He had an alibi. The police let him go."

"You're friendly with him; do you know where he lives?"

"I … he's not a friend. I saw him at the Dortmannhausen pool in the summer sometimes."

"Dortmannhausen, that's it. He lives in the village. Where's your phone book?"

"I don't think we've got …"

"*Deutsche Telekom* delivers them. Where's yours? In the hall?"

Helen blocked his way out of the lounge. "I'm not helping you find the address of someone you want to kill."

"He killed your husband too. He butchered him."

"Stop it, please."

"Don't you want revenge?" He stepped towards her. "Move out of the way. I'll get the phone book myself."

She didn't budge.

"What is it with you, Helen? I'm starting to think there's more to your relationship with Jakobsen than idle gossip. Did you put him up to it, Lady Macbeth?"

In a reflex, she brought her hand up and slapped him.

His face did a tour of shock, humiliation, and anger. For a moment she thought he would hit her back, but he sighed, his anger subsiding, and said: "I deserved that. You're not the type to have an affair. I know the telltale signs. I've practised hiding them often enough. Anyone could see you loved Gary. Can you forgive me?"

She shrugged, accepting the apology as the quickest way out of the conversation. "We're not ourselves at the moment."

Her words triggered another mood change. "We never will be again," he said as tears rolled down his face.

He sank against her shoulder, and she wondered how soon she could break away.

He must have sensed her discomfort. "I'd best be off. I'm on compassionate leave, but I told my deputy I'd go into school this morning."

He looked at the carpet and spoke softly. "I'm sorry about all that just now. You've got your own demons to deal with – worse than mine, probably, as you were the one who found them." He glanced at her as if to check he hadn't said too much. "Anyway, I'm sorry. It won't happen again." He held out his hand.

Helen shook it. "Promise you won't do anything stupid. Let the police do their job."

"I promise. I must have sounded like a raving lunatic."

"Let's forget it." She led him out and stood on the icy doorstep, shifting from foot to foot.

"We could go out for a meal one day this week," he said. Even after everything else, the flirtation made a return to his voice. It was true then; some men couldn't help themselves.

She found a way of letting him down gently. "If you want to take the boys out to tea, I could come and help."

If he was disappointed, he didn't show it. He gave her a cheery thumbs up and was about to head off when they both heard movement at the other end of the road. Sascha emerged with Manfred Scholz from Manfred's house.

"You bastard," Damian yelled, striding towards them.

The cold seeping through her slippers, Helen chased after him. "Wait, Damian, remember what we agreed."

He shrugged her off and kept going. The veins in his neck were pulsating with rage. He reached Sascha, punched him in the face and set about kicking him.

Despite looking dazed from the assault, Sascha – the younger, fitter man – dodged most of Damian's kicks and threw a punch of his own. Damian stopped to rub his forehead and examine the blood on his fingers.

Helen's ears buzzed. The last time she'd seen blood, lots of blood …

Manfred held Sascha back to prevent him landing more punches.

Cello, cheesecake, blood. The noise in Helen's head was deafening.

Damian leapt at Sascha, held him by the throat and dragged

him down into the snow. He sat on Sascha's chest, pinning the man's arms down with his knees.

"Please stop this," Manfred said.

The different voice distracted Damian enough for Sascha to wriggle free. Manfred pulled him back.

The buzzing stopped in Helen's head. She tried to grab Damian's fist but knew it would take more than a woman and an old man to break up this fight. She tried diplomacy. "Can't we talk about this? There's been enough violence in this street."

"And this bastard's responsible for it." Damian lunged at Sascha but this time Manfred let go of Sascha to allow him to defend himself. It was Sascha who landed the next punch and sent Damian reeling. He grabbed him by the collar and hauled him against the wall of Manfred's house.

"So you want justice, do you? Well so do I," he shouted into Damian's face. The back of Sascha's head was soaked in snow, his hair spiking up more than usual. He looked savage. When he pulled back, ready to headbutt his opponent, Helen flinched and closed her eyes. But rather than the sound of Damian's nose breaking she heard police sirens. Damian pushed Sascha off and started thumping him.

Two police officers leapt out of their car and dragged Damian away. The younger of the two fetched out a pair of handcuffs but, instead of cuffing the struggling Damian, he pulled Sascha's hands behind his back. The older one told Damian in English to get himself checked over by a doctor.

"And you also, I think," he said to Helen. Her arms and legs were shaking and she wondered what the hell she looked like.

Manfred said something in German. It sounded like a question but Helen didn't understand it or the policeman's answer.

She saw his face, bleeding and fat-lipped, as he was driven away. It was as expressionless as a police mugshot of a serial killer. Dead behind the eyes.

39

Helen sat stock still, surprised she had breath left in her. So it was Sascha. The swimmer, the smoker, the stalker. The killer.

She was with Damian at the table in Manfred's kitchen. Manfred fetched a bag of peas out of his freezer box for Damian's face, pulled two teacups and a bottle of schnapps out of a cupboard and placed the cups, half-full, in front of them. He took a solitary mug off the draining board and filled it for himself. Both men drank deeply. Helen didn't touch hers.

Manfred folded his arms and rested the mug on his elbow. He shifted his weight from foot to foot.

Sascha, Sascha said her head in time to his rocking. The man she swam with, talked to, defended, had taken Gary from her. If she hadn't spoken to him at the pool; if she hadn't brought him into the street; if she hadn't … She grabbed her cup. The liquid stung her throat but she kept on drinking; the stinging served her right.

"Did you call the police?" Damian asked Manfred suddenly. "How did they know he was here?"

The old man took another drink and said: "He often visits this street. I think perhaps somebody else told the police."

"Why does he visit you?"

He moved his mug in a tight circle, staring into it. "Not me. He stands often in the street. In the wood."

"But we saw him coming out of your house," Damian said.

Manfred's sallow skin grew a shade darker. He moved in front of the sink with his back to them. "Today, yes, but not before. It was a private matter."

Damian slammed the frozen peas on the table. The red swelling on his forehead hadn't gone down.

Alcohol seeped into Helen's head, through her thoughts, but it still didn't cushion them. A long way away she remembered something. "But what about Sascha Jakobsen's alibi?"

Manfred turned to her. "The policeman said the alibi is *falsch*."

Acid came up to her throat. "So now we know," she whispered.

"I've always known," Damian said.

Manfred drank his schnapps.

40

Saturday, 11 December

"You'll share a bottle of red, won't you?" Damian said after he'd placed his order for bolognaise with the waiter. "The house wine is drinkable. Have you been here before?"

"Once." The dreadful time with Gary to make up for a silly row. The Howards had been there and the Mowars, making her sulk behind the fake ivy. She should have made more effort. Time was finite; it ended like everything else. Gary and Helen. Helen and Gary. Gone.

A bark of laughter at the next table; the school admin staff's Christmas party. From the open, trellis-free side of her booth, Helen had a clear view. One was Geoff Barton. No, too fat, and badly dressed. And the woman next to him looked nothing like Karola. An inked salamander crawled on her shoulder.

The waiter was hovering, biting his lip, pen over his notebook. Helen didn't want anything but chose the Parma ham starter as a main and a mineral water. He walked away, not bothering to write it down.

"You have to eat, Helen. After what we've been through, God knows we deserve a decent meal. Besides, with Jakobsen behind bars, we have something to celebrate." Damian finger-combed his hair over the large yellowing bruise on his forehead. Freshly shaved and wearing a silk shirt, he was making her skin prickle.

"You said we were taking the boys to McDonald's. I wasn't planning on dinner. I can't stay long." She'd driven behind him all the way, not realizing the kids weren't in the BMW until he'd got out in the restaurant car park. Tinted rear windows had a lot to answer for.

"The foster family is giving them more burgers than one of Chris Mowar's film-makers managed in *Supersize Me*. Louisa will be turning on her mortuary slab." He puffed out a breath. "Don't pull that face, Helen. Lighten up."

A belch, some squeals, a roar – a man in a flashing bow tie and a reindeer jumper had tucked a bloom of the fake bougainvillea in his hair. Damian talked louder: "I'm not going to avoid mentioning the fact that she's dead any more than I'm going to avoid saying that our marriage wasn't perfect."

When the waiter put down their drinks, Damian took a swig. "I don't see Louisa through rose-tinted spectacles. I know what she was and what I was. Her death doesn't suddenly make us saints. Am I boring you?"

Had he caught her glancing at her watch? "It's just that it's noisy," she said.

"Would you rather go somewhere else? Back to my hotel?"

Her armpits leaked. "Here's fine," she said, but made a point of looking at her watch again. He needed to know she intended to leave soon.

Damian refilled his glass. The wine smelled tinny. "I meant to the hotel bar. We don't have to go to my room." He grinned. Red-stained incisors. Her skin crawled.

The fat man in the big party was telling a joke. "So the inspector said to the teaching assistant, 'Now that's brave.'" Laughter. People applauding like seals. The claret-haired woman opposite him caught Helen's eye and smiled. But then her expression froze. She must have recognized Helen from the gossip grapevine, or from the old graduation photo that the online media had lifted from her Facebook page and used in their so-called news stories.

Helen's cheeks burned. Salamander and Claret gave her inquisitive glances. The heat spread: into her hair, around her neck, across her shoulders. Take her jacket off? No way; Damian's eyes would seek out her nipples through her top.

"This wasn't a good idea. People are staring at us," she said.

He laughed, raised his glass towards the big group and shouted: "Cheers". One or two of the men lifted their glasses in response.

Had he no shame? What must people think, seeing him – them – out drinking while Gary and Louisa lie in a police mortuary? She was about to tell him how disgusting she felt when his tone changed.

"Have you gone through Gary's things yet?" Deep furrows appeared in his forehead.

Helen's mouth went bone dry.

Damian went on: "I don't know where the hell to start with Louisa's. I can't chuck it all out; the boys might like some of it when they're older. Sabine's going to sort out the clothes. She says she'll sell the good stuff on eBay and take the rest to the school shop. Louisa only had good stuff so I reckon the shop's catch will be pretty small." He gulped down more wine and wiped his mouth with the back of his hand. His palm was red and deeply etched. Helen looked away; it seemed indecent.

"I'll keep all the photo albums. She never left photos on the memory card. Every picture was either labelled or deleted if it didn't come up to scratch. Every certificate the boys ever got – from Tumble Tots to music exams – are in the albums too. I must put Toby's new one in there when it arrives, assuming he's passed, but I know he has. It would take more than his mother's murder to put him off his scales." He swallowed more drink. "I keep asking why I wasn't killed instead of Louisa, or Napoleon. God knows I have less integrity than the dog."

215

The food was taking an age to arrive. She thought about inventing a text message that required her immediate return home, but Damian looked desolate, talking about his failure as a husband and punctuating his sentences with gulps of wine. She decided he needed her to listen. It must be hard keeping it together in front of the boys.

But when the waiter brought their meals, Damian asked for another bottle of wine. Helen thought he'd had enough.

He must have read her face. His own expression changed from desolation to defiance. "We have to carry on. It's no good hiding. We can't go back. I'm not skulking around, trying to avoid being seen where I shouldn't be. I'm not lying to Louisa or buying Aldi sweets for the boys and pretending they're from the airport. Marriage should be banned. Who wants an institution based on hypocrisy?"

Helen shrugged. Why argue? She and Damian were poles apart in their views on marriage. He'd even been with someone else on the day his wife was murdered. Was it the babysitter or some other woman? Was he duplicitous enough to have let Louisa invite her to her dinner parties? Helen had seen the way his eyes lingered on Polly Stephens's neat ass and Audrey Garcia's cleavage, but neither gaze seemed reciprocated. Polly only ever had eyes for her baby monitor. Who else? There was another woman who'd visited the Howard house but that had been in an official capacity, hadn't it?

"Have you been seeing Sabine?"

Damian choked on his wine. "The school nurse? She's older than Louisa; why would I go there?"

Helen's mouth opened, about to condemn his ageism, but why bother. Wasn't cheating on his wife the bigger crime? The age of his sleeping partner was irrelevant.

"Don't look so shocked, Helen. A woman in her thirties makes demands, wants commitment. I'd never leave my kids; younger women know the score."

"What about your wife?" Helen snapped. "Didn't she deserve commitment? How could you lie?"

Damian waved his spoon. "Can you honestly say you never kept anything from Gary?"

Sascha Jakobsen: palm to palm. "Nothing important," she replied, examining her fork. The prongs were tarnished.

Damian sucked up strands of spaghetti and washed them down with another drink. He had tracks of red wine imprinted on the corners of his mouth. Dracula after a good meal. Her stomach squirmed.

"And you believe that Gary never kept anything from you?" he said.

She sliced off a corner of ham and pushed it under the rocket salad, ignoring the question. But her head filled with memories of Gary's endless gaming. The sleepless nights, the denial that anything was troubling him.

Damian didn't notice she hadn't answered and fired off another question. "What about Chris and Mel Mowar? I always thought there was something wrong in that marriage."

The second bottle of wine arrived. He refilled his glass, slopping wine over the top. It flowed down the outside of the glass and bled into the tablecloth. Something caught in Helen's throat. Red growing into white. Leaking. Spreading. Swamping. She shook off the flashback to Louisa's bloodied collar and made herself listen to Damian.

"She turns into slimmer of the year and two weeks later her husband is dead. If we didn't know for sure that lunatic did it, I'd be wondering about her."

"You don't mean that."

"She's hardly wailing with grief, is she?"

"Considering she's only just out of hospital, I'd say she's showing quiet determination to get through this."

"It's always the quiet ones. Who knows what goes on behind the façade?" He shovelled more spaghetti into his mouth.

Helen put down her cutlery. "Why are you attacking Mel all of a sudden?"

He looked at her with unfocused eyes. "It's not just Mel. We all have a veneer. Do you know who the biggest phoney was? Louisa, that's who. The Spider Queen spinning her web around us, afraid to drop a thread. What did you think of her?"

Helen trawled her mind for the least damning thing to say, but Damian was off again before she found it. She suppressed a sigh. When would he shut up?

"Let me guess, you thought she was a middle-class, privately educated graduate with transatlantic friends. Isn't that how you saw her?"

Remembering Louisa's outburst when Murdo was missing, how her true accent had leaked through, she suspected her background wasn't privileged, but she nodded. She hoped he would drop it. Instead he raised his voice to compete with the noise on the other table.

"She went to private school – that bit of the image is true – but for all her airs and graces she wasn't middle class. Her parents scrimped and saved to give their only child the finest education they could afford. 'Nothing but the best for our girl.' Louisa died every time her dad said that." He swallowed his gaff, colour surging up his throat. He carried on. "They have no idea how she acquired her upmarket accent or why she called herself Louisa instead of the name they gave her."

"I …" What the hell could she say to that?

Nothing – no need – Damian surged on. "And those girlfriends in New York she kept visiting? They didn't exist. She was in Glasgow with her parents. No matter how ashamed she was of her roots, she was loyal to them, I'll give her that. She went to see them at least six times a year, sometimes with the boys, but always with a different made-up explanation for her absence – shopping in New York, hen weekend at Champneys, school friend's wedding. The old dears are desperate to come out here and look after the grandchildren, but I've convinced them to concentrate on planning the funeral. Let's hope it's not too tacky."

Helen cut off more ham, sliced it and sliced it again, thinner and thinner, imagining it was his tongue and she could silence him. It explained Damian's dig about Louisa's childhood that Helen had overheard months ago, but he repulsed her. His wife wasn't buried yet and he was already betraying her and her family.

Damian went on speaking. "She was a bright girl but she cut her degree short to move out here with me. She lived her career through mine. I'm the head teacher, providing us with a comfortable existence." He counted on his fingers. "But she was the chair of one committee, director of another, trained counsellor, accomplished pianist, charity worker, budding business woman, community campaigner."

He slapped his hands on the table. "The Nobel Peace Prize couldn't have been far behind." He slugged down more wine. "God, I can't tell you how liberating it is to let go of that fiction. It's hard work living with a persona. Marriage wrecks a couple. Do you know what I mean?"

"I …" She sliced more ham. The knife scraped against the plate.

"We're compromised into cardboard cut-outs of ourselves. Don't you agree?"

She pushed her plate away. "I loved my husband. He was my best friend."

Damian dropped his fork. "Come on, Helen. You don't have to pretend you weren't stifled. We all saw how you loathed it here. Your undying love for Gary didn't quite make you a willing consort."

Helen slapped her napkin on the table and stood up to leave.

Damian caught hold of her wrist. "I'm sorry. I have no right to comment on your marriage or Mel's. Just because mine was fake …" Tears rolled down his face.

The claret-haired woman was watching. Her smile was gone now that her mouth was hanging open.

Helen sat down and spoke in a quiet voice. "I don't think anyone's marriage is faultless. We all rub along as best we can. When you've got through this, you'll have the boys to remind you of the good times."

Damian looked at her quizzically, no longer listening. "So you and Gary had problems?"

"Not problems, no," she said. She found herself adding: "Something was troubling Gary. Something long-term, I think. Did he ever say anything to you?"

"Never," he said and drank deeply from his glass.

It wasn't what she expected. She thought she'd shown a weakness that he could exploit but he seemed indifferent.

"I wonder how long Jakobsen will get. I know we're supposed to be terribly British and let the man have a fair trial – innocent until proven guilty – but I don't need a court to tell me he's guilty as the devil," he said.

His face was red with anger and alcohol. Behind the clean-shaven face was chronic tiredness. Probably the only thing keeping him going was his intense hatred of Sascha Jakobsen.

"What did Sascha mean when he said he wanted justice?" she said.

Damian looked away. "Did he say that? I don't remember."

"When you were fighting, he said he wanted justice. He said it to me too, when we were in Austria. I wonder what he meant."

"No idea." He drained the wine bottle and called out for the bill.

***

In the car park she hung back, not wanting to walk with him, fearing a wine-soaked goodnight kiss. But when he slipped on an ice patch and veered towards a departing car, she grabbed his arm and told him he mustn't drive. He blinked at her, lolling from side to side. She wasn't sure he'd heard and she doubted he'd manage to phone a taxi. She found herself offering him a lift back and dreading that he'd mistake the suggestion for a come-on. But he climbed into the passenger seat and fell asleep.

Keen to get rid of him and his booze-breath, she drove fast over the gritted roads. His disclosures about Louisa were at best disloyal and at worst vile. Okay, she took some delight in hearing that Louisa – or whatever her real name might be – was not who she pretended she was. But she sort of admired her too. To reinvent herself and yet to remain loyal to her parents must have taken guts. Had she been too quick to judge her? The woman had made her welcome, in her own way, but Helen had rejected her.

She remembered the argument between Louisa and Chris Mowar at the Christmas market. If they were having an affair, Damian could have known about it. He'd talked about being in a hotel when they died. A moment of doubt pricked her: what if he never left the area that day? The cruel way he ripped apart Louisa's background tonight made it sound like he hated her. Enough to kill? And what should she make of his behaviour tonight: manic, oscillating between fury and despair? Someone that unstable could be capable of anything.

But the snoring drunk beside her was harmless, wasn't he? No more a killer than she was. She gripped the steering wheel. *Than she was.* She'd read about people who'd blotted the most appalling traumas out of their mind. Was her memory fast-forwarding the time between digging her way through the snow into Number Ten and finding Louisa's body? Several minutes could have elapsed between the two events. Then she ran out of the house and into Manfred Scholz. Covered in blood and sweat.

Fiona

A policewoman leant against her patrol car.

"Stay calm," he whispered.

We kept on walking, right past her. Shep even smiled and nodded. So confident.

"How can you ...?" I asked.

"Remember what I said."

No questions. That was Shep's instruction. The bedsit had been arranged in a hurry so there hadn't been time to do a sweep. It was the same in his car; the Syndicate could be listening. But now in the street, in this new town we'd fled to?

Two men came out of McDonald's, eating burgers. Young and stocky. Nice faces, but they were wearing epaulettes and had badges on the top of their sleeves.

I looked ahead of me, not at them.

"Stop pinching me," Shep whispered.

I loosened my grip on his arm. Their uniforms were green so maybe paramedics, not police. But it could be a trap; trust no one.

We turned the corner into the pedestrian precinct.

"I'll be away tonight. I need you to take down codes," he said.

There was an Asian couple with a child in a buggy behind us. Three texting teenage girls approached in front. He must know these people were safe otherwise he wouldn't have mentioned the codes.

"When will you come back?" I said.

"It depends on the terrain."

"And you don't know when you'll call?" I got tired staying awake, and some nights he didn't ring at all.

"Undercover, you know how it is. Codes are vital."

Sometimes lack of sleep made me so dizzy I couldn't feel my limbs.

He put his arm across my shoulders and pulled me close to him. "It'll be worth it in the end."

I smiled at him, my shepherd.

41

Tuesday, 14 December

Should she ring Mel's doorbell? Helen had scarcely seen her since she came out of hospital. They'd shared a shivering doorstep chat when Helen called to invite her for coffee. Mel declined, saying that she wanted to clear Chris's wardrobe. Helen felt as if she'd forced herself on Mel just as Louisa used to force herself on both of them. She set off for the shop without asking Mel whether she needed anything.

***

Aldi overflowed with Christmas display bins: *Stollen* in one, spiced biscuits in another, others with singing Santas and flashing Rudolfs. When the display had gone up in November, she'd told Gary about the range of German delicacies that would make wonderful Christmas presents for his parents. When she thought of Christmas now, it was enough to fracture her heart.

She'd stupidly arrived during the lunch hour and the shop was busy with teachers from Niers International. Despite the English-speaking media's heavy coverage of the outrage, there were still some staff who didn't know her. They pushed their trolleys past without a flicker of recognition. But out of the corner of her eye she could see others making U-turns when they stepped into her aisle. She didn't blame them – what the hell do you say to a woman who'd found three dead bodies? Four, if they counted the dog.

It was like being at a slow-moving barn dance where some potential partners would glide by, while others claimed her for several rounds of the chorus. A woman from Gary's department halted her trolley to offer condolences. Later an admin assistant did the same.

Yes, thanks, she was bearing up. No, no date for the funeral yet. Yes, it's a relief the killer has been caught. No, she didn't know him, not really. Yes, the German police did a good job. No, you don't expect it will happen to you, yes, no, yes, no. "Frosty the Snowman" blared out of the speakers. She grabbed what she needed and left.

***

She pulled her hood up to block out the cold and hide herself from prying eyes. Cars were crawling past. Were they taking it steady on the untreated roads? Or gawping at her through their windows?

A woman called her name. Another tongue-tied well-wisher she would pretend not to hear. But she recognized the accented voice and turned to wait for Maria, her Greek neighbour, to catch her up.

"How are you? No, foolish question. Foolish – it is the word – yes?" Maria asked as they walked home.

Helen pushed back her hood. "I am sorry I cancelled your English lessons."

Maria waved her hands. "Don't say it. I understand, of course. No more lessons; we leave to Athens … er … January. Last week, Dimitris, my husband, ask. Yesterday the school say yes."

Helen knew full well what event had prompted her husband's

sudden request to cut short his exchange posting, when a few weeks earlier he had declared how grateful he was for the English lessons that were helping his wife to integrate into the school community. Nothing like a massacre next door but one to bring on a desperate yearning for the homeland.

"There are going to be lots of changes in the street," she said with false brightness. "Mel and I will leave soon. And I think Damian will move house." Her voice trailed off.

"I am sorry for you," Maria said.

Helen swallowed hard. The Greek woman's simple phrase was more eloquent and better meant than so much of the articulate sympathy she'd received.

They walked on, comfortable with each other. They stayed on the scrubby grass verge that was less slippery than the snow-compacted pavement.

"Four friends leave Dickensweg unhappy or dead: Steve, Chris, Gary and Damian," Maria said.

"Who's Steve?"

"He live in 8, by my house. Now Polly and Jerome live there."

"And he died too?"

She shook her head. "He in Cyprus but he sad because his wife don't go. Dimitris give him Greek lessons."

"A teacher? Was he a friend of Gary's?"

Maria shrugged her shoulders. They'd stopped at the kerb but stepped back when a car sprayed up slush. The task of crossing the slippery road made them silent. Helen didn't resume the conversation on the opposite verge. What Maria said was sticking on her like a scab she wanted to pick even though she sensed it might open up and bleed. Steve? It was an ordinary enough name, but at the back of her mind she knew she'd heard it in connection with something else. They said goodbye when they reached Dickensweg, and Maria went into number 6.

***

226

There was a visitor on Helen's doorstep.

Damian was swaying. "Can I come in?" His speech was slurred.

"I want to make a start on clearing Gary's things. I might not be able to face it later," she said.

"I was hoping you'd give me a drink. The hotel refused to serve me."

He stank of beer and body odour, and there was rusty, unshaven scrub on his jaw. She would have to edge past him without him getting a foot in the door. "The café next to Aldi does coffee and fresh rolls, why don't you try there?" He looked as if he hadn't had a square meal since their restaurant outing.

"That's not the kind of drink I had in mind. Don't come over all disapproving. Why shouldn't I drink? What else is there for me?"

"Your children. Your job." She had trouble sounding civil; children and job were two comforts she didn't have.

He leant against her front door and folded his arms. "I went into school today. I'm fed up of compassionate leave. The way they looked at me – their head teacher – it was nothing short of contempt."

"I'm not surprised if you went to school in this state." She stamped from foot to foot, her toes numb with cold. She hoped she could last the stand-off; no way did she want him in her house.

"Damn it, Helen, don't be obtuse. Booze had nothing to do with it. When your home has been used for wholesale slaughter, you become part of it. It's all right for you; after a decent interval you can pick up your old life in England."

She didn't want England, she wanted Gary. And she wanted Damian to shut up. Would he always be like this now that Louisa wasn't there to keep him in check? She almost missed Louisa.

He was still speaking, his tin-breath misting the air. "I'm unemployable; no one wants a mass murderer in their school." He looked into her face. "It's what they all think. Even my … friend won't answer my calls. She thinks I killed Louisa, did it for her. As if. In her dreams, maybe." He let out a chuckle.

Helen hunched her shoulders and turned away, trying not to listen.

He lolled towards her. "You don't like my jokes, do you? Humour could help us through this."

The word "us" sent a flurry of panic through her. She wanted to flee, put space between herself and any attempt at an "us". But it was her house and it was warm inside. She'd had enough.

"As you said, I'll be moving soon. I have a lot to sort out." She remembered the scab and it itched. "The Greek family at number 6 is leaving. Maria mentioned Steve who lived here. Did you know him?"

Damian's face froze. "I don't think so," he said. "There was a Steve at number 8 for a while. He kept himself to himself. I expect Louisa knew his wife, but I don't recall him well."

He stepped away from the door and didn't try to follow her into the house. Helen closed the door, wondering what Damian was hiding. He had been Steve's head teacher; he'd remember one of his own staff, wouldn't he?

42

Gisela took the bus to the prison. She'd never been to that part of the city before and couldn't trust herself to drive and navigate after the vodka she'd drunk to quell her nerves. She dreaded seeing Sascha. God knew what that place would have done to him. She knew about young men on remand committing suicide. *Nicht nochmal* (Not again). She felt hollow in her chest. She first had it when Mareike died.

The woman beside her got out in Mönchengladbach. When no one took the empty seat, she slipped a hip flask out of her pocket. Slumping low, she brought the anaesthetic to her lips. She tried to bat away an unwelcome thought but it persisted. *If I hadn't been drunk that night, the taxi driver wouldn't have reported me and I could have stuck by Sascha's alibi.* She took another drink. *I sent my son to jail.*

Out of the window a herd of deer posed, russet-red against snow-laden firs. They took the children skiing once in Mayrhofen. Sascha, the natural athlete, joined his father on the steep ridges. She and Mareike sipped hot chocolate from the café terraces and admired the views.

Was Gott tut, das ist wohl getan? What had they done since then to deserve God's wrath?

The prison entrance hall was like Düsseldorf airport. Years ago they flew to Lanzarote for Christmas. Baby Mareike, just able to sit up, spent glorious mornings in the shade of the hired parasol, unpacking and repacking the beach bag: baby wipes, sun cream, formula milk, camera. Her face – hamster cheeks red with teething – a picture of concentration – while, at the shoreline, Sascha and his father built castles and bridges.

The prison foyer, like the airport, was crammed with all kinds of humanity: young mothers with restless children; older, world-weary women; bored-looking teenagers; and men, most of whom seemed intimidating enough for Gisela to think they should be on the inside of the prison rather than queuing to visit.

But at least there had been proper toilets at the airport.

"It's a shack in the car park, dodgy flush. You're best holding on if you can," the woman next to her in the queue said when Gisela asked where the loo was. They stood while prison officers checked ID cards and carried out body searches.

When it was her turn, the prison officer pointed at the notice by his desk that warned that *persons under the influence of drugs or alcohol would not be admitted to the visiting room.*

"MS. It's worse when I have to stand up for so long," she lied. Thank God that vodka carried no smell.

***

In the visiting room, the other people took their places at tables like chess masters awaiting their opponents. Most of the children made for the play area in the corner. Two siblings squabbled about whose turn it was to drive the toy fire engine.

She went to a table when she was directed. A warden appeared, leading Sascha towards her. He was wearing his own clothes but, when she saw his prison-issue felt pumps, she wanted to weep. *My Sascha never wears slippers.*

"Am I allowed to give him a kiss?" she asked the officer.

"No need," Sascha said.

The officer shrugged his shoulders and walked away.

"It's good to see you," she said quietly.

"You don't have to whisper. No one is interested in what we've got to say."

Noise levels were high as prisoners and visitors exchanged news. She shuddered; she'd been charged with providing a false alibi. A malevolent judge might send her to prison too.

"Has Manfred Scholz been in touch?" he asked.

She trawled her memory for two ends of wool to join. The name meant nothing to her.

"Doesn't matter," he said, studying her face. "How much have you had?"

"I'm not drunk. This whole thing is painful enough for me without you insulting me."

"*For you*," he snapped. "I'm charged with three counts of murder and the destruction of a dog, but this is painful *for you*. They can't decide whether I committed a random act and might strike again, or if I targeted the Howards and I'll go back for the father and his children. Either way I'm locked up until the trial."

The police were fools if they reckoned her son committed random murders. *But specific murders?*

"I'm sure the time will pass," she said.

"The next six months until the trial or the thirty years after they convict me?"

"The lawyer can cast doubt on the evidence. It's his job to defend you, whatever the circumstances."

"Listen to you, you've condemned me already. Look me in the eye and tell me I didn't do it."

"Of course you didn't," she said, her gaze slipping from his. The tabletop was a greasy black, years of anxious hands across it. She hated how her gut had churned in the first moment of hearing the gossip in Aldi and how her heart had shattered when he begged her for an alibi.

He interrupted her thoughts. "Mama, *bitte*?" His eyes filled with the same despair as when she had told him Mareike was dead. He had reached out for her then but she'd plunged into her own hell. Mareike was the good child, the hardworking *Abitur* student. The girl was set for university. Unlike Sascha, the naughty one. Two abandoned apprenticeships behind him, blamed at the time on the exploitative bakery owners, but what if his temper had something to do with it?

But she mustn't fail him now. If someone that she had a grudge against was murdered, wouldn't she have constructed an alibi? Sascha couldn't prove he was at a closed-down swimming pool, but it didn't mean it wasn't true.

He was still looking at her pleadingly, a little boy who needed his mama. How much of the plummeting spiral of the last two years was her fault? He had been getting over it, moving on, but in her haze of misery, she'd shown him Mareike's note and his quiet grieving became a clamouring, furious obsession.

"I'll always love you," she said but didn't look him in the eyes.

43

Saturday, 18 December

What would Louisa say? Helen surveyed the lounge of Damian's soulless new rented house three streets away from Dickensweg. How long would it have taken Louisa to obliterate the magnolia walls with savannah yellow or to tear down the floral curtains in favour of Roman blinds?

"I can't face bringing over the furniture from Number Ten. It would be like importing a virus. We won't have Louisa's aromatherapy stuff either. This place will always smell rented," Damian said.

He pointed at the sofa upholstered in a migrainous mix of orange and brown swirls. "Have a seat. It's more comfortable than it looks."

She perched on the edge. "I'll stay for a minute. I only popped round with quiz books for the boys. I didn't realize they hadn't moved in yet." She wished she'd handed the presents over on the doorstep. She wondered if he was drunk again.

"I'll make you a coffee and then you can have the full tour."

She declined both, pointing out that the house was the same layout as her own, but she felt less anxious now he'd offered a hot drink instead of wine.

"Louisa would have had a seizure if she knew her children were going to slum it in a semi," he said.

She ignored the insult to her own house and asked when the boys were moving in. He hadn't shaved but he was showered and dressed. Surely he'd pulled himself together enough to resume his full-time duties as a father.

"Sabine's pressing for me to take them this weekend but they might as well stay where they are and get some semblance of a family Christmas."

"Won't you be lonely?"

"We could have Christmas lunch together. There's no need for either of us to be alone."

"Polly and Jerome have invited me," she said quickly.

"They told me they were going to Center Parcs."

"You could ask Mel. I don't think she has any plans." She drew her arms around herself, feeling a chill, ashamed for offering up her neighbour to cover her lie.

"You must see the bedrooms before you go," he said.

Chill became squirming heat. She moved nearer to the sofa's edge.

"The beds must have been built in a communist factory," he said. "The springs have as much give as a block of concrete."

"Couldn't you get someone to take the beds out of Number Ten for you? I don't think he went upstairs." She swallowed hard, and Damian looked away. They both knew who "he" was.

"I'd best be going," she said.

"No, stay. I want you to know I've stopped drinking." He gave her a pleased expression like a child who'd tied his shoelaces for the first time. "I don't need booze as a crutch. I'm through that now. It's time to move on, don't you think?"

Helen picked her words carefully. "I'm glad you're not drinking, but I think we're all going to take time to put this behind us."

"But we don't have much time. With Gary gone, your days here are numbered."

She stared at him, not sure what he was driving at.

He tilted his head and lifted his eyes towards her. "If you had a sponsor, your status would be guaranteed."

Her mouth gaped. Sponsor?

"Obviously it means moving things on more quickly than either of us would have preferred, but these aren't normal times."

He couldn't be saying that; she must have got it wrong.

"Don't play dumb, Helen. You can't stay in Dickensweg. There'll be a new head of German soon enough and he'll need the house."

Her belly churned with anger and hurt. He was already consigning Gary to the past. He'd replace him like he replaced any teacher when a vacancy arose. Maybe he'd already posted the ads: *Exciting opportunities for Head of German and Head of Art. Due to unexpected circumstances.* And his offer to sponsor her? Did he think Helen would fill the vacancy in his bed?

"I've got to go."

She dashed for the front door. As she reached up for the latch, he grabbed her arm. His grip wasn't tight, but fear froze her to the spot. He stepped closer. The veins in his nose were broken.

"Please hear me out. I'm useless on my own, can't function with Louisa gone. I need someone who understands what I'm going through. And you need a home and a job. I could get you a teaching post at my school."

She found her voice. "You think I'd insult Gary's memory to get a job?"

"Gary's memory?" He let out a hard laugh. "You really didn't know him, did you?" He put his hand on her shoulder.

She jerked her knee into his groin and wrenched the door open as he doubled over in pain.

***

There was a note on her doormat when she got back. Her whole body was trembling so much that she couldn't focus. She sat on the bottom of her stairs in the hall and rocked. The police must have made a mistake with Sascha. He'd warned her Damian was dangerous. In all his stalking, was he trying to protect the neighbours, not hound them? Was Damian the killer? She rocked. No. Yes. No. Did he brood, plot, and covet his neighbour's wife until he could bear it no more? Oh God, did that make it her fault? Was everything her fault?

She rubbed her eyes. The note, torn out of a lined jotter, was from Mel. She had taken in a parcel for her and promised to try her again later.

But why would Damian kill Chris? The voice in her head had a ready answer: Chris must have been having an affair with Louisa. Damian didn't want her but didn't want anyone else to have her so he killed three birds – burdens – with one frenzied knife attack.

But it was four; the dog died too. And how could a father leave a scene of slaughter when there was every likelihood one of his children would find it the next morning? She rocked harder. A man so deranged had no sentiment for animals or children. But his actions weren't those of an out-of-control maniac; he was cunning too. He'd made the hue and cry which had led the police to Sascha. How long had he been planning his crime?

What did he mean about her not knowing Gary? Did he know something or was he making up nonsense to get her into bed? There was one way to find out.

***

She marched upstairs to the computer desk and opened the top drawer. Pens, rulers, hole punch. Second drawer: spare paper. Third: phone charger, scrap paper. It was Gary's room more than hers but there was nothing personal here, no diary, no secrets. She went to their room.

A hollow feeling of grief gaped in her chest as she opened his drawers and parted his Tshirts, socks, and pants. Her hand touched something hard: a mobile phone. But it wasn't the one he used; that had been in his pocket when … The police gave it back to her with his wallet and wedding ring. She kept those things next to her bed. She swallowed a sigh and switched on the phone. Was it the one he'd told her he lost? It was dead but she took the charger from the computer desk and plugged it in. The battery charge symbol pulsed but it was too weak to interrogate.

She made a coffee and told herself to calm down. It didn't mean it was the same phone. Or maybe he'd found it again and felt too embarrassed to tell her. She re-ran the circumstances of its disappearance in her mind. Gary had it on his way to work and by lunchtime he'd bought a new one. She'd thought it odd at the time. And there was the phone call he didn't answer that morning, from Steve C. If the insurance salesman's number was in the phone, she'd know it was the one Gary said he'd lost.

But the phone told her nothing. She knew the pin code: their wedding date reversed – they used it for everything, but there was no call history and no saved numbers. It was either a new phone or Gary had wiped the memory. *Gary's memory* – she thought of the scornful way Damian had said that. What the hell had been going on?

Steve? The thought that had been nagging since speaking to Maria came into focus. Was the person Maria mentioned the same Steve that tried to phone Gary? If he was an exneighbour, it made sense for Gary to have his number stored. So why lie and say the call was from a salesman?

***

The doorbell rang and she went downstairs, expecting to see Mel with the parcel. She opened the door but found Damian. She tried to slam it, but he forced his way in.

Heart hammering, she backed into the hall with her hands frantically searching her pockets but she'd left her mobile in the car. Had he come for her? Like the others? Was it him? Her fingers touched the car key and gripped the fob. Could she stab him in the eye and get past him? He didn't come towards her but he was still blocking the doorway. She would have to advance on him.

"Get lost," she shouted. Bravery was a skinny piece of metal in her trembling hand.

"I want to talk to you." He stepped towards her.

Her hand flew at his face but she dropped the key.

He frowned, picked it up and offered it back to her. "You need to know something about Gary."

Fiona

I'd been awake most of the night, rewinding, reliving the conversation in my head.

My darling shepherd, so attentive these days, let me ring Mum and Dad again. It was completely against protocol; he put his job on the line.

They had asked me so many questions. Where was I staying? What were my French colleagues like? When would I get leave? I had my answers ready, for their sakes, to protect them. My biggest news perched on the edge of my tongue but I reeled it in.

There was a sob in Dad's voice when we said goodbye. I think it had been there for most of the call. He sounded weak and strained. I wanted to cry too but Shep was standing beside me, so I stayed strong. I was sure he would let me ring again. I closed my eyes wondering how soon I could ask. My news wouldn't wait forever. I drifted off into a peaceful dream of the future.

Shep shook me awake, gripping my shoulders hard. He was fully dressed.

"The call's been traced. The Syndicate is closing in."

"How?" I was alert, fear pumping my heart.

"We have to leave."

I reached for my clothes.

"There's no time."

"I'm in pyjamas. I just …"

His face grew pained. He looked helpless. "I can't put you at more risk by letting you pack."

"Let me get my photos."

"Nothing."

"But …"

"We have to go now, please."

I stepped into my trainers. "I'll get my coat."

"Hurry." He opened the door and leant against it. His face was wretched. I'd caused this with my selfish moping, on and on until he offered me the call. I should have let him do his job.

I lifted my jacket from my pile of clothes – two pairs of jeans, a skirt, jumpers, T-shirts, and knickers that no longer smelled quite clean; it was hard to wash them in the tiny sink. A big sigh rolled through me. Of all the things I'd left behind, why did I care about a few clothes?

"We'll get new stuff. Come on," he said.

There'd been times when the Syndicate catching up with me would have been a release. But not now when we had so much to look forward to … A new fear gripped me. What if they reassigned him? But we had to stay together. I vowed never to ask for anything again. I grabbed my coat and went after him.

44

"Have you ever been to Club Viva?" Damian asked. He reached out for the coffee which Helen offered, and held her eye.

She calculated how many strides it would take her to get from the sofa to the front door. She gripped her own coffee, ready to launch it in his face if he moved.

"I'm not going to any nightclub," she said, but the name rang a bell.

"I'm not asking you on a date. I got that message loud and clear." He put a protective hand over his lap. "Club Viva is in the old part of the city. If I'd known what would happen I'd never have gone near the place."

He put the mug to his lips and jumped. The drink was still hot. "I've had affairs, you know that, but I haven't broken the law: no relationships with sixth formers."

He gave a wistful smile as if recalling missed opportunities. Helen poured milk in her coffee and watched the black swirl to beige. What kind of sordid confession was he leading up to?

He fixed her with his brown eyes. "It's important you understand how events spiralled. I'm the only one left who can present any kind of defence. I owe them that much."

"'Them'?"

"Did you know Chris and Gary arrived here at the same time? Four years ago I appointed Chris as the head of art and Gary became number two in the languages department. But that's not the only thing they had in common."

She poured more milk in her coffee. She didn't want to hear any similarities Damian drew between Gary, and Chris Mowar.

"Chris had been here on his own for a year when he announced he'd got married and installed Mel in number 7. Later you appeared on the scene as Gary's wife. It's a coincidence, don't you think?"

Helen gripped her cup. The heat stung her fingertips.

"There are a couple of differences, of course. You and Gary had been married for a while before you joined him, whereas Chris shipped Mel out straight after their wedding. Apparently they had a small registry office do with a couple of witnesses. Louisa put on a wedding breakfast for them as soon as she heard. I expect yours was a big church and family wedding. Am I right?"

"I thought you were talking about nightclubs," she said. No way was she telling him that they got married in Jamaica with two hotel staff as witnesses. Would he ever get to the point?

"Another difference is that Chris and Mel had known each other for a couple of years before they were married whereas, I hope you don't mind me saying, you two had a whirlwind romance."

"What's that got do with anything?" Helen took an angry gulp of coffee.

"Nothing, not yet anyway. You'll see the connection later. Let's go back to Chris. You must have noticed that aura he had about him."

Aura of creepiness, magnetically repellent. Helen coughed into her mug.

Damian smoothed his sleeve. "Some women find me attractive but I had nothing on him."

What was she supposed to say? She wouldn't have hopped into bed with either of them.

"He got random women to reveal things about themselves that they'd never disclosed to anyone else. Their fears, phobias, and ambitions. How do I know this? I heard him in school. Age was no barrier to him – a girl in Year 9 or a thirty-something teacher's wife, it made no difference to him."

His face coloured. One particular thirty-something wife must have been Louisa. But it was the Year 9 girls that concerned Helen more.

"And you let him teach in your school?"

"He assured me his motives weren't sexual. I found out about the nightclubs when Steve told me." He paused to look at her. "You asked about Steve. As well as being my next-door neighbour, he was my head of science before Jerome. A salt of the earth type; what he lacked in teaching ability he made up for in crowd control. Anyone who can keep a lid on the Year 10 bottom set deserves a job. He was married to a German woman. Louisa took Beate under her wing and included her in her various social activities."

His eyes were steady. Was he telling the truth? He couldn't get away quick enough when she'd mentioned Steve before. Had he taken time to concoct a story? She wanted to ask for Steve's surname, but doubted he'd tell her the truth.

"Steve overheard Chris talking to a couple of lower sixth girls about going to Club Viva," Damian said. "He came to me concerned and wanted me to challenge Chris. I know you'll criticize me for it but I was more interested in finding out how the hell Chris Mowar did it."

Helen glared at him. Criticize? Utterly condemn more like. Was this irresponsible creep really a head teacher?

"I persuaded Steve that we should go to Club Viva, catch Chris there with the students and confront him. We roped Gary into driving us and told Louisa and Beate it was a teachers' night out.

"The nightclub music was bollock-throbbing loud and we couldn't see two feet through the gloom, but we found Chris with a gaggle of German girls in a quiet area at the back. Except for their four-inch heels, you'd have thought it was a group of children in an audience with Santa Claus. The girls were hanging on his every word. When he saw us, he said something to the girls and they moved away, throwing us filthy looks and making it clear we'd ruined their evening. He was angry too and accused us of interrupting his research interview.

"I demanded he show me his research methods in action."

Damian picked up his coffee and settled back in Gary's chair, at home in his narrative. Helen again mentally rehearsed the sprint from her armchair to the hall. Whatever he was building up to was bound to be sleazy. What then?

He put his mug down. "I pointed at a smart waitress who was collecting empty glasses from the tables. I told Chris to interview her.

"He shook his head and said it wouldn't work. The woman was too busy. The subject had to be in the mood. He said his research was about female dependency and the woman didn't look the dependent type.

"Gary pointed out a girl walking past our table. She was young, skinny and had pokerstraight blond hair like a lot of German girls. We watched until she disappeared into the toilets. Chris said she was a loner because in-crowd girls go to the ladies in packs.

"'She might be the pack leader,' Gary said, his eyes glued to the toilet door.

"'You saw the way she hunched her shoulders. What does that tell you?' Chris said.

"'Self-conscious, weak, vulnerable,' Gary said."

Helen shuddered. It was obscene to hear Gary through this mouthpiece. He wouldn't have said those words.

"When the girl emerged from the ladies, I told Chris to bring her over so we could observe his so-called interview technique. He refused at first but I reminded him I could land him in a heap of trouble if he couldn't prove to me his interest in the other girls had been innocent.

"She seemed startled when he approached her but as he talked to her, she loosened her folded arms and lifted her head to look him in the eye.

"He led her back to our table. It was like watching a duckling waddling after its mummy. When she saw us, she was shy again, head down, arms wrapped around herself. Chris reassured her we were good guys. She'd known him thirty seconds longer than she'd known us but she took his word for it and gave us a nervous smile. Steve offered to buy her a drink. She said she wanted a beer.

"Gary asked her name and gave her all ours. She pulled a face and said she never remembered names especially English ones. I can hardly blame her as I can't remember her name – Angelica, Petra, who knows? We all laughed about it and she relaxed. I nodded at Chris to get on with his research. I have to give him his due because that's what he did."

Damian paused to raise his coffee mug. It seemed to be a toast to the dead film-maker. Helen didn't raise hers.

"He would ask her a question and, depending on how she answered, he would know what to say next to draw more information out of her. Through her broken English and with Gary's help at translating, we learnt that she wanted to go to university after she'd finished sixth form, but she'd be the first person in her family to go on into higher education. She was worried how her working-class parents would react. She didn't think they had the strongest marriage."

He looked at her. "Do you see what I mean, Helen? In five minutes Chris knew about her family set-up, her education, and her fears for the future. The guy was a genius and kept on probing. I bought us another round of beers and later someone – Gary, I think – got us on vodkas. He stayed on light beer because he was driving. We found out about her childhood, her school friends, her first boyfriend …"

The doubt grew in Helen. Gary would never have plied a schoolgirl with vodka. It was all a ludicrous preamble before Damian admitted his fling with this German girl.

"It got late and Chris, feeling that he'd gleaned all he wanted from the girl, switched off the charm, shouting across her to talk to the rest of us. She tried to re-engage him in conversation but he shrugged her off. He could be a cold bastard when he wanted. We felt sorry for her. Steve said he'd call her a taxi and went out to the car park to get a mobile signal. She went with him. She was pretty unsteady on her feet. Gary got up too and said she could wait for the taxi in his car as it was too cold to hang about outside." Damian hesitated. "Do you want me to go on?"

She swirled the dregs in her mug, the milky taste still strong in her mouth. She thought about walking to the door and holding it open, giving him no option but to leave. But curiosity got the better of her and she decided to hear him out to the punchline.

"Chris and I got talking to two women at the bar. We lost track of time, but it was ages before the others came back. When they did, Steve was white as a sheet. Gary was dabbing a scratch on his face, and he made it clear that if we didn't leave immediately we'd have to make our own way home.

"No one spoke in the car. I thought Gary and Steve must have had a fight."

She scrutinized his face. His cheeks were flushed and his nose was verging on mauve. He said he'd stopped drinking. That would have been his first lie of the day. They'd been mounting up since then. She hadn't even met Steve but Gary never fought with anyone. Gary was everyone's friend. Her best friend. She swallowed but couldn't shift the ache in her chest.

"When we went back to work on Monday, Gary and Steve avoided each other. One would leave the staffroom whenever the other walked in. After about two weeks, Steve came to me in an agitated state. He showed me the front page of the *Tageblatt*. There was a photograph of the German girl from Club Viva.

They'd blocked her eyes out – like the German press always do – but there was no mistaking her. Steve's wife had translated the article. The girl had been found dead, having slit her wrists. Neither her family nor her friends could explain why she might have taken her own life."

Something prickled across Helen's neck. She needed the story to end. She provided her own summary. "So you think she was so humiliated by Chris that she killed herself?"

"Don't be naive, Helen. Do I have to spell it out?"

Helen's jaw tightened. "I've heard enough."

"Let me finish. I feel partly responsible. If I hadn't taken Gary to that nightclub—"

She stood up. "Enough."

Damian stayed in the chair. "As Steve described it, she came on to Gary while the three of them were in his car waiting for her taxi. She was pretty drunk. Any chap would have reacted. Steve left them to it and had a couple of cigarettes in the car park. He saw her climb out of the car and run away. It was too dark to see much but he heard her crying. He opened the car door on Gary to find him dishevelled, with his face bleeding."

The word "dishevelled" thundered in her ears. She shook her head to dislodge it from her vision of Gary. "You're lying. I don't believe it."

"Steve believed it. That's why he made his wife translate the local newspaper every day. He expected to read that the police were investigating a sexual assault outside a city nightclub. Instead he read about a schoolgirl suicide."

"What kind of sick joke is this? If the police ever questioned Gary about something like that, it would have got out. You can't keep secrets here."

"I think she was too humiliated to report the attack and, after a few days of keeping her secret, couldn't cope with the shame."

"Steve must have made it up," Helen said. "You said yourself you thought he and Gary had a falling out. He must have tried to frame Gary."

Damian shook his head. "Steve begged me to recommend him for a move to another school so that he wouldn't be around if the police made the link. Rather than tell the police what he'd witnessed and land Gary in trouble, he chose to flee the country. I got him a job at an army school in Cyprus."

Her whole body shook. All kinds of thoughts raced – protests, ideas, fears. She grabbed one, an explanation, and said: "He probably fancied a change of scene and came up with this cock and bull story to make you release him from his contract."

He shook his head again. "Because he needed Beate to translate the newspapers, he had to tell her what happened. She gave him an ultimatum: tell the truth or I'm leaving. Steve chose to protect Gary. The day after the newspaper article appeared, she took the kids and went to her parents in Bavaria. She never came back."

Helen didn't care about Steve or the bust-up with his wife. It had nothing to do with her. Smoke and mirrors. "If Gary had done something like this, I would have known. I'd have sensed a change in him, seen guilt in his behaviour."

"With respect, Helen, you hardly saw him in those days apart from the odd long weekend. What did you really know about him?"

"How dare ...?"

"Besides, you did see a change in him. Wasn't it about then that he proposed to you?"

"What's that got to do with it?"

"Gary, the confirmed bachelor, proposes marriage to a woman he's known for all of three months. I'd say that was a seismic change, wouldn't you? Did you ever wonder if he really loved you?"

His neck was red like a turkey's wattle. He wasn't the affable neighbour with a wandering eye; he was a twisted liar. She raged over him: "Get out of my house."

He went into the hall. "I'll come back when you've had time to take it in," he said in a voice meant to pacify her. It enraged her more.

"Never come near me again." She was about to close the door on him when Zanders and Simons drew up in front of the house.

"When's the trial?" Damian asked as Zanders got out of the car. "I want a ringside seat when that bastard gets sent down for life."

Zanders shook his head and told him Sascha Jakobsen had been released. "A new witness. Someone saw him scaling the fence into the swimming pool."

"That's complete bollocks. He must have paid them to say that," Damian shouted.

Grim-faced, they ignored him and walked towards Helen.

Even before Zanders spoke, she knew. His eyes, his head, his body, everything was level, emotionless, detached.

In a flat voice, he told her she was under arrest for murder.

PART THREE

45

"Try to calm down. It won't help your case to overreact," Karola tells her, suited and professional. She's Frau Barton now, dog breeder reverting to trained lawyer to brief her client in the interview room.

Helen slams the table. "The police can't arrest the first person on the scene and call it case closed."

Karola picks up her papers. Her chapped knuckles are the only clue to her spaniel-walking other life. "The police interviewed everyone who attended Louisa's swim club party. They know about the argument."

"Christ, I can't even have a row without one of the bystanders becoming my defence lawyer. Did the police interview you too?"

"They talked to Geoff and me last week before you became an official suspect. But they aren't basing their case on that one incident; I can still represent you. Neighbours say there was long-term animosity between you and Louisa, and they claim you were aggressive towards Chris Mowar."

"They said that?"

Karola shuffles her paperwork. Is she even listening?

Helen clamps down her anger and keeps her voice steady. "What motive would I have for killing Gary? I never touched … I didn't get his blood on me." She rubs her temples, trying to banish the vision of his lifeless body slumped over the dining table, the back of his shirt wet and red.

"Raised voices were heard from one of your upstairs rooms a couple of hours before the murders," Karola says. There's no pity in her eyes. "Are you sure no one saw you go over to Number Ten? They could confirm the time."

Helen wonders whose side this woman is on – hers, the police's, or the school Stepfords'. "It was snowing a blizzard so no one else was outside." She sits back on the hard interview chair. Even her own lawyer wants to interrogate her. Isn't it enough for Zanders and Simons to poke holes in everything she says?

"I'll come back later, Mrs Taylor."

Helen watches her pack up her briefcase. She'd be more reassured if she still called her Helen.

46

Sunday, 19 December

Helen curls up on the bed, feeling shivery. She craves the coarse duvet that smelled of industrial washing powder but the guard took it away hours ago when he brought in her breakfast.

She wraps her arms around herself, gripping her shins and forcing her folded legs against her chin. She's still trembling from Karola's latest visit. Why the cross-examination about Sascha?

Did it have anything to do with Zanders placing the see-through evidence bag in front of her? *Do you recognize this, Mrs Taylor?* She admitted it looked like one of her green teardrop earrings. Had he found it at Louisa's house two weeks after the murders? Would it have been in her best interests to lie to Zanders? She hasn't worn the pair since one of them disappeared in July. She tries to conjure up the mess and disarray of her ransacked bedroom instead of the gruesome chaos of Number Ten. But she can't stop herself from fast-forwarding. Toby's snapped cello fingerboard, Louisa's crimson collar, Chris's gaping crewneck sweater. Images vie for her attention. Neck and Neck.

She stands up and imagines the guard at the custody desk peering at her on the CCTV screen. She wants to pee but isn't desperate enough yet to crouch on the toilet in the corner. She's used it only once in the early morning. No doubt the cell camera has infra-red but she convinced herself the guard couldn't see her in the dark. She didn't sleep at all. Time became endless without her watch, which the custody sergeant confiscated. They took her wedding ring too. She almost cried at how easily it slipped over her knuckle.

Her head aches with thirst. She's avoided the drinks they've brought into the cell, to keep her bladder empty and because German herbal tea stinks like rotting undergrowth. She walks to the breakfast tray which still hasn't been taken away. The white roll and slice of liver sausage lie untouched alongside the cup of now cold, pungent liquid.

A sense of defiance takes her. Why should she starve herself? She breaks off a chunk of the dry roll and pushes it into her mouth. It's hard and scrapes her throat. She washes it down with a swig of tea. Before the foul taste can take hold, she shoves in another mouthful of bread.

She chews on the meat and she thinks about how bogus Damian's story is. And yet. She feels a sharp pain as a piece of sausage gets stuck. She thumps her chest and drinks the last few dregs from her cup. The pain eases but leaves a scratching sensation in her gullet. *And yet.*

She falls back on the bed, winded at where her thoughts are going. She can't suspect Gary of rape. She won't. And is Louisa, the unquiet ghost, still spinning her web of control? Why else would the surviving neighbours see Helen as a mass murderer?

Club Viva. She tries not to think of where she first heard the name, but she knows it was in Louisa's cellar. The men playing pool, Gary looking worried, Chris assuring him Club Viva was in the past.

Had Louisa known about Club Viva too? It would explain why Gary was quick to defend her, afraid that if Helen pushed her too far she'd blurt out the story. But many a time she and Louisa drove each other to the limit. If Louisa had a story that would have shocked Helen, she'd have told it months ago.

Mel is too low in the pecking order to know, but Chris had some kind of hold over Damian. It could have been over Gary too. Why would Gary associate with Chris, the arrogant creep, and Damian, the raging philanderer, unless there was a secret bond between them? A bond of silence? No, she knew Gary; there would have been signs.

The countless times she found him gaming in the spare room. But that must have been her fault. He was unhappy that she hadn't settled down in Germany. That was bad enough, but that was all it was, wasn't it?

A whirlwind romance. What panicked him into marriage? He proposed about the time Damian claims the girl committed suicide.

She makes it to the toilet in time to throw up the undigested sausage. Her eyes stream with tears – the first since she ran into Manfred Scholz outside Number Ten.

She hears the door bolts deactivate and Karola's voice is back.

"Good news; the police are letting you go."

Helen stays over the toilet and spits up bile.

47

"How did you find me?" Sascha asks. His eyes are tiny, black beads that skitter over her shoulder to the foyer.

Helen surges inside. She expected his flat to be grubby and untidy but the hall is uncluttered, stale tobacco tang neutralized by air-freshener. There's a painting of the Madonna and Child on the wall. It makes her falter. His walls, his territory. Roman Catholic.

"My mother is a believer," he says, catching her gaze. "I have no god." His mouth is set thin and pale. She trembles; she shouldn't have come.

"How did you get this address?" He sounds uncertain and it makes her determined again.

"What's it like to be on the receiving end?" she says. She steps towards him and his eyes dart to her hands. "Does it make you feel stalked and hounded? I hope so." She puts her hands in her pockets.

"You know what I said to the police?" There's a tremor in his voice.

"You told them we were together at the closed-down pool for an affair. What kind of fantasy is going on in your head? I've been released from custody on the strength of a lie that insults my husband's memory."

"You didn't kill. Louisa Howard irritated you but that is all."

"Isn't that for the police to decide? I thought Louisa was controlling, but wherever I turn it's you standing in the way."

Sascha rubs his hand through his hair. She moves closer, making him look at her. "And now you've convinced the police I was unfaithful to my husband."

"When the police see a possibility, they want to prove it. I stopped that happening to you." He smiles at her, apparently pleased with his argument.

It's all that she can do not to punch his face. She presses on with what she came to ask.

"How long have you and Manfred Scholz been friends?"

"Scholz?"

"He gave you your alibi. My lawyer told me. He's the witness who came forward to say he saw you climbing over the pool fence. And now he's corroborated the one you gave me."

Sascha's face colours as if she's hit a nerve.

"And Scholz says he saw you dropping me off in Dickensweg less than ten minutes before I ran out screaming from Number Ten. No time for either of us to barricade bedroom doors and commit four murders." She starts a slow hand clap, moves it closer, towards his face. He pulls his head back but she keeps coming. "What makes Manfred Scholz so ready to lie? And how did the police find my earring in the *Freibad* grounds? The last time I saw that earring was before the burglaries in July. How about I tell Zanders that?"

His body sinks and he drops his gaze. "The police already know. It's not true but they have evidence. A little blood and a thumbprint."

She pauses for a moment, processing what he's telling her. An exploding wave of anger crashes through her. "So it was you? I never believed it, but I should have listened to Louisa. We all should have listened. They'd be alive if we had."

He backs away until he reaches the wall, his head below the Virgin Mary. "I'm no burglar."

"You're so much more than that," she yells.

"It …" he fidgets, tucking that stupid hair strand behind his ear.

She brings her hands up. To clap again or to slap him? She doesn't know but he grabs them. Her wrists collide and burn. She sucks in saliva and launches it at his face. Her spit speckles his upper lip. He flicks his head towards her and she braces herself for a headbutt.

But he presses his mouth over hers. She breathes in nicotine and tries to cough. The spit rubs from his lip to hers. She tries to pull away but he spins her round and presses her against the wall. Her hands are crushed, prayer-like, between them. She shakes her head, shakes it with rage and disgust and fear.

His hand threads through her hair and clamps her still. Her gums hurt from his pressure. Their teeth grate and her jaws open in pain. Their tongues touch and something else ripples through her. Her legs buckle. He finds her zip and she shrugs out of her coat. Her palms are pressed against his chest. He's shaking and urgent. He doesn't smell of cigarettes anymore; it's a scent of heat and Gary when … *Gary*.

She struggles but can't move. She forms "No" but it's not there through kiss and tongue.

He grips her shoulders. Her head catches the picture frame. He kisses her throat.

"Stop," she shouts.

His hand moves back behind her head, forcing her mouth on his.

She's alive. There's been no human touch since …

They are kissing now, her tongue as eager as his. His hand is on her throat, pressing up under her chin. Thunder through her ears; his pressure is choking her. Her eyes are open but all she sees are bubbles of light that burst to dark. She can't feel her lips.

Sascha lets go of her head and the movement is enough to break the connection. She snaps her face to the side.

"No!" she chokes.

The pressure on her throat is gone. Her vision returns.

He's staring at the picture above her head, The Holy Mother.

He shrinks off her. "Oh *Gott*, I'm sorry. I swear I wouldn't …" he says. "I swear it on Mareike's grave."

The winter air bites Helen's tender neck as she sprints to her car. She puts her coat back on but it's soiled like everything else she's wearing.

48

Tuesday, 21 December

Helen grasps the armrest as the taxi driver accelerates around a hairpin bend. The football key ring on his rear-view mirror flies trapeze-high. One half of her brain screams slow down, the other half wills him faster. They agreed on €80 from the airport in Larnaca but the final fare to Episkopi depends on the time it takes. If he slows, she's bankrupt. If he speeds up, she's dead.

There are hills on one side, haggard and flaky. Every so often houses and olive trees poke up through the rocky plains on the other. The only structures with plan and order are the shrines by the roadside. Orthodox thanksgiving or in memory of those that didn't make it? Her head bangs into the passenger window as the driver jumps another bend. She lolls onto the seatbelt but it's slack against her breastbone, no spring left in the coil.

She had a terrible night, consumed by disjointed snatches of Damian's story. Did she, at some level, believe him? Why else would she have let Sascha kiss her, put his hands on her throat? By 2 a.m. she convinced herself she'd never sleep again unless she put her doubts about Gary to rest. She had to know the truth even if it meant finding out her marriage had been a sham and her husband had been a predator.

But how could she disprove Damian's version of events? Four men met a girl in a nightclub two years ago. Three of the protagonists were dead, one was long gone and one blamed Gary. If only she could find an independent witness.

She sat up in bed: Steve, the one that got away. According to Damian, he left to shake off the guilt by association with Gary. But what if Damian was lying, would Steve tell her the truth? A Google search for army schools in Cyprus led her to St Joseph's School. If it's the right school, she'll find him there.

***

There are ninety minutes of jolt and lurch before the cab sweeps up a steep, modern road to the front of St Joseph's School. Apart from the sea view and the scattered palm trees, she could be looking at Niers International. Whitewashed concrete walls, pillars propping up a porch, brown front entrance. Architects must have come up with a one size fits all for international schools.

A hard-looking woman with pocked skin sits behind a window in the foyer. She has blond hair but the peroxide is a vain attempt to hide the years. She ignores Helen, when she approaches, and only looks up to answer the ringing telephone. Her responses are monosyllabic, and she ends the call without putting it through to anyone.

"I'm here to see Steve Chadwick," Helen says. Any chink of nervousness and this receptionist will demolish her. She silently thanks Birgit, Damian's school secretary, for being the woman's polar opposite. Birgit gave her Steve's surname when Helen phoned her this morning. She didn't even ask her what she wanted it for, which was just as well; how could Helen have explained she was on a crazy trip to Cyprus to prove her dead husband wasn't a monster who preyed on schoolgirls?

The St Joseph's receptionist says: "He's teaching."

Helen asks if a message can be sent to him.

"Are you a parent? There are proper channels to go through."

Now what? Hang around the school gate until home time? She doesn't know what Steve Chadwick looks like, and she's got to do this now. She thinks herself back into her role as head of PE, produces her passport and pushes it towards the woman.

"My name is Helen Taylor. I'm from the Niers International School, Germany. Please send a message to his classroom. I can wait until break-time."

The woman opens her mouth to speak. Helen gives her a senior teacher stare. It works.

"Take a seat in the foyer," the receptionist says.

There is a procession of kids through the corridor. Some stop at the receptionist's window, and she bats them away. "Cover for 9S? Speak to Mrs Bowers. … Mr Knighton? Have you looked in his office? … Feeling sick? Toilet's next left. Hurry."

Has the woman sent the message and will Steve come if she has? The mention of Niers International might whet his curiosity, but if he realizes she's come about Gary, he won't want to see her. School holidays tomorrow. If he gives her the slip and leaves without speaking, this whole trip is an expensive failure.

The break-time bell goes and children swarm from all directions. She's back in Shrewsbury Academy. Happy times. Her chest gapes, this time yearning for her old, old life.

"Mrs Taylor? You wanted to see me."

A stocky man stands in front of her, holding out his hand. The handshake is moist and firm. There's a tremor in hers. Does this man, as unremarkable as countless other teachers, have the power to save her? She must be expecting too much of a knight in rolled-up shirt sleeves and beige trousers.

"I'm so sorry for your loss. I saw it on the news." He sits down beside her, landing heavily on the plastic chair. Friendly eyes full of concern. How they will change when she tells him why she's here. She can still leave and make up some stupid explanation for her visit. In the area, just passing, Damian Howard sends his regards.

But she thanks him for his condolences and gets to the point. "I have to ask you about Club Viva."

The friendly eyes snap away. He shuffles in his chair.

She thinks he's going to bolt but she presses on. "Damian Howard told me what happened but I find the whole thing impossible to believe."

"He told you? Why the hell would he do that?" His raised voice attracts the attention of two passing pupils. They grin at each other and slow down, growing elephant ears for more. Steve glares at them and they hurry on. "He swore to me it never happened." His eyes narrow and he seems to be seeing something that isn't there.

"Mr Chadwick? I have to come to terms with this. Will you help me?"

He scans the corridor. The receptionist is paying them more attention than the queue of pupils in front of her window. "Let's go outside," he says.

They go through a different exit into a courtyard full of children. A few boys are chasing around, throwing their sweatshirts at each other. Most of the girls have tied theirs round their waists. Steve finds a bench in the shade. He wraps his arms around himself. Out of the sun, even a Cypriot winter can nip. The children are out of earshot and making their own noise. Helen slips on the coat she's lugging over her arm and asks what he can tell her.

"It sounds like you know it already. I can't see why you need to hear it from me."

"Please. I'd like your version of events."

"It won't make it sound any better. A girl still dies."

So it's true. Until this moment she's clung to the hope that Damian made the whole thing up.

"Mrs Taylor, Helen. I didn't mean … Have I said too much?" The eyes are friendly again. She shouldn't have come. She can stop it now and not have to see his pity. She'll head back into the sun and find the waiting taxi. But she can't make her legs stand up. She has to know.

"Please tell me about the girl."

"Are you sure that's a good …?"

"Tell me."

"If that's what you want." Steve sighs and loosens his tie. His throat shines blotchy-red. "She was sixteen years old. It was no defence to say she looked older because she didn't. He plied her with drink. By the time I noticed how long they'd been gone it was too late. I knew he was a sleaze but *that*. He made me sick to my stomach."

An icy hand reaches inside Helen and squeezes. She bends over her knees but can't clear the din from her head.

Steve's face comes into focus. Her dizziness clears. "How do you know it was assault?" She knows it's a mistake before she's finished the question but it's out. She grips the side of the bench, preparing for his answer.

He shakes his head. "I couldn't see much in the dark but I heard her cry. I still hear her." He kicks at a clump of grass by the bench. His voice becomes bitter. "He refused to accept what he'd done. He was used to charming his conquests into bed and couldn't comprehend he'd forced one."

Conquests? Gary had other women? She is trembling. "Could you have misunderstood, do you think? Is that possible?"

He puts the weight of his foot on the grass and twists it. "Even when I confronted him with the news that she'd killed herself, he said it had nothing to do with him. I blame myself. If I'd noticed that he'd taken Gary's car keys, I might have been able to stop him. If I hadn't been addled on beer and vodka …"

Helen stops listening. "Didn't Gary take the keys with him?" she asks.

"Gary must have put them on the table when he got his wallet out to buy a round. Damian picked them up when he went off with the girl. Gary followed afterwards but I'm guessing he was too late."

Helen feels hope for the first time in weeks. She wants to savour it and let it smother the lies she's been fed. "Are you saying it was Damian who took the girl outside and attacked her in Gary's car?"

"Who else did you think it was? That's why I'm shocked he told you."

"Damian said it was Gary."

The colour darkens in Steve's face and he looks angry. He grips her elbow and turns her towards him. "Believe me, it was Damian."

Relief dances through her. She can leave now. Go and face Sascha and the rest of them, then back to England and pick up the fragments of her old life. How could she have doubted Gary? All the evidence of Damian's sleazy ways was there; even his latest conquest is a 19yearold babysitter. Only just legal. But she needs to know it all.

"Why didn't the three of you report Damian to the police?"

Steve's hands cover his face. "I wish to God I had." He looks straight at her. "But I had no proof, only suspicions. When we saw the girl running away, all Chris said was, 'I wish I brought my camcorder'. He said I had an overactive imagination."

Low-life scum. She sees his severed head, bile rising in her throat, but she's glad she kicked it.

"I bought the *Tageblatt* every day expecting that the girl would report the crime. I told myself that if the police appealed for witnesses, I would come forward. When I saw her photo two weeks later, the eyes were blocked out, but I recognized her. My wife translated the article, and I found out we had her death on our hands.

"I asked Chris and Gary to come with me to confront Damian. But Chris said my conclusions were a complete fantasy. I think he had his own agenda."

Helen sighs. The conversation she overheard between Chris and Damian about Chateau Petrus wine falls into place. Damian's dirty secret was Chris's cash cow. Why back up Steve when there was an opportunity for blackmail?

"You and Gary could have gone to the police without Chris," she says.

"Gary didn't know what the hell to do because he saw how the whole thing was destroying my marriage and he was scared for himself. He'd started a relationship with you and he was afraid you'd react pretty much as Beate had. In the end we agreed that we wouldn't jeopardize your future together for the sake of something we couldn't prove. It's a decision that's haunted me ever since."

The sleepless nights; it had haunted Gary too. How would she have reacted if he'd told her? Was it her fault that he'd kept silent?

She remembered the call Gary deleted before he "lost" his phone. "Did you ever contact Gary after you moved here?" she asks.

"I sent him a few texts and phoned him every few months to see if he'd changed his mind. But I never pushed him very hard. I doubt I'd have had the guts to come forward even if he'd agreed. In the end he must have got sick of me phoning; his number became unobtainable a while ago.

A shiver runs through her. So Gary lied to her, changed his phone to make sure she didn't find out about Steve. Damian had been truthful about one thing: *You really didn't know him, did you?* She freezes as another thought occurs to her. Two years on, had Gary's conscience caught up with him? That was it. He must have warned Damian that he was about to tell her.

Gary. Louisa. Chris. Did Damian silence them? Got his girlfriend to give him an alibi?

"I can see how this is eating at you," Steve says, studying her face. "Go home and mourn your husband."

They stand up and shake hands. He pats her arm. She touches

his and they embrace. His shirt smells of fabric softener and his arm is plump and undefined. She feels held by a friend or an uncle. Not Sascha. This is guilt-free human contact. Finally someone on her side. She'll have to go to the police about Damian, before he knows what she's discovered and comes after her.

The school bell's gone but Steve walks with her to the taxi. It's the calmest she's been since Number Ten.

"It was good to hear the truth. Thank you."

He holds the car door for her. "You've done me good too. I needed to say it out loud. There have been times when I thought I might explode. When I close my eyes I can't stop seeing that newspaper photograph: Mareike J (16), Dortmannhausen. I'll never forget her."

49

Tuesday, 21 December

"*Ja*?" It's a woman's voice on the intercom. Then a click. In the background Helen hears a male "*Nein*", but the woman's already buzzed Helen through to the foyer.

She bangs on the apartment door, thumps it with both hands. "Let me in, you scumbag." She grabs a wreath off the door and chucks it to the floor. "I know you're in there. I'll stay here until you face me."

The woman opens the door. Small, thin as death, black hair with aged, blanched-out roots. She must be Sascha's mother. Helen pats her jacket pocket and feels the outline of the vegetable knife. She wishes the woman wasn't here. Her grudge is with Sascha. This is for Gary. Eye for an eye.

Sascha in a torn housecoat appears behind his mother.

"Why did it have to come to that?" Helen screams. "If you'd told me what happened to Mareike, hell, I would have helped you."

"*Was sagt sie?*" the woman says. She must have made out her daughter's name in the tirade of English words.

"*Nichts, Mama,*" Sascha says and pulls her away. She goes into a room at the back of the hall but leaves the door ajar.

Helen barges past Sascha and gets into the hallway. "Was it me? Mareike died two years ago. What the hell did I do to trigger you off now?" She knows her skin is red, both face and neck. She let him kiss her neck once. Never again. "Answer me."

"I didn't know it for many months."

"Speak up, Sascha. I want to hear you explain it while I look you in the eye."

His eyes are pinpricks, burning into hers. "How much do you know?" he asks.

Is it a threat? She doesn't care. She'll attack first; she's got nothing to lose anymore. She puts her hand in her pocket and touches the hilt of the vegetable knife. "I want to hear you say it. All of it. From the beginning."

He glares at her. His pupils are still tiny but there's fury there now. "Mama found her body and has to face every day through a schnapps glass."

The woman's shadow moves across her door. Helen knows she'll be out in the hall soon. *Mareike* and *Mama* are all the decipherable words she'll need. Helen must act before that, but she needs the whole truth first. She folds her arms. Her coat's zipped to her throat. Her unkissable throat.

"Mareike kept our family together. Afterwards, my father left. Mama and I argued. Always the same: I told her to stop drinking; she told me I would drink too if I lost a child. One argument went too far and she showed me Mareike's suicide letter. I knew then."

He softens his glare as if searching her face for sympathy. She hardens hers.

"She'd hid the letter to protect my father and me, and she burnt it after she showed me. I couldn't prove anything."

"So you decided to avenge Mareike."

"I found Damian Howard, one of the men from the nightclub. He saw a child in danger and did nothing to help her. I destroyed his garden and told him I knew. He said he didn't understand

271

but we both knew he did. I thought if I pushed him hard enough, he'd tell me the truth, tell me which man was responsible. By the time I met you at the *Freibad*, I was ready to try a new tactic."

Helen steps closer. There's a tiny mole below his eye. She noticed it when they kissed. He moves back up the hall. She matches his movements, a menacing quickstep. "So I was in the wrong place at the wrong time?"

He nods. His mother comes into the hall, swaying, as if she's been drinking.

Helen glowers at Sascha. "I thought we were friends. I defended you."

"It was for Mareike. Any means possible." His voice is hard.

Even through her raging anger, she feels a twinge of rejection. So she was his means to an end. Her stomach clenches, by God what an end.

"Was Gary in the wrong place too?" she says quietly.

"I don't …?"

"Why would you hurt him? What did the suicide note say?"

"Mareike said one of four men from the International School attacked her but the only name she remembered was Damian. I discovered Damian Howard was the head teacher. I don't know if he attacked my sister, but at the least he stood by and let another man do it."

She leaps at him. His mother screams and sways again.

Helen grabs Sascha's shoulder, her nails wanting to pierce the nylon material of his housecoat and dig into his collarbone. "You're telling me you didn't know that Damian attacked her, or that Gary and Chris were two of the other men? They were just random victims who got in the way when you killed Damian's wife and dog?"

She feels his body stiffen. He pulls her hand off his shoulder. "Are you saying Damian Howard did it?" He shakes her. "Howard attacked Mareike? Killed her, as good as?"

She yanks herself away, feeling her upper arms bruising up

from his grasp. "They could have helped you bring him to justice. Instead, three people died while the real culprit is free."

She's crying now, and Sascha's mother puts an arm around her. The woman's breath is tinny and smoky, but mostly it smells sad.

Sascha's not looking at them. He's pacing the hall, his face twisted in a snarl.

Helen sobs harder. Real tears that won't stop. Why does she finally have to cry now? It's all gone wrong. Everything. She slips away from his mother and dashes out of the flat.

50

It is one in the morning when Helen gets to Dickensweg. She's driven back sweating and crying and shaking. She parks and leans over the wheel. She wants the fire in her to reignite so she can carry on hating. Her eyelids droop and her head lolls against the steering wheel. She forces herself to get out.

The cold air takes the edge off her sleepiness. There's a light on in the kitchen next door and through the window she can see Mel filling a kettle at the sink. So she doesn't sleep nights either. Across the road at number 8, Jerome Stephens is in his kitchen with what looks like a glass of whisky in his hand. She walks up her path but at the last minute goes to Mel's door. She taps lightly and prays Mel will answer. She's heavy with everything she's learnt in the last twenty-four hours. Mel can share the burden.

Mel is chalk white when she opens the door. She lets out a breath when she sees Helen.

"Were you expecting someone else?" Helen asks.

"I thought … Chris used to tap the door like that. I thought for a minute … I expect you think I'm crazy."

"Of course not. Sometimes I think I can hear Gary playing computer games. It must be part of the grieving process."

Mel's expression is blank, not taking the trouble to either agree or disagree. It's a face that shuts Helen out. United in tragedy, divided in mourning. She's wearing the mustard kaftan that once strained at the seams, but now gapes at the neck and hangs off her narrow shoulders. Her cropped hair has swapped its ingénue chic from the swim club party for sticky-up and greasy. Three weeks ago they were normal, now they are freaks.

Helen apologizes for her late visit and says she's just back from Cyprus. "Do you remember a teacher at school called Steve Chadwick?"

"No."

"He was a friend of Chris's."

Mel shakes her head. "I barely knew Chris's friends, but it doesn't matter now." She coughs. Her breath stinks. Like a homeless person.

"Are you eating?" Helen asks.

"Are you? I thought you were in jail," she replies.

Helen explains she's been released without charge. "I know now that Sascha Jakobsen had a strong motive," she says. "Damian attacked Sascha's sister."

Mel's eyes flicker to Helen and she manages a flat "Oh".

"Doesn't that shock you?"

Mel gives a hollow laugh. "The shock-wagon has already rolled."

"But don't you think that makes Sascha the prime suspect?"

"I told you that."

"He got Manfred Scholz to lie for him. Could they have been in it together?"

Mel looks at her. "Isn't that a bit far-fetched?"

Helen feels foolish under Mel's sceptical gaze. But what if she's right? Damian authorized the demolition of Manfred's cottage. Did he seek revenge?

"And Damian has a motive," she says, her brain racing to the next possibility. "Gary, Chris and maybe Louisa knew about Sascha's sister. Damian might have wanted their silence."

"He might have," she says but she's staring out at the street towards Jerome in his window.

51

Wednesday, 22 December

Helen is on her third coffee of the morning when Mel knocks on the door. She brings her into the hall. The woman's a chameleon. She has showered, blow-dried her hair and swapped the yellow parachute for jeans and a tight-fitting polo neck.

Mel tells her that the police have finished at Number Ten. "I'm going over to clear out Louisa's things for Damian. He can't face it alone."

Helen's coffee comes back to her throat; the mention of Louisa's clothes triggers a flashback to the blood-soaked bib of her final outfit.

"Damian told me Sabine has done most of it. I don't think there's much left to do in the house," she says.

"He held onto some things of sentimental value but now he's decided to sort through everything. He phoned me this morning and said it's hanging over him and it needs to be done."

A dark thought occurs to Helen. What if he's … luring Mel to …?

"Are you sure you want to go into Number Ten?" she says. "On your own?"

276

Mel shrugs. "Come with me if you want."

"Me?" Helen backs away. "I haven't been inside there since …"

"We can't let this blight the rest of our lives. We'll get through it quicker if we face it head on."

"I … Do you even have the keys to get in?" Helen asks.

"Damian's meeting us there."

Helen's heart belts. "Don't you remember what I told you about him last night?"

"If there was any proof of that, he would have been arrested months ago. What's your problem, Helen? The days of your aloofness towards the Howards should be long gone."

Helen cannot speak. Has Mel blanked out how Louisa used to humiliate her? Her weight, her cooking, her phobias – everything about her was fair game to Louisa.

"I'm sorry if that sounded harsh," Mel says. "Louisa and Damian were good neighbours. I'm not going to let Damian down."

"I don't think … It might not be safe."

"I know about his string of girlfriends. I'd bet Louisa did too. But he isn't about to jump on me. He treats me like his kid sister. So are you coming?"

Mel's confidence almost persuades her to accept, but "kid sister" jags out thoughts of Sascha and his revenge.

"You go on ahead, I'll catch up with you later," she says, a sense of dread settling on her shoulders.

52

Sascha scales the Howards' back fence. The hoar frost suckers his bare hands and burns them. He lands in a frozen flower bed and puts his hands in his pockets. His blood pounds. It's the sound of fury. *Damian Howard*. He surveys the summer house, still fit for an Inuit despite the partial thaw.

The house is shabby, hunched up in the cold. The painted brickwork is chipped as if a spray of bullets has passed over. One of the shutters is off its hinges. *Verschlampt*. No. that's not the word; not slutty, just lifeless. Death has claimed this house, but not entirely, not yet. His jaw tightens.

He peers in through a window. Posh sofas. Poncy candles. Polar bear rug. Howard has it all. Sascha bangs a fist against the pane. The frame moves. He puts his fingers round it and pulls it towards him. If he could get high enough, he could get through there. All he needs to know is where the bastard is living now. There could be a letter from his school left behind or a forwarding address somewhere. Unlikely but worth a try.

The canvas gazebo on the lawn has buckled under the weight of snow. But the table underneath is dry and he drags it to the window, yanking and lifting it over the compacted snow. He stands on it and notices silver and pink speckles of glitter on the palms of his hands, remnants of Louisa's party. But the party's over. He climbs in.

53

Mel's not in a rush; she doesn't think Damian will be there yet. She makes herself another cup of tea – a dash of milk, no sugar. It has taken some getting used to after the syrupy stuff Chris used to make her, but now it's a beverage she savours, alongside her daily perusal of the *Telegraph*. Aldi stocks British newspapers because of the international school being nearby, but they are ridiculously expensive. Still, she allows herself this luxury. She's feeling stronger today, back to normal. She could even make that phone call she's been putting off although her stomach clenches when she thinks of it.

She scans a headline about a murder in Yorkshire. It's a thump in the chest. A reminder of where she's going next. She hasn't been to Louisa's place since it happened. But it's just a house. She's not scared of ghosts; living people are more threatening.

When she went out earlier to buy the newspaper, she became Moses, parting a Red Sea of sympathetically smiling shoppers. Parents and staff from the school regrouped in murmuring waves behind her. She caught one of their hushed conversations: "My money's on the German they released … got one of his lot to lie for him."

So they've gone off Helen as their prime suspect. When she

was arrested, the school jury was swift to reach a verdict: "Always thought there was something not right about her … She had a massive row with poor Louisa the night before …" So resolute were their convictions that Mel found herself believing them.

She sips her tea and contemplates the stalker's resurgence as public enemy number one. It is feasible, for sure. He hasn't done himself any favours with the pestering and garden vandalism. He might as well stick an "I did it" sign on his back. But why blame him for murder just because he wrecked a garden? Besides, a couple of weeks and one swipe of Damian's credit card later, Louisa's garden was restored to its former glory.

What state is that garden in now the snow has melted? Black leaves rotting in scrawny flower beds. Moss sprawling across dark, frost-brittle lawn. Tendrils of unpruned climbers clawing into masonry. She could do the neighbourly thing and give it a bit of a tidy. The ground's rock hard but she could get rid of the decaying leaves. Technically it's still Damian's place. He might appreciate her efforts.

She drains her tea, grabs a coat and goes out to her shed. She hasn't been in it since the summer. It's dank and smells of old grass mowings and creosote. She picks up the rake and wonders what other school-issue implements would be useful. She sees the secateurs on the ledge that runs round the top of the wall. To get closer, she moves the bag of compost Chris bought the previous year in a fit of enthusiasm but never opened. The floor wobbles where the heavy bag stood. She lifts up one of the floor-boards.

54

Even after everything that's been strewn around this house, the Howards' sofas are creamy clean. He sits down, depositing his oily fingerprints on the expensive fabric. Damian Howard left his marks on something far more delicate. Sascha gags. Acid up to his nostrils.

He throws a cushion across the room and topples an unlit candle. He walks to the hall and sees a discoloured patch of parquet. Whose job was it to scrub this house? Damian on his hands and knees, like a post-war *Trümmerfrau*, picking through rubble from British acts of terror.

He sniffs the potpourri on the telephone table. It makes him think of the scent on Helen's neck. He clenches his fists.

He hears movement in the street outside. Someone approaching the house? He freezes and listens hard. *Scheiße.*

55

Helen drives, not caring where she goes. She chucks the vegetable knife out of the window, not even able to get that right. Revenge isn't something she's good at. And who's responsible? Sascha? Damian? Manfred? She might never know.

She yawns. If she closes her eyes and opens them again much later, she'll get her old world back. She'll mark the A level PE projects by Christmas Eve. She'll order the last few presents on Amazon and buy some bits from Waitrose to take to Gary's parents. She'd rather be at home, cooking duck for the two of them, but it means a lot to Gary, so mother-in-law turkey it is. At least they'll have their New Year break in Gran Canaria to look forward to and a lovely long, sleepy rest.

Her eyes open. She slams on the brakes, just missing an Opal van in front and she slews into the layby near the *Freibad*. She climbs out of the car to get some air and wake herself up. Slush spatters her jeans where the sun has managed a puddle-sized thaw.

Without thinking, she approaches the swimming pool fence and finds a foothold, then another and a third. She lands in a gnarled tree root protruding from the ground on the other side and jars her knee.

The pool looks different from how she remembered it in the summer. It's naked now – sun loungers, tables and parasols packed away and the float cage empty. Ice sheets drift on the water. There's an ethereal quality which draws her closer, but she slips on the frosty poolside and lands on the same knee. She lets out a yelp that echoes across the expanse of cold. Is this where it started? She rubs her throbbing leg. If she'd never come here, would Gary still be alive? If she'd taken up jogging with Louisa. If she hadn't befriended Sascha. Her hand goes to her throat.

Her throat. Her shame. She will lie down, close her eyes and leave this place. Pay the ultimate price for her betrayal. She thinks about Mel calling her aloof towards Louisa. Does Mel hold her responsible? Does everyone? She kneels down and the cold ground acts as an ice pack for her leg. She started it here so this is where she should finish it. Everything forever. The End.

No way. She sits up. Her knee kills but she gets to her feet. In spite of the hell she's seen, she wants to live, to mourn Gary. He's all that matters now. Not Mel or Sascha Jakobsen or Damian Howard. Mel's a grown woman. She thinks Damian's harmless. It's up to her if she wants to go to the house. But Helen is getting out.

She struggles back over the wall. Flights will be busy so close to Christmas but she'll drive to the Channel if she has to. She can stay with her brother until her Shrewsbury house is available. The police can contact her there.

Changing gear on the drive back is agonizing. She hopes there's a flight as she doubts she's up to the four-hour drive to Calais.

***

Back at home there's a note from Mel stuck on her front door. She's found Chris's missing DVDs in their shed and wants her to go over to Number Ten to watch them while they clear Louisa's stuff.

Her body clenches at the thought of going there. And then to have to watch Chris Mowar talking rubbish into a camera lens while his widow sobs her heart out beside her. She hasn't got the stomach for this, nor the time. There's flight availability to check and packing to do. She could say she never got the note; it blew away. But is she that selfish? It's Mel, not Damian, who wants her help. She's leaving anyway so watching one quick DVD won't hurt. She postpones her escape until the afternoon.

At the other end of the street Manfred Scholz comes out of his house. He tugs on his hat before the sound of his snow boots thuds away to the main road. She thinks of going after him to demand to know why he gave Sascha an alibi. But the fight has left her. It barely matters.

She limps across the compacted snow to Number Ten. Damian's BMW is parked half up on the kerb. A prickle of fear comes over her. She'll stay outside, call Mel on her mobile and make some excuse to get her out of the house and away from him. But what's her number? Come to think of it, she's never even seen her texting. The front door is ajar. She calls out for Mel, but there's no reply. She gathers her strength and goes inside.

56

"Mel? ... Hello? ... Damian?"

She sees the faded patch of flooring in the hall. Napoleon. She breathes in meat and decay. The house has ignited her memory, vivid and cruel. The real smell is of bleach. She chokes.

The coat rack is empty but there's a bowl of potpourri on the telephone table. She doesn't sniff it in case it brings back too many memories of Louisa. There's a film of dust on the stair rail. Some of it is fingerprint powder.

"Mel?"

The lounge door is pushed to but not closed. She hears a fast, rhythmic noise beyond it. *Jesus*. Pain tugs in her knee, daring her to run. She stays put and reasons it might not be Damian. It must be a radio left on or a ticking clock. She rubs her temples and is surprised how sweaty her hair is. She puts her shaky fingers on the door handle.

She rushes in, her whole body tensed, and smiles with relief. Mel's sitting on the rug, surrounded by scattered felt-tipped pens. She's working one furiously over a child's colouring book, it's the noise that Helen heard. Helen breathes out and thanks God that the sliding doors to the dining room are shut; Gary's in there.

Without looking up, Mel asks: "Do you ever think there's a colour missing from the spectrum?"

Helen doesn't know how to answer and homes in on the colours in the room – yellow and gold wallpaper, regal blue curtains. The room is still habitable, only the art prints have gone, but it seems barren. It's Louisa that's missing, not a colour.

"I don't know," she replies.

But Mel has moved on. "I've put the first DVD in."

Mel launches herself backwards into the sofa next to the DVD player. "I dragged the player out of the music room in case you're wondering," she says. "Louisa wouldn't allow TV in the lounge. Are you going to sit down?" She pats the cushion beside her.

Helen looks at the sofas. There's no chemical cleaning smell in here. It's the same soapy lavender fragrance she first encountered at her welcome party in April.

"Where is Damian?" she asks.

"Not here yet. He dropped the keys through my door."

"His car's outside."

Mel shrugs. "Are you sure it's his? Sit down."

Helen's pretty sure the BMW belongs to Damian. He could walk into his old house at any moment. He'd have them cornered then. She perches on the edge of the other sofa, resisting the comfort of the deep cushions. She keeps her ears primed for the sound of the front door.

Mel fiddles with the remote control. Her expression is composed. Was she so calm when she pulled the TV out of the other room, knowing what had happened to her husband in there? Maybe she didn't take it in when the police explained it. A shudder runs through Helen. Maybe you have to have seen it – to have been there – to know. To still see it now.

Mel says: "We're lucky nothing's been stolen. I found the window in here wide open and the floor's wet. You'd think the police would have taken more care. Anyone could have got in." She waves her hand towards the window. There's a dark patch on the parquet where it's wet. The meat-smelling memory of the hall flashes through Helen.

"I've paused the disk at the start of Chris's documentary. Or we could watch on the flat screen in the cellar if you prefer?" Mel asks.

Access to the cellar is through the kitchen. Louisa's in there, crumpled, hand pressed between her body and the worktop, her manicure still intact. Helen trembles. "In here is fine."

Mel presses play. Chris's head and shoulders appear on the screen as if detached from the rest of him. Helen fights off a surge of nausea. A dead man talking. She glances at Mel, ready to move in next to her and take her hand to comfort her, but she's leaning forward, looking curious rather than sad.

"*Welcome to Mowar Matters. Tonight's programme is about con men. What you're about to see is the most ground-breaking investigation ever undertaken. After painstaking research over a five-year period, I present to you the definitive insight into how and why even intelligent, rational people fall victim to the most outlandish cons.*"

The queasiness is gone and she feels the same nasty taste in her mouth she had whenever Chris pontificated. If he hadn't been murdered, he would have died of hyperbole. He must be reading a script off to the side of the camera. It makes him look as if he has a squint. His thumb and index finger are pressed together and move in circles as he conducts his delivery.

"*Let's take a look at gullible people.*"

The screen changes to an image of Louisa Howard walking Napoleon. Helen shoots a look at Mel but she's still focused on the TV. The next scene is Damian Howard climbing out of his car. Helen folds her arms, resigned to viewing whatever farcical hatchet job Chris Mowar has got planned for his neighbours. Damian isn't gullible. Would he fall for a con? Or Louisa, or … Helen gasps. She's watching her own image as she mows her back lawn. The creep must have filmed her from his bedroom window. Still Mel stares at the screen. Her eyes don't seem to blink.

"*Which of these people would make the best victim? To discover that, you must study them. Observe their lifestyles, find out what motivates them. Take time to learn their secrets, their indiscretions, and their weaknesses. This woman, for example, is a loner who doesn't follow the crowd.*"

Helen's throat narrows when there's more footage of her, this time going up her path with an Aldi carrier bag. No reaction from Mel. No apology. She wants to yell at her: *your husband was a filthy peeping Tom*. The film plays more video of Damian and Louisa: he's getting a crate of wine out of his boot; she's running past the Greek family's house in her sport clothes. Chris's voiceover continues. "*This man is in a position of power but his secrets could topple him. This woman is a control freak who keeps up appearances at all costs …*"

Helen recalls Damian's rage when he pummelled Sascha. If he saw this …

"*Which one is the perfect victim? The man? He would make a prime target for blackmail. The con artist could pull his strings.*"

Helen's eyes are wide. Is he admitting he blackmailed Damian? If Chris talks about the nightclub, it could be evidence. It could vindicate Gary. She waits for the next line. This could end up being the one decent thing Creepy Chris has ever done.

"*What about the loner? She's bound to be vulnerable surely? But a loner is only weak if she's on the outside yearning to get in. This woman never wanted to run with the pack. She's alone but strong.*"

A blush heats her face and she can't believe she's taking a compliment from this sleaze.

More footage of Louisa in her sport kit. A distance shot of her hands pressed against her front door, stretching her calf muscles.

"*The victim in this trio is the control freak. Underneath her outward show of dominance, this woman – let's call her Tracey – is running scared. She's terrified her husband will leave her and destroy the world she's fabricated.*"

Bastard. All of Louisa's secrets broadcast. Was Tracey her real name? Helen's glad Chris is dead. She's glad Louisa is, too, and spared this humiliation.

"*For the purposes of my investigation, I assumed the role of the con man,*" Chris announces on the screen.

"You arsehole," she shouts, not caring what Mel thinks. But Mel sinks back in the sofa, as if settling in for a good David Attenborough.

"*I started with the 'seduction'.*" He makes inverted commas with his fingers. "*I pressed buttons that made her feel good about herself. I was attentive to her in a way that her womanizing husband was not. When I'd gained her trust, I told her a secret. Disclosing confidences to a woman like Tracey is like feeding best steak to a lioness. She thrives on control and knows that information is power.*"

Helen rubs her eyes, tugging at the skin below her sockets. What makes it so bad is that he's right. Every cruel hole he pokes is a perfect puncture in Louisa's façade.

"*The secret I told her …*" There's a beat and he looks straight into the camera. "*was a lie.*" There's another beat as he smoulders with smugness into the lens. Helen relives every dignity-destroying dinner party she attended with Chris at the table. It's a wonder she didn't decapitate him herself.

"*Every con artist knows that to tell a convincing lie, you should tell the most outrageous one you can. I told Tracey I was an undercover intelligence officer, monitoring security risks to the British community in Germany.*"

She doesn't bother looking at Mel, sure that even this revelation won't rock her. Maybe it isn't news to her; maybe she knew her husband was Walter Mitty.

"*I confided in Tracey that it was becoming difficult to do my job because of my wife's mental problems and bouts of paranoia.*"

Mel folds her lip over her teeth and scratches her nose. These are tells, but Helen can't read them. The woman's eyes stay on her husband.

"*I appealed to Tracey's sense of her own self-importance. It seemed to her entirely apt that a woman such as herself, who ran every committee in her community, should be co-opted onto a forum of national importance. I asked her to keep an eye on my wife while I was out on 'missions'."*

Another set of inverted comma fingers. Helen's own hands itch. She wants to grab his fingers and shove them down his throat. Wait until Damian sees this. If Chris wasn't already dead, he soon would be. Damian would never have let Chris trash Louisa. Helen looks away but not before seeing Chris's face break into the smug grin she found so repugnant when he was alive.

"To keep her convinced, I arranged what I call a 'tableaux of authenticity'." More inverted fingers. *"I organized for her to meet me coming out of the police station near where we lived. I told her I was on a liaison assignment with the Germans. In fact, all I'd done was ask the desk officer for directions to the cinema."* His nostrils flare, triumphant in his own ingenuity. A thoroughbred tosspot.

Helen shakes her head; the whole thing must be a crappy spoof. No wonder he was apoplectic when the DVDs went missing. He wouldn't have wanted anyone seeing this. Mel said it was the first DVD. How much more rubbish is there?

No way would Louisa have fallen for this. She was a snob but not an idiot. Louisa was all for pretence as long as she was the one making it. She'd have seen straight through Quentin Tarantino here.

The screen goes blank.

"That's the end of the first disk," Mel says, jumping up. How sprightly she is these days.

"Is that all you can say? Aren't you shocked?" Helen asks. "Did you know about any of this?"

Mel tilts her head, as if weighing her up. "Yes and no," she says. She puts another disk in the machine.

57

Sascha sits on the cellar steps. His body aches from straining against the door into the kitchen. He heard voices and now someone has put on a TV or a radio. A man's voice. A police radio? *I'm screwed this time.*

He should have held his ground when the front door opened instead of running into the cellar. The visitor could have been Howard himself. It would all be over by now if he'd got him, put his hands around his throat and squeezed. But there'd been shouting, too muffled to make out. A scream? Then silence.

The new voices must mean the police or a witness. Revenge just got complicated.

58

"*Now onto the scientific element of my research — a step-by-step guide to selecting and manipulating a victim.*"

The camera pans across a bar full of people. It's The Britannic, the town's attempt at a British pub. Helen loathes it, but, as Chris's filming shows, it's popular with most school families. She picks out two of the gap-year students and what might be the claret-haired woman from the Italian restaurant, although her hair is dyed black in the film.

"*So first find your victim. A good place to start your search is a nightclub. Young people out on the town let down their guard. They'll be happy to pass the time in conversation with a friendly, older man. Gradually some will melt away — no doubt finding the older man rather boring.*"

The camera is back on Chris. Helen ignores his stupid mock-modest grin. She waits for the next line. Nightclub. He's going to do it. He's going to talk about Club Viva.

"*The friendly, older man will be left with two or three. He'll ask them about their families, their relationships, their aspirations. In no time, he builds up a picture of who is vulnerable and suggestible. He gets their Facebook details and takes it from there.*"

Helen leans forward. This is it. *Say it, you creep, say it.* She unbuttons the top of her jacket. Christ it's hot. The heating's still on despite the house being vacant.

"*An excellent potential victim is the student. Young people with a naive curiosity for life. The con man installs himself in a university town and seeks out the pubs that students frequent.*"

She undoes another button and glares at the screen, willing him to get the hell on with it. The scene changes to views of several cities. She recognizes Oxford and London. Another cityscape wobbles and falls away, leaving a view of the magnolia-painted wall. The faker filmed it in his bedroom. He's holding up postcards to the camera. What an amateur.

"*Sit at the bar and be on the look-out for the straggler in the group: the prissy one who can't keep up with the drinking games; the nerdy one who talks about finishing essays; the unattractive one who gets left out as the others pair off.*"

There's acid in Helen's throat. This is what Damian said happened at Club Viva. She braces herself for the whole sordid story.

"*I found Fiona in a pub in Southampton.*"

Images of what Helen presumes is Southampton city centre appear. But why is it Southampton and not Düsseldorf?

"*She was the quiet one in a bawdy group but she didn't have the strength of character to find more suitable friends. Instead she attached herself to me. She told me she was in the final year of her French and Business degree and had spent the previous year as a language assistant in Lyons. Her parents doted on her, and she worried about their health.*"

Helen shakes her head again. It's a fairy story. Mareike was German and still at school.

"*With the groundwork in place and a considerable rapport established, I revealed that I was an intelligence officer sent to root out a drugs syndicate at the university. They were believed to be Western European with links to major terrorist groups worldwide.*"

Chris steps closer to the camera. His skin is flushed and shiny.

A real film-maker would have dabbed on Max Factor. His eyes still squint to the side.

"*Most of you watching this will refuse to believe that anyone would fall for a line like that from a bloke they met in a pub. That's why choosing the right victim is so crucial to the con man's plans. Fiona didn't take what I said at face value. She searched the Internet and asked me questions, but I'd prepared my character well. I had sufficient answers to reassure her.*

"*It was time to move in for the con.*"

A dramatic soundtrack blares as Chris holds up a card with the words "The Con" handwritten on it. Presumably he intended to add graphics to his masterpiece later. He holds up another card: "Create Anxiety". His expression is primary school teacher doing flash-card phonics.

"*Stage one of this con meant making Fiona feel frightened.*"

Helen's skin itches. It isn't the Club Viva story; it doesn't feel like a story at all.

The image changes to a ransacked room – sheets ripped off the single bed, desk drawers open, books and papers torn and strewn across the floor.

Helen throws up her hands. It's a story all right, or a re-enactment. "Mel, that's … Is that your house? … Mel?"

"It's our spare room. He used it as a studio," she replies but her eyes don't leave the screen.

"*I staged a break-in at her halls of residence. I made sure I was with her when she found the mess. I told her that my bosses had discovered that the drugs ring was French and that she had unwittingly made contact with them during her year in France. She was now in danger.*"

Helen rolls her eyes when she hears more of the dramatic music. Chris's film-making skills are amateurish, and sick. It's like watching a 10-year-old pull the legs off an insect he's captured.

He laces his hands together across his chest. One finger stands proud of the other digits. It's his pointing baton to emphasize his words.

"*From this moment on, the con gathered speed. I knew she wouldn't contact the police because she was utterly convinced of my status as an intelligence officer.*"

He holds up another handwritten card: "Social Isolation". "*If you've laid firm foundations in stage one, the transition to social isolation will be smooth.*

"*I told her I was putting pressure on my bosses to find her a safe house. I would request permission to become her protection officer but it would take a few days.*"

The camera angle changes to a full-length shot. He has adopted the persona of a policeman: feet apart, hands behind back, mono-tone delivery.

"*I stayed away for a week and in that time made silent phone calls to her mobile. By the time she saw me again she was barely venturing out of her room. She was ready to accept anything, so I told her I'd managed to get her a flat in Manchester. I said my bosses had taken some convincing but I'd called in a couple of favours. She was to tell her parents that she'd been headhunted for a trainee journalist job in France.*"

Helen tries to remember Chris ever mentioning Southampton, or Manchester. Is it true?

The screen goes blank and then comes back with a close-up of Chris's face. "*Within three months of meeting Fiona, I'd convinced her to give up her degree, lie to her family and go into hiding.*"

The screen darkens and Chris reappears further away, holding up another card: "Control Communication".

"*I convinced her to avoid anyone in uniform, warning her it could be a trap. Pretty soon she would hide in the bathroom if there was a knock at the door. I didn't tell her to; she worked it out for herself.*" His face has the punch-pleased expression of a dog owner whose mutt has won an obedience class. If Fiona were beside him on-screen, he'd pat her head.

He waves another card: "Financial Dependence".

"*I convinced Fiona that the drugs syndicate would trace her through her cashpoint withdrawals. All she had to do was give me her bank details and I'd take care of everything. From that point on she had no access to money. If she needed anything, she had to put her plea to me."*

He holds up another card but drops it. He swears and then the screen goes blank as he stops filming.

"This is criminal, Mel. Did he really do this?"

Mel's eyes stay on the fuzzy image, waiting for her husband to reappear.

"Mel, is this true? Answer me."

Mel puts her finger to her lips, shakes her head at Helen and snaps her gaze back to the TV.

When the screen comes back on, he's holding the card in place. "*Stage five is Physical Manipulation. The weak victim is a malleable victim. I deprived Fiona of sleep. I would ring her in the night with important codes to write down. She had to stay awake, never knowing when another call might come through.*"

Helen puts her head in her hands again. She wants to leave, to unknow his sick fantasy. But her gut says it's not a fantasy and she's already complicit. She stays.

"*There are two more stages to achieving total dominance over the victim. Stage six is to make the victim abandon their past. I let Fiona ring her parents again. She played her part well: the trainee journalist on a chance-of-a-lifetime internship.*"

"You sick bastard," Helen says. Mel waves her silent.

"I woke her in the early hours in a state of alarm. I told her the call had been traced. The drug barons were closing in."

Mel's fidgeting. She folds her arms, unfolds them, bites her nails.

"*By 9 a.m. I was driving her away from everything she'd ever known. I told her that in order to protect her parents she couldn't call them again.*"

He has another card but it's blank. He taps it in his hand. His face beams with joy.

"*The final stage – stage seven – came about unexpectedly.*" He turns the card round as if he's an archaeologist revealing a Viking treasure. It reads: "Shatter Reality".

Helen stands up and presses the player's off-button. "I'm not watching this. To dream up this kind of fantasy and pass it off as a documentary is vile."

Mel is still staring at the blank screen. "It's real," she says quietly.

"How real? You mean to tell me that Chris went to Southampton to brainwash a girl into leaving university and going into hiding with him?"

Mel looks at her now. Her blank face is the polar opposite of Chris's animated onscreen features. "You never liked Chris, did you?"

How can she ask? Of all the nosy neighbours, Chris was always the biggest creep and, after what she's just watched, even his wife must see it. "If you knew about this, why didn't you tell the police or at least leave him?"

Mel stands up. "I'll make a start on sorting Louisa's stuff. Come up and help." She goes upstairs. Her steps are light and brisk.

Helen rubs her knee. It's hurting again and she's too outraged to move. The intrusive questions, the pronouncements he made on her marriage. Chris Mowar preyed on women and saw them as fodder for his pseudo-documentary. Poor Louisa. Helen accused her of pulling the neighbours' strings when in truth Louisa was the one who was manipulated and humiliated.

Chris Mowar justified his behaviour in the name of a documentary. The charm, the flamboyance, the arrogance, the cruelty, it was all there. And Mel had lived with him. Why the hell did she do nothing?

Helen goes to the front door. If Damian turns up, Mel can take her chances.

She calls out: "Something's come up. I've got to go."

There's no reply.

"Pop round for a coffee later if you want."

Still no reply. Her skin tingles. What if Chris's film has shocked Mel more than she let on and she's up there sobbing?

Even though Helen thinks Mel has shown more resilience in the last few weeks than anyone else, she finds herself walking back into the lounge. She'll stay a bit longer, for Mel's sake. She sits on a sofa, needing a minute to prepare herself before going upstairs. To Louisa's stuff. She imagines the chiffon blouses, the tailored trousers, and the designer exercise clothes standing to attention in Louisa's wardrobe, like faithful retainers awaiting their mistress's return.

The DVD player is still lit up, with Chris's disk inside. No way is she watching any more. She was right about his attitude to women. Didn't Steve Chadwick say Chris wanted to film Mareike straight after she was attacked at Club Viva?

Damian Howard and Chris Mowar – some double act. It gives Sascha one hell of a motive for wanting them both dead. Her heart races. Now that the DVDs have come to light, it's only a matter of time before Sascha finds out about Chris's predilection for snaring girls. The hairs on Helen's arms stand on end and she has the urge to flee. As soon as she's warned Mel, she's getting the hell out of Number Ten and Germany.

When did Mel first see the film? Her reaction – or lack of it – suggests today wasn't her first viewing. What if she first found the DVDs in early December? How would she have reacted then? Helen snaps a lid on her thoughts, not liking where they're leading her. She takes a deep breath and wills herself to stop imagining all sorts.

But what if, despite her lack of emotion, she did watch them for the first time just now? Helen lets out a sigh, predicting that Mel might spend the next several hours crying on her shoulder. But Helen needs to leave. The film was disgusting but there's nothing she can do about it. Mel will have to come to terms with it in her own way. She limps across the hall, trying not to put weight on her injured leg and opens the front door.

Mel appears on the stairs. She's slipped one of Louisa's Lycra tops over her clothes. Although she's lost weight, she hasn't reached Louisa's diminutive proportions. The shirt is straining across her breasts. Her pallor is corpse-like against the salmon pink. She stops on the bottom step.

"Where are you going, Helen?"

59

It's gone quiet. For the thousandth time Sascha tells himself he's a *Vollidiot* for not stepping forward as soon as he heard the front door close. But there are at least two people in the house. He doesn't know their whereabouts and can't take them by surprise. He isn't sure whether the man was on a radio or in the house. There was a woman's voice too and above his head a herd of elephants. Now nothing and he needs to pee.

His legs ache from crouching on the cellar steps behind the kitchen door. He backs down into the cellar and accidently kicks a child's bag on the stairs. He stamps on it to stop it rolling and holds his breath. Nothing; no one's heard him.

He doesn't dare switch on the cellar light in case it shines through to upstairs. Winter gloom from the street comes through the grilled windows at the top of the wall so that he can make out the decor. Dark wall tiles and flat-screen TV: it looks like a porno cinema. Damian Howard drooling over images of underage girls. Sascha kicks out at a popcorn dispenser and cracks the plastic casing. He freezes and listens hard. *Scheiße.*

60

"I was letting in some fresh air," Helen says. "It's warm in here."

"Why are you shivering then?" Mel asks.

Helen closes the front door. She doesn't see how she's going to get out now without offending her.

She rests one hand on Mel's arm. "I think we should leave. Damian's obviously not coming. I don't like it here."

Mel's eyes are on her. Helen can't read them. "Let's watch the rest of the DVD first," she says.

"Can't we just …?"

"Please, watch with me."

She follows Mel back into the lounge. She'll give her ten minutes, make herself stomach that much more of Chris's poison. Then let Mel down gently and leave.

Mel presses play. Chris reappears on the screen with the "Shatter Reality" card. "*I was the only person that Fiona had spoken to for four months. I became not only her protection officer but also her lover.*"

She rolls her eyes but Mel, chin in hands, is totally absorbed. Helen gives a loud sigh to distract her but she doesn't react. How can she be sucked into this tripe?

"*When she became pregnant she was happy – for the first time since I convinced her she was mixed up with the drugs syndicate.*"

Helen wants to stick her fingers in her ears but Mel doesn't stir, not a flicker of movement. She sits on Louisa's sofa in Louisa's shirt, watching her dead husband say he got a girl pregnant.

"*Fiona's delight gave me an unexpected opportunity to achieve the final stage. I told her how thrilled I was and attended every hospital appointment – which wasn't easy as I was working overseas by then.*"

Still Mel doesn't move. How much more can she listen to without reacting? How much sicker can Chris's fantasy get?

"*Twelve weeks into the pregnancy, I told her devastating news. The drugs gang had tracked her down. Intelligence reports suggested that they intended to kidnap the baby and force Fiona to testify in their favour.*" Chris turns as if addressing an invisible Fiona beside him. "*Sobbing, I said, 'My bosses are arranging your new identity but while the Syndicate is after you, no baby of ours can ever be safe.'*" He looks into the camera and sighs. It's a ham actor's attempt at regret.

Helen shakes her head. Not that. No way could he have made a girl do that.

"*The clinic gave Fiona every chance to change her mind. But she stuck to the script: we were too poor to provide for a child; the time wasn't right; there would be other chances.*" The camera refocuses on a close-up of his face, pink and puffy like undercooked chicken. "*You must decide for yourself whether she showed great strength of character or utter stupidity.*"

Helen hisses at the screen. "You disgusting, little—"

"Listen," Mel snaps.

"*A week later I told her about her new identity. She was a former telesales worker who would become my wife, and live with me in Germany.*"

Helen's blood is hot then cold. She stares at Mel. "You?"

Mel's expression is blank.

"You? You're Fiona. He did this to you?"

"That was Chris for you." Mel sighs, as if she's complaining that he never did the washing-up.

Helen catches her breath. "You lost your baby? He made you do that?"

"Watch this bit," Mel says, pointing at the screen.

Helen wants to switch it off and talk to Mel, listen to her, give her comfort, but like a rubbernecker driving past a traffic accident, she's drawn back to the screen. It's another view of Dickensweg filmed from an upstairs room. Mel crosses between two parked cars and emerges on the far side, with a pushchair. Her pace is trudging. Helen has forgotten how big she used to be. When Chris's voiceover starts, Helen can't stop herself from trembling.

"To prove to the 'Security Services' that she had put the loss of the baby behind her, and that she could handle our assignments, she had to walk around the neighbourhood with an empty buggy."

Helen wants to puke. Chris was a total psycho. What kind of sadist forced a woman to get rid of her baby and made her relive the agony? "I'm so sorry," she says. She knows she sounds pathetic.

Mel's mouth twists. Helen thinks her triteness has made her angry, but she's glaring at the screen.

There's a camera close-up of Chris's manicured fingers. He has a €10 note in each hand. *"Düsseldorf Airport was another test. I left her there with hardly any cash and a suitcase full of shoes. I told her it was a vital training exercise in case she ever had to go on the run without me."* The camera moves to his face. *"Do you know how hard it is to stay at an airport without a flight ticket and not get arrested?"*

Mel pushes her thumb in her mouth. Helen thinks she's seeking comfort. But, no, she bites it, drawing blood. It mingles with her saliva and blobs onto Louisa's shirt. Helen looks back at the TV to stop herself remembering the last time she saw blood on Louisa's clothes.

It's Damian on-screen now, filmed from above, a glint of red scalp through faded boyblond hair. He's staggering up a garden path with a suitcase. Mel appears in shot behind him. Filthy T-shirt, sweat patches at her throat. She takes the case from Damian and drags it forward out of view. Helen's seen this before, live and from ground level. She was watering her garden. Damian, red wine in hand, on his doorstep. Mel shuffling towards them. She'd been to Lanzarote. Except the poor woman never went on holiday.

"When I went back to get her, I was her saviour. It didn't matter that I'd put her there in the first place. I told her that my bosses had one more test. I dropped her at a service station on the A61. She had to walk 10 kilometres along the side of the motorway without a police patrol spotting her."

"Oh, Mel, I don't know what to say." Helen puts her head in her hands, ashamed of how wooden she sounds. But it's the truth, she hasn't a clue how to speak to this abused woman.

"Be quiet. It's not finished yet." Mel licks the blood from her knuckle as she keeps looking at the film.

"My bosses told me my operation was costing too much." He doesn't bother with inverted commas this time. Perhaps he was deluding himself by now that the bosses were real. *"They would decommission me unless I raised €3,000 in three days. Fiona had to contribute 10 per cent."*

More street footage. Mel is staggering across the road with a pile of clothing to the Stephens's doorstep. The door opens and the pile is passed to the figure in the obscured doorway, presumably Polly. Then the film speeds up and shows Mel whizzing across to other houses with more piles. Her fleshy backside quivers in blue striped leggings. With a Benny Hill soundtrack it would be comical but there's no music and Chris's words are chilling.

"Fiona washed those clothes as if her life depended on them."

"Didn't he know he'd get arrested if anyone ever saw this? This stuff could have put him in prison for years," Helen says.

"He would have edited it. He was good at editing." There's a tear on her cheek. She lets it reach her chin and fall away.

Helen kneels in front of her, ignoring the pain in her leg. The coldness of Mel's skin seeps into her own when she touches her hand. "I … Mel. I don't know what to say, I …"

Mel faces her. "How old do you think I am?"

"I …"

"I'm 26. Five years ago I was a student studying French. Now I can't remember a single word."

What can she say? Even after the weight loss, Mel looks late thirties. The skin, the mouth, the face – washed out and knackered.

Mel leans forward, shaking off Helen's hand and presses the eject button on the player. "That's the end."

Helen moves back to the sofa. Five years. It's been going on for five years. "I didn't know any of this. I …"

Mel's back is ramrod straight. The short sleeves of Louisa's top dig into the sleeves of her jumper below, so tight her arms must hurt.

"He taught me to trust no one. I had to report to him any unidentified cars outside our house and sweep every room I entered for listening devices. You caught me once, looking in the drawers in your hall. Didn't you guess?"

"I had no idea," Helen whispered. She'd thought Louisa had put her up to being nosy. If only that was all.

"I had to practise surviving interrogation. You must have heard splashing through the wall." She's staring at Helen now, it's the same empty stare she gave the TV screen.

"I … don't … didn't know what it was." The gasping and coughing, Helen on the toilet trying to pee quietly so the bather next door wouldn't hear her. She should have known.

"When you came to my door last night I thought for a moment it was Chris. He'd go off for days, leaving me with no money and not much to eat. If I didn't hear him tap on the door when he came back, he'd leave again. If I didn't listen, I didn't get fed."

"Didn't you ever think of leaving him?"

Mel narrows her eyes, focusing on Helen. "How could I? He was shielding me from a drugs syndicate. He was the shepherd, protecting his flock. I couldn't walk away; it would be a death sentence on my parents. Then I saw the DVDs. I realized the sentence was lifted because I'd already died."

Helen wants to embrace her, tell her she has a chance at a life now, but she glances over the parquet to the door, to the windows. She has one more question and sits on the edge of the sofa, in case she has to run. "When did you find them?"

"In July, after the burglary. We all went out looking for Murdo. Everyone thought I'd just flown back from Lanzarote but I'd walked miles. I couldn't keep up with the search so Chris sent me home. Our house had been ransacked. The burglar had smashed open Chris's locked cabinet in the spare room. The DVDs were on the floor. I watched a bit of one and then hid them in the shed," Mel says.

She pulls a piece of paper from her waistband. "I found this too. At the time I couldn't understand why he kept it. I get it now." She throws it to Helen but it flutters to the floor between them. "Go on, read it."

Helen reaches for it. It is a newspaper cutting. *Missing Girl Phones Home.*

Mel says: "Do you know how it feels to make a call like that? Hearing your parents' voices after so long is like having your innards ripped out. And every day afterwards, when you wake up, you feel eviscerated all over again." Her shoulders sink and she chuckles. "Good word: eviscerated. It's a Fiona word, not one of Mel's." She stiffens again.

Helen holds the piece of paper out to her. She can't stop her hand from trembling. "The DVDs, this cutting. They're evidence. We could go to the police. Get help for you. Why didn't you go when you found them?"

Mel takes the paper, folds it and tucks it up her sleeve. "I had to work out my exit strategy."

307

Helen shivers. Should she work out hers? "We ought to go now."

Mel turns back to the blank TV screen and continues her monologue. "I pretended to have a nervous breakdown after the burglary. God knows I'd earned one after what I'd discovered, but I was only faking it. Whenever he went out, I left my bed and exercised. By December I was ready. Chris might have called it Stage Two. But I'm not as good a planner as Chris. I got something wrong."

"What? What did you get wrong?" she asks but dreads the answer.

"I overheard Chris and Louisa arguing at the Christmas market and thought Louisa was in on it. I started thinking it was real again." She pauses to suck more blood off her thumb. "I went back to bed. You see, I hadn't watched the part where Chris introduced Louisa as a victim. If I'd seen that, things might have been different, but I wasn't to know, was I?"

She looks at Helen, twisting her head to one side like a manipulative child who's done something bad and thinks peering through her fringe will make it all right again.

Get the hell out of here. It doesn't matter how. Just get away. Helen snatches at an idea. "Let's talk about this somewhere else. Do you remember what I told you last night about Damian? We're not safe here. Phone him and say you can't face clearing Louisa's stuff. Then I think we should go to the police."

Mel glares at her.

Helen flinches and tries to qualify her mention of the police. "They'll be able to reunite you with your parents."

Mel stands up, and Helen cowers. Oh God, she's made it worse: Mel's parents. Pandora's Box.

But Mel walks to the colouring book. "I suppose it's because we use the other colours so much that there's a need for one more."

"Mel, shall we …?"

308

"I phoned my parents this morning. God knows how I remembered their number after so long. My father wasn't there. He died two years ago."

"Oh God, I'm so sorry …"

"You think I should call Damian? Let me show you something." She walks over to the sliding doors into the dining room, pushes them open and points at the music room door beyond. "In there. Go and look."

Helen hesitates behind Mel. The last time she saw Gary, he was slumped over the Howards' dining table. And she found Chris in the music room. Dead Chris. Headless Chris.

"Go on." There's fury in Mel's voice.

Helen pushes the music room door ajar and sees a pair of legs on the floor. One brown loafer is unhooked from the heel. There's a Christmas tree pattern on the sock.

61

Helen ducks out and grips the dining table to stay on her feet. She can't see whether Damian's bleeding, but blood from Chris and Louisa and Gary cascades through her mind.

She clings to her wreck of an escape idea. "We have to get out of here," she gasps. "It's not safe."

Mel saunters back to the lounge. She selects a felt-tip, goes to the wall and scrawls on it. Helen feels dizzy. The pen is red, it had to be red.

"I always hated this wallpaper," Mel says. She presses so hard that she splits the nib.

Helen still clutches the table edge. How easy is it to open the patio door? How fast can she move with her injured knee? How will she get out? How? How?

"Come and sit down," Mel says. She goes back to the rug for another pen. "I said sit down."

Her heart in her throat, Helen moves into the lounge again and sits on a sofa, the one nearest to the hall door.

As she tests other pens on the colouring book, Mel says: "Louisa was fine playing spies, but as soon as Chris asked her for money, he lost her. He misjudged how important her marriage was.

Damian promised to stay with her if she economized; there was no cash for spy games."

She goes back to the wallpaper and stabs it with purple dots. Her arm moves with rhythmic precision. She returns to the rug when the pen has bled out.

"The argument I overheard was Louisa telling Chris she'd had enough. It panicked him into thinking she might expose him." She selects a black pen from the pile and scrawls a wavy line on the colouring book. "Chris told me his bosses were preparing to move us again."

She wraps her arms around her body and rocks back and forth. "Another bedsit, alone, no food, only tap water. Crying for my baby. Phone going, no sleep. A knock at the door, hide, hold my breath." She stops rocking and shakes her head. "Not again. He wouldn't do it to me again." She selects a different pen. Her expression remains hollow.

"Mel, I think it's time to—"

"White could be the missing colour. I don't use white when I'm colouring." She turns the page and begins filling in Marge Simpson's hair. Her pen strokes are quick and neat. "There were a few snow flurries when I went over but, half an hour after I left, my footprints were buried under a good six inches of white."

"Mel, I think I heard something."

"I had Chris to thank; he taught me stealth. He said it was on his bosses' orders but he never did say why. I had to practise creeping up on him. If he heard me, he would spin round fist first. I learnt to be stealthy."

"But it's over now. No one will hurt you if we go somewhere safe," Helen pleads.

"Louisa was leaning over a pudding, piping on whipped cream. Stealthy. Stealthy. Stealthy." Her pen moves back and forth to the same rhythm as her words.

Helen stands up, feeling giddy. Her knee is throbbing but she continues the pretence of hearing someone else nearby. "There's that noise again. We should ..."

"I've always thought cheesecake was upside down fruit crumble. Louisa's was a bit of a mess afterwards to be honest." She continues colouring as she speaks. Her voice is monotone, matter-of-fact. "When Chris played stealth, I learnt to be quick. Into the dining room, quick. Knife into Gary, quick. But Chris was quicker. The big-I-am special agent ran like a frightened girl into the music room and shut the door. So I came over hysterical: 'Help me, Chris, please. I didn't mean to.'"

Helen squirms as Mel's voice goes up in pitch. She sounds like the ineffectual Mel she's always known – the one Chris created. She can imagine how it would have convinced Chris he still had a hold over her.

"He opened the door; he thought he'd won again. But the knife was in his neck before he knew it." She grips the pen in her fist and gouges into the paper. "All the dread and humiliation of the last five years fell away. Fiona came back. I saw the kids' musical instruments and smashed them up. I'd switched off to everything for so long. It felt good to have a normal temper tantrum."

Normal? Helen can see the stairs through the open lounge door, and the edge of the telephone stand. The potpourri is out of sight.

"Sit down," Mel says.

It's a few steps to the front door, but Mel is quick. Knife quick. Helen sits down.

"Napoleon came in wagging his tail. I watched him for a while, licking up Chris's blood. I hate dogs. One of Chris's loyalty tests was to enter a disused classroom block at the back of the school. He said there were guard dogs patrolling. There weren't but I believed him. I was so scared I soiled myself. He wouldn't let me bathe. The sores took weeks to heal."

She finds a clean page and decorates Homer in olive green.

"Napoleon followed me into the hall. He let me tickle his tummy. I overcame a lot to do that, you know." She glares at Helen, demanding some kind of acknowledgement.

"It must have been hard. I know you don't like dogs," she says, playing along.

"He made the most bizarre noise when I slit him."

Sweat pools in Helen's armpits. Mel can't talk forever. What next? She points at Louisa's fireplace. "The police said they found traces of men's clothes in this grate. I thought it could be Sascha Jakobsen."

"No, you didn't. You never thought that. Don't bother saying it now. I arrived in some of Chris's clothes. They got bloody so I burnt them. I put on Louisa's coat from the hallstand when I left. I can wear it now I've lost weight." She smooths out the hem of the Lycra top.

She puts down her pen and lifts up the rug. There's a knife. Damian's blood has seeped from the blade into the parquet, Napoleon red.

She moves forward, the knife held upwards, the point glinting.

62

Helen leaps into the hall but the blade catches her, metal slashing through her jacket, ripping into flesh. Pain screams down her arm. Her palm throbs and her arm won't move. She cups her elbow and blood percolates through her thumb and fingers.

Helen's good hand forms a fist and drives up into Mel's belly. That hand hurts now too, differently, a snap, a bruise. Mel staggers backwards, blocking the front door, giving Helen time to run upstairs, blood from her wound spotting the treads. Which door? Her lungs lag behind and she pauses for too long, giving Mel time to lock the front door and come after her. She is halfway up before Helen lunges into the bathroom. The bruised hand, clammy with the other arm's blood, bolts the door.

She must find a weapon. Razor blades? There's a vast wood-panelled cabinet, polished as a coffin. But there's nothing on the bottom shelf except deodorant-can-shaped rings of talcum powder. She feels her bloodied fingertips along the top shelf. They come away white. Red and white. Like Louisa's cheesecake. She gags. Acid up to her nostrils.

Thud. Mel hits the door.

Helen's in a cage of white enamel. How to hide? How to run?

She'll lower herself out of the window with the shower curtain. But there's no curtain to degrade this deluxe suite. And her bad arm is a dead fish, slippery and oozing blood down her elbow, forming rivulets in the lines on her palm.

Thud.

She goes to the bathtub, dirties its sleek surface with a rusty handprint. She catches her reflection hovering in the polished chrome tap and looks down before she can focus. Is there a plug on a chain? Flick it into Mel's face. Distract her long enough to get past her. But there's no chain, it's lever release.

Mel slams against the door again. The lock won't survive the onslaught. She must slow it down.

"Why didn't you tell someone?"

No reply. The door judders against another attack.

How will she fight her off? There isn't even a loo brush, and the top of the cistern is tiled into the wall.

"Why didn't you tell?" she asks again.

Mel shouts: "Tell who what? How would a neighbour know any better than me about the intelligence services? The only person who knew was Chris."

There's a shower spray attachment with a massive showerhead. Swing it fast and hard?

"You could have told me. You must have known I never trusted Chris."

"I didn't care what *you* thought. I believed *him*. He wasn't after my money. He took that in the early days." The door handle rattles and then there's another thump. "If he'd wanted to con me, he wouldn't have come back, would he?"

The wood behind the lock splinters. The first screw drops. Helen yanks at the shower attachment with a desperate scream. Adrenaline triumphs, the attachment pulls free of the wall bringing tile and plaster with it.

If she's going to die, she'll die with answers. "I get why you killed Chris and even Louisa. But why Gary?"

"He knew. You all knew that monster made me kill my baby, made me miss the last years of my dad's life."

Thud.

"You're wrong, Mel. No one knew. We couldn't have—"

"Liar! I saw them. The whispering in corners, the sudden silences when I walked in."

Helen speaks faster. "That wasn't about you. It was about what Damian did to that poor girl; I told you."

More wood splinters. The second screw falls and skitters across the stone-tiled floor. Helen's defence is a coil of shower tubing. "And you never doubted Chris? Not once?"

"Sometimes when he nearly drowned me, I'd think I'd be better off dead. But he'd turn on the charm and I accepted everything all over again. He was my shepherd … What? Who's there?"

The thudding stops.

"Wait there. I'm coming down," Mel shouts.

Helen tries not to breathe. The stairs are creaking. Mel's heard something in the house, but one more assault on the door and she's in.

No thud. No sound. Helen trembles and waits, freezing and pouring sweat. She loosens her grip on the showerhead. Two minutes? Five? She gets down on the floor. It smells of jasmine. There's a new pain as she kneels on one of the fallen screws. She peers at the narrow strip of light under the door. No movement, no shadow.

If she opens it, there'll be an ambush. For the first time, Helen thinks about getting help. She could open the window and scream to passers-by. But the neighbours have joined the Christmas exodus; no one would hear her. Even Manfred has shuffled off somewhere. The police then. The number is 112. The only thing she got out of Sabine's welcome briefing in April. Damn. Her phone's at home. She pictures Number Ten's layout – there's a phone in the hall – but even if it hasn't been disconnected, Mel will get to her before she reaches the handset.

Helen winds the shower tubing around her goodish arm. She reaches up to pull what's left of the bolt. Her clammy fingers struggle to grip it.

She's out on the landing.

Nothing. All the doors are shut. She tries to remember if they were like that when she ran upstairs. She holds her stance, expecting one of them to fly open. Nothing. She creeps to the stairs. The staircase has grown to be the longest in the world and every step creaks louder than the previous one. An eternity later she reaches the front door. She pulls and yanks and fights it but knows Mel locked it.

Where next: patio or back door? The patio means going through the lounge, and Mel might have gone there to annihilate more wallpaper. The back door was unlocked the last time Helen was here. She'll have to hope the police – and Mel – have over-looked it. She darts past the lounge. Out of the corner of her eye she sees the colouring paraphernalia but no sign of Mel. Mercifully, Damian isn't visible when she passes the dining room.

She pushes open the kitchen door and stops dead. Instinct detects something – a sound or a movement. She winds the shower coil tighter but Mel doesn't leap out. She holds her breath, straining to hear. But she can't bear the limbo state any longer. She dashes through the kitchen and utility room to the back door. She yanks the handle up and down. Up and down. Up and Up. It makes no difference: it won't open. She senses the shadow approaching. She prepares to swing the showerhead but finds her arms pinned to her sides. She bucks and rears and kicks but the grip is too strong. She waits for the blade.

"Relax," Sascha says, "I've locked her in the cellar."

He lets go of her arms as she stops struggling. She takes hold of him and hugs his sinewy, boyish body into hers. He must feel her trembling.

"You're safe now," he whispers into her hair. "But I think she may have tripped on the steps."

317

63

Saturday, 25 December

Helen lays a coat on the thin layer of snow and sits down by the pool. The cold seeps through to her thighs. She pulls another coat tighter across her shoulders. Gary's ski jacket.

One last Christmas with Gary, or with his jacket at least. It's their wedding anniversary in three days' time. She'll be alone with him for that too. Their second anniversary and their last. It might take months or years to get through her mourning but she knows leaving this place will start the process.

She draws up her knees and cups her arms around her legs. One leg still feels sore. At least the climb over the fence was better executed than last time and she hasn't made her injuries worse. She rubs her knee and then her hand travels to her arm. The coat is too thick to feel the bandage. Fourteen stitches where Mel's knife caught her. A cheerful, overweight doctor at the police station patched her up. She witnessed mental cruelty, violence, and murder, but her body will leave this place with fourteen stitches in her arm and a stab of anti-tetanus in her thigh.

The winter sun comes out and she shields her eyes. Unbidden, an image of Toby's bloodied, broken cello drifts into view. She fixes her gaze on the iced-up water. Her mind skips back to May. That first tingling dip, balmy on her naked limbs, after the hit of cool spring air. And the more she trained, pumped, kicked, the hotter her body became. Gary used to love it when she came home pink-faced. He had to kiss her, touch her, and whisper cool breaths on her neck.

Tears sting her face but she doesn't wipe them away.

A car door slams and the perimeter fence creaks and sways. There's a thud onto the ground.

When Sascha sits down beside her, she looks away so he won't see her tears.

Neither of them speaks for a while.

Eventually he says: "I didn't push her."

"It doesn't matter."

"She heard me come out of the cellar. I saw her eyes before I saw the knife. She went for me but stumbled through the open cellar door. There was a child's bag on the steps. I'm sorry she fell."

Helen says: "I'm glad it ended then. She'd suffered enough."

"I swear on Mareike's grave I didn't push her."

She scrutinizes his face. He looks older, more her age. The all-out, hell-bent fury in his eyes has dimmed to something else. Sorrow, acceptance, maturity? There are lines etched at the side of his mouth and visible through the stubble. He's a man now, and he used her, but all she wants to do is mother him.

"Don't you think it's time to let Mareike rest in peace?" she says.

Sascha nods. "Mareike was the first tragedy. I will always remember but I think I must not look only backwards."

"Will you tell me why you robbed us in the summer?" she asks. "I just want to know."

He glares at her, some of the fiery youth comes back. "You still think it was me?"

She shrugs. She doesn't care if she's offended him. Too many people have watched their words. Too many secrets. Too many lies. "Wasn't it you?"

His expression relaxes, the fire dies even quicker than it ignited. Perhaps he doesn't care anymore either. "On that day I was in the wood by the Howard house. The street was deserted and I found out later you were looking for a missing child. Manfred Scholz came out of your garden. After he'd gone, I went round the back of your house and saw the broken glass in your door. I cut myself. That's why the police thought I was the burglar but they dropped the charges when there was no evidence I went inside. Your earring was on the path. I meant to drop it into your bag when we met for swimming but I didn't get the chance. It stayed in my pocket until I left it here in the snow as an alibi to get you out of jail."

Helen rubs her face; her head is starting to hurt. Can there be more revelations? After everything else? "Why would Manfred Scholz burgle my house and three of my neighbours?"

"I had reason to hate the British so I figured he did too. I said nothing and silently wished him good luck. Then it went too far. Murder. I had to confront him. You saw me coming out of his house when Damian Howard attacked me."

Helen shakes her head. "Did you suspect dear old Manfred of a killing frenzy? I can barely believe he ransacked my house."

He glares again, his eyes flashing with the annoyance she remembers from their first meeting months ago, when he'd just seemed grumpy, before she knew his temper.

"What do you know about Manfred Scholz?" he asks.

She shrugs again. "After what's happened, isn't it obvious that I didn't know much about any of my neighbours?"

"The Niers School demolished his cottage to make way for a sports centre."

"Somebody – Louisa, I think – told me that months ago. Apparently, the cottage was in a poor condition. The school re-housed him and his wife in Dickensweg."

Sascha shakes his head. "Moving onto an international estate broke Christa's heart. In Manfred's eyes, the foreigners were no better than the Russians who expelled his parents from their homeland in Silesia. When Christa died of cancer, he knew who to blame.

"All his life he had been a man of honour. But now he didn't care. He hated the international teachers with their stupid cocktail parties and noisy dogs. He attacked with – how do you call it – paint on walls and signs?"

"Graffiti? Manfred Scholz was responsible for all the '*Ausl nder Raus*' spray paint?"

Sascha nods. "He told me that wasn't all he did. He broke play furniture in children's playgrounds."

"We thought it was kids."

"I think he was drinking too much. He wanted to do more than smash playgrounds; he wanted to smash houses and shops. He had a tactic. He told me he set a toy bomb and trashed your houses. He also took the boy. He knew what the residents would do."

Helen kneels up and faces him. "You're telling me Manfred Scholz kidnapped Murdo Howard to create a diversion and ransack our houses? I can understand a bit of vandalism but Murdo is five years old. Scholz should be arrested."

Sascha raises his hand to calm her. "Manfred said they played marbles and listened to his Kelly Family records. He left the boy watching *Raumschiff Enterprise* when he broke into the houses. He took him home to his mother afterwards. The child was not harmed."

"I'm truly sorry he lost his cottage and then his wife, but that doesn't excuse what he did. What's to stop him doing it again?"

"He won't. When I went to see him, I told him I knew about the burglaries. I made him look me in the eye and tell me he'd done nothing else. I was talking about the murders but he confessed to the bomb scare and to taking Murdo. He said his campaign stopped the moment he ran into you outside the Howards' house. He saw your terror. It made him realize where his own vengeance might have led if someone else hadn't got there first. His rage is spent. He'll harm no one, except himself with alcohol." Sascha looks away and seems distracted by another thought.

"So you blackmailed him? He got you out of jail with a false alibi and in return you said nothing about him kidnapping Murdo?" She scoops up some snow and hurls it at the pool railing. "Is everyone I've met here a criminal?"

"Not me. Not really. I was at the *Freibad* that night even though Manfred Scholz didn't see me. I'm glad I made him lie for me. But I regret I destroyed the Howards' garden. I was trying to get at Damian but I only hurt Louisa. I thought she was a bad person too but I was wrong."

Helen sighs. "Louisa wasn't a bad person. I see that now. She was manipulated like everyone else." She glares at him. "Manipulated like me."

"I'm sorry that I lied to you. I would have done anything to get to the truth, but I shouldn't have involved you."

She throws more snow. It misses the railing and spatters on the frozen water. No, he shouldn't have lied, but then so did everyone else, including her own husband. The only one who didn't lie, except maybe about her childhood, was Louisa.

"Are you going to stay in Dortmannhausen?" she asks.

"My mother has promised to get counselling. Bereavement help at first but I hope one day for alcohol too. I will stay with her. I've decided to go back to the *Hochschule*. To study English. What will you do?"

"You'll do well; you have a flair. I'll get a teaching job in England, but first I have to find Mel's mother."

"Shouldn't you leave that to the police?"

"They'll tell her that her daughter murdered four people. I have to explain why it happened and that there was a far crueller person than Fiona behind it." She pulls the ski jacket tighter.

They are silent for some time. She looks at the water again. Will the pool open in May next year now that Louisa isn't around to wave her petition at the town hall? Louisa deserves that legacy at least.

She thinks of the elderly woman swimmer in the flowery cap. What's she doing now? Cooking Christmas Day goose while her husband reads the newspaper? Or do they have the grandchildren round? Normal life. Louisa would have adored that role one day. They'd have been Leo's children. Toby, on the international classical concert circuit, wouldn't have had time to marry. And Murdo … Leo's kids would have loved their funny uncle whom Granny Louisa fussed over.

Sascha says: "I think we must try to live our lives. For Mareike and for Gary."

"Yes" she replies, "for Mareike, for Gary … and for Louisa."

They both hold up a hand, and their palms press together.

Acknowledgements

Thank you for reading *The Perfect Neighbours*. I really hope you liked it.

Without the help of many people, this novel wouldn't have seen the light of day. I'm grateful to my editor Finn Cotton at HarperCollins and to my agent Marilia Savvides at PFD who believed in me and in this book, and helped bring it to a publishable standard. I'd also like to acknowledge the painstaking work of copy editor Janette Currie. A big thank you must go to my husband Nigel who proofreads my early drafts and gives me the space in our lives for me to write. I must also mention my former tutors in the Creative Writing department of Lancaster University. I thank Sarah, Eoghan, Conor, Tom and Zoe for their expert thoughts on technique. This novel is dedicated to fellow writers Fergus Smith, Gillian Walker, Jenny Sanders, Peter Garrett and Karen Pegg whose constructive criticism on several drafts and wise encouragement kept me going when I might have given up.

I twice lived in a cul-de-sac in Germany like the one featured in the novel and I used this experience as the backdrop for my setting. However, my real neighbours were nothing like the characters I created in *The Perfect Neighbours*. They were invariably warm, friendly, kind and witty. I thank them for the many times they helped me and my family, and for making our time as expats fun.

If you'd like to keep up to date with news on my writing and reading, please visit my website at:

www.rachelsargeant.co.uk

And I'd love to hear from you on Twitter:

@RachelSargeant3

KILLER READS

DISCOVER THE BEST
IN CRIME AND THRILLER

Follow us on social media to get to know the team behind the books, enter exclusive giveaways, learn about the latest competitions, hear from our authors, and lots more:

 /KillerReads 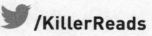 /KillerReads